JET'S 20 Albums

D1346049

*Janet Jackson*

*Luther Vandross*

**Artist and Label**

Title

# THE UNFORTUNATES

## J K CHUKWU

J K CHUKWU is a writer and visual artist from the Midwest. She holds an MFA in Literary Arts from Brown University and was a 2019 Lambda Fellow. Her work has appeared in *Black Warrior Review*, *DIAGRAM*, and *TAYO*.

# THE UNFORTUNATES

# J K CHUKWU

THE BOROUGH PRESS

The Borough Press
an imprint of HarperCollins*Publishers* Ltd
1 London Bridge Street
London SE1 9GF

www.harpercollins.co.uk

Harper*Publishers*
Macken House,
39/40 Mayor Street Upper,
Dublin 1
D01 C9W8

First published in Great Britain by HarperCollins*Publishers*
1

A catalogue record for this book is available from the British Library

HB ISBN: 978-0-00-847801-8
TPB ISBN: 978-0-00-853878-1

Printed and bound in the UK using 100% Renewable Electricity
at CPI Group (UK) Ltd

This book is produced from independently certified FSC™ paper
to ensure responsible forest management.

For more information visit: www.harpercollins.co.uk/green

For anyone who was told they were too much.

**Stumbling is not falling.**

—Malcolm X

# CONTENTS

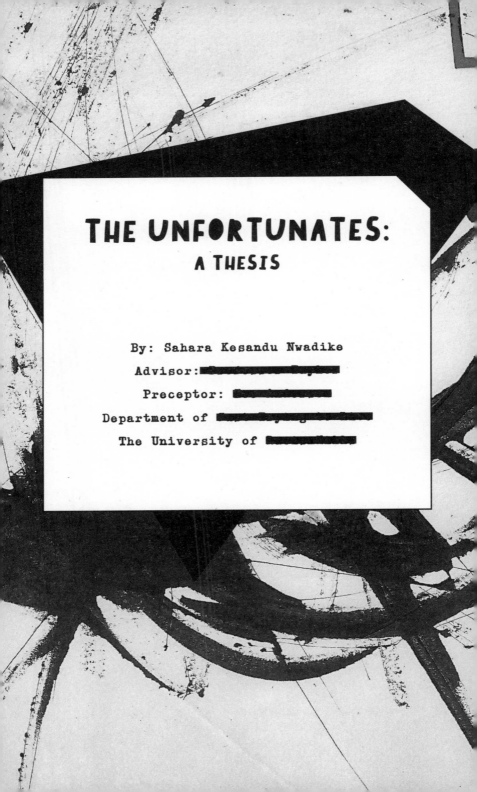

# THE UNFORTUNATES:
## A THESIS

By: Sahara Kesandu Nwadike
Advisor: ███████████████
Preceptor: ███████████
Department of ████████████████
The University of ███████████

# DE(A)DICATION

Dear Thesis Committee,

It has come to my attention that smoking kills, along with police, loner white boys, and looks. While embroiled in the process of trying to live, I have written this honors thesis.[*]
It[†] is dedicated to the first-years who haven't yet died from alcohol poisoning, exhaustion, or overdosing. This work has been a labor of love and of hate. In it, you will find juxtaposition, verisimilitude, French, Freud, and anything else I've wasted $60K a year to learn.

 I would like to thank my advisors: Mr. White Supremacy, Mr. Capitalism, Ms. Racism, and, of course, my Life Partner for all the guidance they have provided during this process.

Yours Truly,
Sahara Kesandu Nwadike

---

[*] *Ma lettre d'adieu.*

[†] When writing an honors thesis, you can get away with vague antecedents.

# BLACK (GIRL) RAGE

In 1994, the year of my birth, my aunt Nita died from AIDS-related complications. My earliest memories are Mother saying: "So much of my sister is inside of you."

\*　　\*　　\*

Growing up, I tried looking for her. I spent minutes gazing into mirrors, staring down my throat, pulling open my mouth till the corners of it hurt, rubbernecking up my nose as I tried to see past the hairs and boogers. Aunt Nita wasn't in my eyes or throat or even up my nose.

After every failed search and rescue attempt, I remember wishing things worked the way they did in *Cinderella* or *Anastasia*, where lost things were always found in ninety minutes or less. If I were in a movie, I would've seen Aunt Nita in my eyes, and she would've looked back at me, smiling. Toni Braxton would've screamed in her three octaves and Aunt Nita would've told me to *Carry on, my child, and fight the good fight, so you can live for both of us.* And if not a good movie, then a good book would've also worked. Because, if I were in a good book, pages of beautiful description would've compared us to one another while using literary devices I still have memorized for no reason.

No movies, books, or metaphors could've helped me escape and find my aunt. I was stuck in Southfield, searching for a family member who was allegedly inside of me. I would never enter an altered reality where I could pick my aunt out of the lining of my cheeks, so I guessed she was in my head, and in Mother's head, and Father's head, and my brothers' heads, but not my bigot of an uncle's head.

But, of course, I was wrong—the white people stole her!

To be exact, my college library had her zine in the bookstacks. The zine,* outside of holding little ole me, was one of the few things that brought her joy during her dying months. With the help of Mother,

---

* According to Mother, before Aunt Nita was fired, she worked as a classroom assistant in elementary art, science, and literature classes. Someone at work found out about my aunt's AIDS diagnosis, that someone told another, and another, until they forced my aunt to quit because she posed a health risk to the staff and students.

Well, on her last day, Aunt Nita asked Mother to pick her up from work a little later than unusual. Patiently Mother waited until she saw my aunt running out the school's front door with Mother's metal shopping cart filled with art supplies, a giant cream-colored Epson printer, ink, snacks, and new science textbooks. Aunt Nita only stole most of the supplies that the school bought from her fundraising efforts. She figured if the school wanted nothing to do with her, then they should have none of her things, including the fruits of her labor.

While en route to Mother's AMC hornet, the cart's wheel flew off. The principal saw my aunt dragging the cart, and chased after her. The principal tried, while of course keeping his distance, to stop her. He even threatened to call the police. At first, Aunt Nita listened to Mother's pleas to ignore him, and just go. But then, as Mother loaded up her hatchback, my aunt cussed out the principal, then screamed as she helped Mother finish loading, "Y'all don't want anything I got. So, leave me the hell alone."

Mother believes that the shame of getting fired caused Aunt Nita to rarely leave her and Father's apartment. Aunt Nita's favorite pastime was pestering Mother. One day, Mother had enough and accidentally told my aunt, *go and write a book* instead of *go and read a book*. Stuck with boredom and a hoard of stolen school supplies, Aunt Nita did just that, and made her zine.

Aunt Nita published the zine, and even had a "book signing" before she died.

Fast-forward a decade and a half later, a white graduate student decided to write a thesis about AIDS crisis art, post-WWI German art, and Freud. Somehow during his hunt for sources, he found my aunt's work and used her as a citation.[*]

Because I am supposed to be grateful for this ivory tower that is the fifth best in the nation, this is the part where I say maybe all the bullshit, the crying spells, the nineteen extra pounds, and the all-nighters I experienced last year were worth it, since I found family and part of my history at my University. Oh, and according to an email the president sent in August, the University is making strides **EVERY DAY** to become a much more inclusive, diverse, and comfortable learning environment without sacrificing its academic rigor.

I only said that because I felt obligated to.

Hopefully, the previous two sentences will ensure that you, the Thesis Committee, see me as worthy enough for recognition.

Hopefully when some college student is writing a thesis about this thesis years from now, I will seem a little well-rounded and not too much of an Angry Black Girl. But I *am* an ABG. There are no other words or thinly veiled metaphors I can use.

From my anger, I have realized that I don't want to be here anymore. Years after pledging to a flag, after learning about Pilgrims while making turkeys with my hands, after learning every moment in European history, after learning only of Egypt during its era of pharaohs for

---

[*] He called her a misguided anarchist who needed to take drawing classes. Despite using it as a source, he didn't see the point of the zine and what he described as its "flat, ineffective" language. I hope my aunt is haunting him and sneaking typos into his dissertation whenever he's not looking.

African history, after reading books that use descriptors such as Nigger Black, I remember that my history goes unreported, and I am left compiling fragments of it. My history is in Father's Igbo conversations, which I cannot understand. It is with Mother's murdered ancestors, who worked this nation's fields for men whose descendants have University buildings named after them.

Despite my resentment, I'm going to classes inside these buildings. I'm living in a dorm where I'm too ashamed to wear my bonnet, and I'm graduating with classmates who want to wear cornrows and FUBU because they need that "ghetto" look for a '90s-themed frat party.

So yes, I am an ABG who is accumulating tears, debt, and trauma just for the possibility of surviving to graduation and getting a piece of paper that is mostly in Latin.[*]

---

[*] Who am I, Ovid?

# ALL ALONG THE WHITETOWER

Dear Thesis Committee,

If you have any students under your tutelage who are looking for ways to survive college, tell them to play games. They are the best ways to keep the mind and time moving. You can trust me on this, I'm an expert. Last year, I thought too much, I cried too much, I tried too much. Today, the first day back in Chicago and on campus since summer break, I have decided that I'll make everything into a game. I'll play hide-and-seek with my professors. For breakfast, lunch, and dinner, to ensure I have enough carbs bottoming my stomach so I can drink, I'll play Meal of Fortune and pick one meal a day. Ah yes, praise be to Rum Almighty, I'll play Russian roulette with shots of vodka, Everclear, and silver tequila, so that for this year, the fun will never die.

\* \* \*

My wisdom about games took me some time to attain. When I entered college, I was a serious student. I even bought the optional textbooks from the campus bookstore. But then in my first year, the other Black students started disappearing. To be exact, we lost four of the seven

Black students who lived in my dorm. Two transferred, one dropped out, and the other, Alicia, "graduated early.'"*

After the initial mourning, while the students began laughing off their grief, I could only listen. I was finally ready to hear the alarms I snoozed with my denial. When Alicia joined The Unfortunates, I began to realize I wasn't the only one, that my pain in this place was real, and worthy to fix in any ways I saw fit. Though I barely knew her, after she died, I kept searching for traces of her. I reimagined the ways she sat in the dorm's study lounge. I walked the different paths she might have taken to reach the dining hall, and when I reached the dining hall, I scratched the laminate off the wooden table, the same way that I remembered her doing so.

Thesis Committee, I want you all to remember that she always put her dishes away after eating at the dining table, she held doors open for frazzled first-years, and she was a political science major who didn't want to become a lawyer. She <sup>was</sup> is a good person. She <sup>was</sup> is another Black student at this University, and we stick together even after we fall one by one.

I want to keep her memory out of hopes that karma will make sure someone keeps my memory when I inevitably join The Unfortunates. Only to you, my readers, will I admit that during the pauses of my games, a growing part of me is preparing to leave like her after one good quarter. During the walks to lecture, I wonder what Mother will

---

* Here, among us, the best of the best, the smartest and burgeoning, there is a slight division on what we call our fallen comrades. For most, whenever a student leaves the iron gates for the pearly ones, and an email titled *Unfortunate News* signals the recent departure, classmates quip that another dead student has graduated early. However, when Black students talk to another about one of us dying, the deceased has not graduated early. They have joined The Unfortunates. There's no other way to describe surviving quarters of social deaths in this ivory mausoleum only to die before graduation.

say when I leave, and what other Black students will say, knowing that another has disappeared?

I'm tired. I no longer want to perform. Most days, I want to use my energy to take a power drill with a 7mm drill bit and drill a hole into my head so the thoughts I have

l

e

a

k

o

u

t.

I can't say this out loud. I can't be the Black girl who is always angry, mad, silly, and depressed. That's too many diversity quotas checked. I need to find more games to keep moving and going around and around in circles, so these thoughts don't catch up to me. The moment my thoughts are trapped inside of me, I cannot move, and the pressure builds within, causing time to stand still. To survive, I need time to move. I need for minutes to keep accumulating until they turn into hours, hours to days, that to weeks, then that to months, and finally my last quarter here is over.

I want to say goodbye, but I can't. Obviously, I can open my mouth and feel that echo in my throat as the letters *G O O D B Y E* come out and my lips move up and down. But the letters don't become a word with a meaning. My language folds into itself and produces nothing satiable.

As I'm stuck in the **GOODBYE**, I will take the escapes anywhere I find them.

# All These Tears Got To Be Going Somewhere

## By Nita Smith

# READY OR NOT, HERE I AM

After the six-hour train ride from Michigan, the 126 bus and then the transfer to the packed 6, after missing my final bus stop, then lugging my dad's old black suitcases with green tape wrapped around the handles an extra block, and then after dragging my over-stuffed Ghana Must Go bag up two flights of rubber stairs, I finally arrive at my dorm room. I'm sweaty, and hella tired, but hey, I made it in one piece, right?

I hand fan myself and peer at a note written on Vera Bradley stationery, which sits on my bed. What could this be? A welcome-back note that has a voucher to Chipotle, a preloaded bus pass, no, no, a get-out-of-finals-for-free card. Let's see, let's see! Drumroll, please.

\* \* \*

Sadly, there's nothing with it, but a message that reads, *Hey, hey Roommate! Gone for a camping trip before classes start. So excited to meet you. P. S.—They didn't give us any toilet paper for our bathroom. Please get some when you can. XOXOXO.*

Instead of a first-name basis, I guess Roommate and I will go by Roommate. It's fine. I'm terrible with remembering names. Plus, this roommateship won't survive a second year. I crush the note, slip it into my jeans' pocket,* and then close my eyes as I try to situate my body in this room. I wait for a feeling of elation that I'm no longer back home for the summer, and I am free to live my college life. But that buzzing excitement for my freedom away from home only thunderbolts me when I think of drinking.†

I continue counting seconds, hoping that time's accumulation will result in even the smallest compounding of my slightest joys. I don't know what I'm trying to imagine with my eyes closed. This mind is mostly filled with school. I don't know if I have the capacity to imagine a new place that exists outside of books, dead white men, and dirty coffee cups. When I sense my hope's failure is imminent, I open my eyes, then take in what will be my new home for my last months.

Though this room is in a different dorm‡ than last year's, it still feels and looks the same as the one before. I stand between two twin XL beds, and perpendicular to me are two beige writing desks to toss your backpack on, study, or mix drinks. A little light can enter through a tiny window that faces an ivy-covered brick wall. I feel the dread and anxiety from last year entering, braiding into one another to create rope

---

* Now we wouldn't want Roommate finding the crushed note in a trash can, which would then lead to a passive-aggressive fight, which would then lead to an RA intervention, right?

† I know. I have a problem and it's that I think too much. The only solution is drinking, which slimes my thoughts enough to slip out my membranes.

‡ My previous dorm was an insane asylum turned rehabilitation center turned dorm. This new dorm is a gentlemen's club turned hotel turned dorm. So far, the only perk of this dorm is that all the rooms have a private bathroom.

that tightens my chest. I shut my eyes again. I remain still for a little longer. I press my feet harder into the faded carpet. Hell, I even click my heels twice as I try and hope that somehow, somewhere under this rainbow* of spackled ceiling, I'll find my home. Outside of the dread and my baseline of depression, the constant feeling is my fracturing between leaving home, now being on campus, and always being in the void of these places.

FYI, when I say *void*, I'm not only indulging in poetics. I'm using one of my least favorite aliases for my depression aka my Life Partner who lives in my head rent free. LP† has been my bestie since third grade‡ and sees my life in 20/20. Since we've known each other for so long, she can't just live in any ole place. Her mansion, which could unseat Frank Lloyd Wright as the greatest architect, is constructed with everything I see, feel, think, or remember. To keep her happy long enough before her takeover, I curate the mansion with whatever she desires. Tonight, as we roll into the weekend, I suspect she'll need her beer, vodka, and tequila shots, her Capri Funs, and the sips of Cook's if I'm feeling a lil' fancy. She'll need her anything—and my everything—just to keep her occupied long enough so that I won't finally say fuck it and skip into traffic, a lake, or out an open window of a high-enough building.

\*       \*       \*

---

\* Dear Thesis Committee, here's a fun fact about this America. In 1939 three of the top five songs were, "Somewhere over the Rainbow," "God Bless America," and "Strange Fruit." #themoreyouknow

† Life Partner.

‡ In third grade, Father was away at work. Mother was in the basement helping Brother 1 cut clovers for his school's Saint Patrick's Day celebration. I remember leaning against the Creamsicle-colored kitchen island, feeling a desperation to escape my life as I pressed a butter knife against my wrist. To much disappointment, nothing red appeared. Eventually, I joined Mother and Brother 1 in the basement. That day in third grade began the cycle of attempting to escape, failing, and then returning to my family.

Let's stop this spiral before I'm sobbing against the carpet, sucking in my snot and dead skin cells from every student who's passed through this room. I just need to get back in it, tiptoe toward my happiness with complete gratitude. Yes, I'm happy to be here with my friends, free from Mother screaming my name for the TV remote or helping find her phone. Yes, I am overjoyed and oh so very honored to be one of the University's tokens. I'm here at one of the top five universities. A degree from here will open a door anywhere. Even though I'm studying with classmates who scheme to become the nouveau colonizers in this digital era, how could I not be grateful to learn at this premier institution? If I am going to fall into *happy to be here, Sahara*, the palatable character that hides my rage and pain, then I must set the stage.

**Step 1: Make my bed.**

I take last year's ratty linen. The sheets are covered with whitehead-size fuzzies, and the blue dye stains my skin. Sure, these sheets are shitty, but I'll worry about them when the concerns about the carcinogens of blue dye start trending.

**Step 2: Unpack clothes.**

\* \* \*

My side of the room is made. The one-two step is completed. There's no running away from this year. As I shove my empty suitcase into the small sliver of space that's left underneath my bed, I hear a knock on my door.

When your best friend is your soul mate, you feel their presence in your bones. I open the door and ROD, my Ride or Die,* shouts, "Welcome baaaackkkk!" as she's carrying a red-and-white-topped cooler. Her screams are so loud that a student across the hall opens his door. He pokes out his needle head, which irritation threads. To this intrusion and stitched-up eyebrows of annoyance, my immediate reaction is to smile and then mouth *sorry*. ROD glares until the door is closed again. "Nosey fuck."

"God, I missed you too."

"Does it feel good being back?" she asks with a half-smirk. She's the only person I texted throughout the summer while sequestered in Michigan, the mitten of the politely racist. So, she already knows the answer.

"Yup, like I've gotten slightly better real estate in hell."

---

\*   The first event that solidified ROD and her mother in dorm folklore occurred during freshman orientation. Day two of move-in, ROD's mother found a condom wrapper in ROD's jacket. This discovery led to a screaming match that drew the attention of first-years, their siblings, their parents, and the ill-equipped RA, who watched and tried to remember if any of her summer training had notes on how to handle a family feud that wasn't an icebreaker.

The fight ended with ROD alone in her single, sitting on a bed that didn't have sheets because the fight with her mother ran longer than the pickup window for her bedding at the college bookstore. Desperate for a friend, she called the guy she'd met last night. They started having sex on her dorm-room floor, but fights with mothers aren't the best aphrodisiac, and before his second pump, ROD started crying, I mean bawling. (She's a crier that could give Viola Davis a run for her money.) Not knowing what to do, he slipped out of her and then the room.

Fast-forward to the third week of first quarter. After the graduate student leading the discussion section finally got out of "traffic," on a traffic-less day, ROD's *Power and the Being* discussion was set to start. As the grad student scribbled questions on the board, she overheard the guy whispering to his friend that she's a crier, not a screamer. Embarrassed, ROD dashed out, tripping over Marc Jacobs and Michael Kors backpacks as she left. She retreated to the bathroom, where I saw her mid–ugly cry. Her cropped black hair was tousled in the direction of North by Northwest, and snot smeared her glasses. Immediately, I hugged her so tight that I hoped I would squeeze out all her tears. As I washed her glasses, she tried to compose herself and fix her hair. (Her attempts only resulted in a new direction of South by Southwest.)

We stayed in the bathroom, bonding over our intensely religious mothers, hating frat parties but needing them for the alcohol, and feeling alone ever since move-in. Before we left, we decided there was no turning back, we were friends for life.

"Oh come on, hell's extreme, maybe purgatory. We're here together, another year closer to graduation, and there's this feast." She opens the cooler, then hands me stuffed Vons bags. "I told my mom you were also coming in today. She made me haul so much food that I had to bring this cooler all the way from California."

"I didn't even know you could bring a cooler on the plane."

"Neither did I, but it's my mom, so of course she found a way."* She sits on my bed and begins scratching lingering neon paint splatters off her wire-framed glasses. "Seriously, I'm happy you're back. This place is shit, but—"

"God, don't say it."

"You bring a little heaven to it."

"It's because I'm already dead."

"Damn, Sahara. Classes haven't even started yet. Let's at least try and be a little happy. At least until Monday."

To her request, I sing out, "*It's because I'm already dead*" in a happier, show-tune aesthetic. I laugh at myself and then say, "Seriously, I

---

\*  On top of five stories of ROD's mother's persistence is the tale of how her mother, with the help of two other Korean moms, led a successful coup in their church. The tale is as follows: ROD's mother, tired of boring sermons where the pastor always loses his place, and annoyed with listening to the former Mrs. ██'s constant complaints of always seeing her ex-husband and ex-brother-in-law at church, recruited two other mothers for her campaign to replace the pastor.

Two whispers turned to four, four to sixteen, on and on until the majority members in the two hundred–plus church now felt the pastor's sermons weren't a blessing anymore, and quite possibly the cause of Mr. ██, the pastor's brother, deciding to leave the former Mrs. ██ for someone younger.

With tensions running high and the church wanting the current pastor gone, ROD's mother hoped that a special Wednesday Bible study could help calm the growing anger. A few weeks into this special Bible study, she just happened to invite a new pastor who coincidentally needed a new church home. The packed attendance at the special Bible study, the new lack of attendance at Sunday services, and the decline in donations left the church committee members with no option other than asking Pastor ██ to step down to then replace him with the new Bible study pastor ROD's mother just "happened" to invite.

don't know what I would do without you. You're one of the many reasons I won't transfer."

"That and Sallie Mae."

"Ugh that succubus," I respond as I open the bags. ROD flops on my bed and discusses her latest art adventure, which included almost forgetting to apply Vaseline before placing plaster strips on her arm. Though I'm concerned, this food is too distracting. Underneath the heaps of clementines, the two Tupperwares of chive pancakes, are her mom's iconic fried wings with her homemade red pepper paste. "I love your mom."

"Let me know when you're ready to trade."

"As if you're trying to start every morning with T. D. Jakes."

"Who?"

"Never mind." From the depths of my Ghana Must Go bag, I pull out a twelve-pack of Heinekens that I smuggled from home.

"How did you get beer so quick?"

Unsure of how ROD will react to drinks on the ready, I reply, "My roommate left me a pack. Nice, right? We have wings, beer, and fruit. It's a feast for the gods old and new."

ROD opens her hand for her beer, which I already opened. As she's drinking I try to figure out which of the wings is the biggest.* I'm torn between one in the middle and another just to the left of it. Just when I'm ready to pick the one in the middle, ROD swoops in and snaps it up.

"I was about to take that one."

"You took too long."

---

* One of the things that makes ROD my Ride or Die is that she's one of the few people I'm able to eat in front of, and when I say eat, I mean I can go to town on a burger, milkshake, and chili cheese fries, half a panini, sugar cookie, then buy a donut for later, and there's no judgment.

"I thought your mom made these for me."

"Sharing is caring."

"Mhmm."

I lay down a towel on the ground, and then ROD and I set up our food and beer as if we're in the Loop about to enjoy an end-of-September picnic at Daley Park. Sitting across from her, I can feel the idea of a possible home edge through the cracks of my door. If every day could be this, if I could no longer live in a character of respectabilities' creation, then maybe I could survive this place.

While in the onset of our food coma, ROD scrolls through her phone. "*Goddamn,*" she says before she passes me her phone. Its screen is open to the current conversation happening in the EAA* group chat that she's in. One member, wanting to showcase her birthday party, sends her receipt for $408.13 from De Quincey's Liquors, our on-campus liquor store. She then sends her address and the note that everyone is invited. ROD smacks her lips and calls the party a waste of money and just time with the fakes.

"True, but it could be an amazing distraction from the quarter starting."

"Why have a distraction? It's starting no matter what."

"Okay, true, but think about the assholes, all the annoying assholes that could influence your next art piece," I say, trying to appeal to ROD's artistic sensibilities, which are always on the hunt for the next inspiration. "Remember the last piece you made.† It was hit at the campus show."

"Yeah, yeah, and I need more stuff like it. Is there anything more pathetic than a one-hit coffee gallery wonder?"

---

* East Asian Alliance.

† ROD's last piece, titled *Fraternizing*, was a collage of every racist remark she'd heard from frat brothers during parties.

"A no-hit coffee gallery wonder?"

"Fair."

"So, we're going."

"Sure."

"Yes," and we then recommence finishing the last of our feast.

Bones, clementine peels, and beer caps fill the Tupperware. As we are splayed on the floor, plastic bags crinkle underneath us. Before more exhaustion hits, we talk in bursts of half thoughts. Although ROD's company distracts LP, between the bursts of conversations, when there are no words or giggles, LP regains control.

As my thoughts float in and out of ROD's excitement for applying to art shows, I plan how joining The Unfortunates will come about. The plan and then backup plans always begin with the guilt of leaving Mother, Brother 1, Brother 2, Father, and ROD. This guilt, which sputters my determination, makes me question if my death is actually something that I could undertake myself. Even with the guilt that compounds to doubt, I always continue planning. My death's beginning so simple—a night of celebration gone too far, sleeping on my stomach after one drink too many, a slip in front of the L train. All are possibilities for a passive death while living in a school—no, state—no, *country* that hates—no, kills—no, *destroys* so much of us.

\* \* \*

Desperate to escape out of myself, I grab ROD's hand. I pick off the lingering plaster that encrusts her nailbeds. "I love you so much."

She stares, confused. I'm uncomfortable, attempting to remember if my *I love you* sounded too desperate. LP's convincing me that it did and have ruined this moment. It's only day one. How else will I fuck up in these next coming days? ROD squeezes my hand. "Duh." She groans as she struggles to sit up. "I know that once classes start, we're off to the races, but we got this. We just have to—"

"Fake it till we make it."

"And remember—"

"C's get degrees."

# PASS THE COURVOISIER,

## PART III

ROD left to change into her party fit, which for her, means changing out of her Vans, and into her high-tops. While waiting I mix some vodka and some Crystal Light. The taste shivers the hair on my arms and tickles my ears. These are the kicks I need to get me going for this year's first night out. I'm playing my Daft Punk station on Pandora radio. The techno beats circuit my mind to excitement then pleasure. By the third drink, I'm fully ready. I shove a handful of Altoids into my mouth, crunching on them till the mint shears my tongue.

My excitement diminishes when ROD texts:

> ROD: shit, sorry, I can't make it tonight

> ME: why?!

> **ROD:** I lucked out and got hours at a studio for tonight

> **ME:** ugh, fine, Warhol, go on ahead

> **ROD:** 1, fuck that guy. 2, thank you, see you tmrw ☺

Part of me suspects she's lying. Her distaste for snobbery out-weighed any taste for free inspiration or booze. I keep my suspicions to myself and restart my pregaming. At least without ROD, I don't have to eat tablespoons worth of mints to hide my breath's scent. And yes, this means I'm still attending the party. I have the address. This vodka has me thirsting for more of her, her cousins, and friends.

Dear Members of the Committee, don't count this decision to at-tend against me. There's no need to add parties on the list of entities to gatekeep. I assure you that I still am an intellectually sound student, simply building on what I know. When my drinking began at fourteen,* then, like now, I was alone. While Mother and Father were away at a graduation party, wedding, or wake, I drank Father's alcohol that he kept underneath the kitchen sink. Though Father ~~was~~ is a busy man and ~~didn't~~ doesn't notice the missing reserves, I ~~was~~ am still smart with it. I only ~~took~~ take what he drank the night before. The perfect gaslight-ing, always letting him think that it was him who had those extra gulps and glasses.

Back home while sipping, I reimagined my favorite memories of Father. He wears his *isiagu*, and dances with an uncle. A crumpled napkin is in his hand to wipe off the sweat dripping. They are shimmy-

---

* I don't know whether this age is young, old, or within the standard of deviation.

ing, their hands clap together, and gold watches rattle on their wrists. Father's wide smile reveals metal crowns that sit on three of his molars. When Father and the uncle are too hot from dancing, they roll up their sleeves, showcasing their BCG* scars. Every part of them is drunk off cognac and the smell of fried puff-puffs, fried goat meat, jollof rice, and Prince Nico Mbarga.

"Sweet mother, sweet mother."

When my imagination turns to a different, sharper note, which screeches me to my other reality, I see sweet Mother who never drinks during the parties.† She sits next to me, focusing on the selected whispers of the Naija women, listening as her ears try to preemptively protect me from snickers concerning her children, the half Nigerian, half Black American mutts. One night the loaded question "Are you even Nigerian, my girl?" leaves me in the bathroom crying. Mother finds me and locks the bathroom door. She wipes the tears away and presses a wad of wet paper towels against my red eyes. "It's okay," she promises.

---

* Scar from a TB vaccine.

† Mother has always hated parties, and the snickers from these Naija women didn't help. When she was growing up, parties were a gateway drug, and they were to be avoided if you wanted to protect your soul. Grandmother took Mother and Aunt Nita to church, hoping to protect and help them escape from their house on Gratiot, a house of rotting ceilings and broken doors. Grandmother's tactic worked on Mother, but not on her youngest. When Grandmother wasn't looking or busy listening to Martha Jean "The Queen," Aunt Nita snuck out of the house, and only returned when she had stories of all the loves she secured for the night.

At first like Grandmother, Mother tried using religion to protect me from anything that could be a getaway to a life I had no business living. At church, I never listened and instead read books, wrote thoughts on church newsletters, or recommended ways that Jesus could have done his job a bit better. When Bible stories failed, she switched to traumatic stories from her childhood, and asking, *What business do I have doing x, y, and z.* On me, these tactics worked, but if she tried them on my little brothers, B1 and B2, they weren't as effective.

Brothers 1 and 2 learned how to play Mother and Father against one another. They would complain to Father, which would lead to Father complaining to Mother that she needed to "let her sons be men, o."

"They don't understand what they say." With smiles cuing that start of our next performance, Mother and I return to the hall; however, this is the last Naija party I will ever attend.[*]

In college, I have no home. And so, I drink to remember the parts of it I need. Since Father's silence[†] about his childhood and Igbo culture left me halved with the knowledge of my ancestry, I learned how to drink like him. At dinner while rolling fufu in my hands, my eyes tracked what Father decided to pour into his tall glass. Cognac and Vernors soon became one of my favorites, and then I learned to love the breadiness of stouts.

\*    \*    \*

I enter the party. A student screams she wants to dance her tits off. Her shouts lead us to a present problem that you will have to solve within twenty minutes. This problem is as follows:

**Problem 1:**

Student A is in an east-facing, overpriced apartment with slanted floors and a succubus landlord. The music is blaring at a speed of 117 bpm. She is five foot three and 125 pounds and gyrating at a rate of twenty-two twerks per minute. If said tits were danced off, would they:

---

[*] While I stayed at home, there were nights Father dragged B1 and B2 to accompany him. Because they were Nigerian boys who would go on to become Nigerian men, they needed to know about their culture. Every night I and Mother were left in the house. I remained in my bedroom, jealous of B1 and B2.

[†] His silence is understandable. Growing up during a civil war would snatch away your tongue that is too connected to your haunted histories.

a. Roll underneath a couch
b. Fly off into an empty cup
c. Be picked up and taken to the fridge for safekeeping

Please show your math and reasoning for the correct scenario. For your reference, included is a diagram of the apartment.

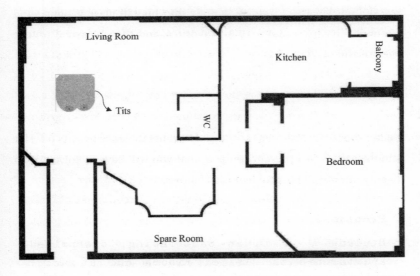

Answer:

*       *       *

Although I don't like most people and think hairless cats should re-place them, and although this party is terrible and the students scream *nigga* whenever it's on a rap track, the booze is still here, and anywhere is better than a dorm room that will never be home. I wander as I drink, and I peek inside one closed bedroom with a homemade sign that reads OPPY DEN. There, I spy with my little eyes: students a-snorting, and a-smoking, and a-rolling. Someone sees my spying little eyes, another slams the door in my face. I search for a new drink. With every step into this petri dish of privilege, as I squeeze between slim bodies that stand stoic, or hear debates on why it's not called wintering, but we have summering, and as I realize that instead of soirée this is a séance of dead personalities with the medium of liquor, I wish I had ROD's wisdom of bailing.

As I stand alone and type thoughts into my phone,* I notice a girl, one who snorted inside the self-proclaimed OPPY DEN. She keeps smiling at me, and though I don't know if I'm sober enough to carve a smile into my face, I know I can talk. Drunk words have no weight beneath them. I could announce, *I want to murder myself and every person in the room*, and an evangelical soror would say, *Omg saaame, girlfriend.*

The girl moves closer and towers over me. This is good, no great. A body standing next to me makes it seem like I belong here. Her gray eyes glow against her skin. She moves even. Her smile, as it reveals her canines. Her stare is the closest one I've felt since ROD's.

"Hi."

"What's your name?"

"Sahara."

"Like the desert?"

"Sure."

---

*   Last year, while attending parties alone, I learned typing on my phone is the perfect way to seem important. While onlookers think you're texting your friends about the next party, you're writing down all the things you hate, and, of course, number one on the list is you.

"Cool."

"More hot than cool."

"Funny. Have you ever been there?"

"No."

"How are you named after a place you've never been?"

"Ask my aunt, she named me."

"What?"

"Nothing. What's your name?"

"██████. I haven't seen you around. Are you a new Donor Kid?"*

"No, I normally don't get invited to parties like these."

"Who invited you to this one?"

"The Grapevine."

"So funny."

"Who invited you?"

"The host is a friend. I haven't seen her in like a year."

"A year? Were you on—"

"Oh no, I wasn't on leave or anything. I was in Rome. No way I was spending my second year, here, you know. What year are you?"

"Second."

"Good luck. Second year is always shittier than the first. And mine was hell."

"What happened?" I ask, wondering if—let's call her C1, since she's the one person who seems to see me at this party—is as displaced as I am. Perhaps, last year, a year of looking for escapes, places us in the same boat. Well for me, a raft, and her, a yacht, but still a boat, nonetheless.

"Ugh, everything. I had a falling-out with people who weren't my

---

* Donor Kids are universities' Brat Packs. While still gestating in the womb, their parents began their donations to top universities, effectively securing their children's spots here.

real friends and didn't know how to have fun. Only this place could make me, a prom queen, into a loner." C1 hands me a cigarette. I smoke and watch her as she talks. I'm not exactly sure whether she's here for my ears or lips. I want a kiss—maybe even six. C1 is beautiful, the type of beauty that 1920s blues warns you about. "My white friends talked about me behind my back. The people who I thought were my friends in the Black Student Coalition kept trying to tell me how to live my life. Then some bitch in the Coalition left my perm in for too long and ruined my hair." She's steamrolling this conversation, and I'm still here sipping and slipping into every detail, relishing in this taste of her life. She's rich, fabulous, and yes, she's a dime a dozen at this University, and yes, of course I believe we should all eat the rich, but—she's the first person like her to ever give me the time of day and right now I'll play therapist, hell I'll even sing out the *DSM-5* as a lullaby. Thesis Committee, I'll do that and even a little more, if it means she approves of me. Talking to her allows me to bite into the life scenes of the upper crusts. "So, I said fuck it and went abroad. I hate it here. This quarter hasn't even started, and I'm already trying to find my way out."

"You've been there and back again," I say in quick agreement. I'm desperate to keep having this conversation. I've been alone all night, waiting for tonight's libations to take effect. It could be nice to talk to someone just as jaded.

"Yep. And here I am, back in this hellscape."

"Could be Mordor."

"Excuse me?"

"There and back again, Bilbo Baggins."

"Huh?"

"*The Hobbit. Lord of the Rings.*" I raise the beer in my hand, pretending that it's a staff, and say in my best Gandalf, "You shall not pass!"

"Oh, are you like a Dungeon and Dragons type?"

The dip in C1's voice alerts me that this type is something that she doesn't want. I finish my beer and laugh off my previous weirdness before responding, "No.* Just a lame joke."

"You're weird, aren't you?" This time, C1 grins after saying *weird*. "I like weird. Weird ones are loyal friends." C1 tosses her cigarette off the balcony. Someone below screams, *what the fuck*. She doesn't notice and opens her Chanel purse. "So, if you don't like fantasy, what *do* you like?"

"No—" Before LP can fully emerge into the conversation, I shift my words. "Nothing, major. Music, books, basic stuff." In an attempt to rid herself of the cigarette's smell, she sprays herself with floral perfume, then chews on a stick of gum. Before too much time of her chewing in silence can pass, I step closer and ask, "Do you want to grab a drink?"

She checks her reflection in a pocket mirror from her purse. Her eyes avert from the glass and to my eager grin. "Oh, uh I'm waiting on someone I'm here with. He said he'll get me a drink. *He* should be coming soon." C1's constant emphasis of *he* heats me with embarrassment. I take a few steps back, then reach for my phone to fake an important text. While I'm typing, she adds, "You can come with me to find *him*, if you want." She reapplies her brown lip liner, then shines her lips in berry-tinted lip gloss. To match her energy, I tussle my braids.

We move from the apartment's balcony toward the party's nucleus—the kitchen. Most students crowd around the countertops covered in a mix of half-full bottles of vodka, pop, rum, gin, tonic water, and tequila. She offers to get a drink for me, and before I can tell her what I want, she departs for the fridge. I remain near the back door, which

---

* That's a lie. If I had the patience, I would hatch into a D&D chick.

exits toward the balcony. I lean against the wall and wait, praying for the alcohol to slime my thoughts.

*      *      *

C1 returns with a beer and a boy. He has khaki-colored skin and an ass chin. His sunken eyes are the color of whiskey and above these whiskey eyes are his bushy eyebrows, filled with the bushmeat of dead skin. The front of his lime shirt reads in black letters CAUTION: STUDENT LIVER.

He asks, "What do you have planned for the rest of tonight?"

"Nothing," C1 replies.

"We should hang after."

"Sahara, come with us? This party's dead," C1 says.

"Thanks, but I'm waiting on a few friends," I lie. As they talk with one another, I'm the spare tire, only referenced when their conversation needs new momentum. Every chance he gets, Student Liver tilts himself sideways to graze his hands against her back. I finish my beer and the next kick of the drunkenness temporarily washes the scum of discomfort and jealousy off me. Student Liver's hands walk farther down C1's back. He's telling her that if she's on break with her boyfriend, anything that happens doesn't matter. Tired of being in the trunk of in their moment, I tell them, *I should go.*

"Don't leave, we just met." C1 steps away from Student Liver and pulls out a small glass bottle from her purse.

"What is it?"

"A popper for relaxation."

While holding the cap between her glossed lips, she sniffs first. Then Student Liver, then me. Heat rushes to my head and I tilt it back. All my thoughts are at rest, and for a moment, the intensity of the alcohol and popper freeze my involvement with time. I stay out on the balcony and listen to C1 and Student Liver flirt. As they talk, I think,* growing anxious and restless. I wonder what would happen if I jumped off the balcony. The fall wouldn't kill me—it would break a femur at most, maybe the sounds of a bone breaking would shock Student Liver, best-case scenario he's a little traumatized.

A question from C1 retrieves me from my wondering. I ask her to repeat herself because I don't understand. After her words are restated, there's still nothing. Her words are too disjointed by the time they enter my minefield of a mind.

Student Liver says slowly, laughing at the rate he has to speak in order for me to understand, "C O M E back to MY"—he points at his chest—"APART-MENT." His antics snap me into the present, I answer *no*. "Come on, Sahara, it'll be fun." I'm here enough to tell this fucker, "No."

"Come on, Sahara, he'll smoke us out," C1 says, grinning, and rubbing Student Liver's back.

"It'll be fun, Sahara." Student Liver tips toward me, then raises his index finger, as if he's instructing me on a crucial lesson, "And according to the president we are crème de la crème. And I say the best of the best needs to play harder than they work."

*Next time*, I promise. I leave C1 and Student Liver. As I exit the party unnoticed, I steal a bottle of gin that sat forgotten in the spare bedroom turned coat room. With gin hiding under my fleece, I walk to my dorm, chanting to myself yes, I'm the best of the best, I deserve all the fun.

---

* This thinking won't ever end. Even when my brain shuts off to sleep, I dream my thoughts, spiraling down into that day's word worlds. One remedy for heavy dreams that I picked up last year is two pink Benadryls and two beers. Pop two bennies, down those beers, and bam, you're a sleeping beauty.

## CRÈME DE LA CRÈME

*With closed eyes, Me, a prototype Black, stands in a giant glass case. Her hair is in a perfect Afro and her skin is the right shade of brown, i.e., not too dark. She is naked, and a Chelsea Smile is cut into her face. Next to her are four other prototype people of color who stand with closed eyes inside glass cases. They too are naked and have Chelsea Smiles.*

*The Academy Leader enters the stage, and other members of the Academy follow him. They all wear vibrant Victorian suits and dresses. The Academy Leader's right hand is a giant white cane with a golden tip. He is the proudest showman in all of academia.*

*Once the Academy Leader and members of the Academy enter the stage, the people of color inside glass cases open their eyes. Me's hands are sewn together, stuck open in the begging position. Me repeats, "I'm just happy to be here. I promise I'm one of the good ones." Tears of "gratitude" walk down her cheeks.*

*The next person in the second case has a war bonnet sewn onto his scalp. He cries throughout the play.*

*The third person is coated with glitter that has been applied with rubber cement. His hand rests on his hip as he repeats, "Yas, hunty. I'm hereeee, your neighborhood queer."*

*The fourth person has two guns glued onto his hands. He screams out, "I've seen some shit. Shit you can't even believe." He continues to scream. His exhaustion causes his eyes to water.*

*The fifth person has two money bags glued into her hands. She is naked except for her shoes. One of her feet is kicked up to display her red-bottomed Oxfords. She says in a 1920s posh accent, "You see, I'm different. I descend from the original members of the Niggerati. I read Langston Hughes's grammar books in Mompsie's air-conditioned womb."*

**THE ACADEMY LEADER:** *(His voice is amplified by a microphone, drowning out the showcase's screams, crying, and repeating.)* Come one, come all! Come see the diversity showcase. According to New News and You, we have the fifth best in the nation. Come close and see! Look at this progress! Isn't it grand?

*Members of the Academy clap and scream huzzah. They knock on the glass cases, examining what's inside.*

**THE ACADEMY LEADER:** They are the crème de la crème. The cherry-picked, the curated, the best of the best.

**ACADEMY MEMBER 1:** Do you have ones from the hood?

**THE ACADEMY LEADER:** Why, yes, of course, madame! Just turn to your left and you'll see one straight from the jungles of your scariest hood. *(Runs over to the fourth case. Leans toward Academy Member 1 and whispers in her ear.)* Rumor has it that they were born and bred in Chiraq.

**ACADEMY MEMBER 1:** Oh, my.

**ACADEMY MEMBER 2:** Do you have any Native Americans?

**THE ACADEMY LEADER:** *(Gallops over to the second case.)* It took some time. They're a little hard to find, but we were destined to manifest one. Now look and see!

**ACADEMY MEMBER 3:** Any gay ones?

**THE ACADEMY LEADER:** Sir, we are the fifth best for diversity in the country. Of course we have gay ones. *(Somersaults toward the third case.)* We've been told that straight is so passé, so we kicked out some of the straight models and added in new gay ones. *(The Academy Leader snaps feistily.)* Aren't they so glittery?

**ACADEMY MEMBER 4:** *(Huffs as she pulls up her pants and wipes clean the spectacle that is infused in her right eye, causing for puffed, infected skin to bevel over the lens.)* This is great and all, but do you have traumatized ones?

**THE ACADEMY LEADER:** *(Looks disgusted.)* Ma'am, we are still the Academy. We DO NOT admit them unless they have been traumatized.

*All five faces in the cases fall into Elmer Fudd frowns. The Academy Leader bows. Members of the Academy wander around the glass cases. Member 4 taps on Me's case and it topples over. Both the glass and Me shatter into pieces.*

**ACADEMY MEMBER 4:** Oh no, I think I broke it.

**THE ACADEMY LEADER:** Unfortunate, but it's okay! It happens all the time. *(He looks to the side of the stage.)*
We have a code blue, again. *(Two new members of the Academy enter the stage. They are dressed in blue hazmat jumpsuits. They sweep up the pieces of the glass and Me, then exit the stage. Seconds later, one of the jumpsuits wheels in another glass case. Inside is someone who looks just like Me—#twins.)*

**THE ACADEMY LEADER:** You can't even tell the difference! Now, let me take you to the classroom to show what our curated crème de la crème learn while they are with us at the Academy.

# AMERICA
## THE TERRIBLE

I wake up at seven in the morning.* I turn to the side and see Roommate isn't there. Even though it's 2013, and from overheard news conversations, I'm learning that the terror and trauma never ends, I'm not curious enough to tell my RA. Roommate's probably fine. Best-case scenario she demanded another dorm room closer to campus.

I'm praying that my headache and nausea go away. A few *Dear Lords* pass, my prayers go unanswered.† The only response from the universe is the DADS.‡ I drag myself out of bed and as I sit on the toilet, I stare at myself in the mirror. Cellulite pulls my thighs, and the only

---

* One of the many things wrong with this body is that it's never able to sleep after a night out. It wakes up early, trying to piece together whether it had fun with the rest of me the night before.

† God must be saving His intervention for when:
  I need salvation from alcohol poisoning.
  I need an extension for a midterm.

‡ Day After Drinking Shits.

interruption is the cutting scars that started around 2006. The dried blood from my last night's afterparty of cutting sits at the center of my left thigh. After washing my hands, I drench the last wad of toilet paper on my skin. Dab, dab, dabbing at the blood till it's saturated with water. I try to peel off the scabbed patches of skin. These scars—a combination of dashes and dots—are the evidence of me searching for ways to unzip this body and see where the wrongness rests. Is it in my thighs, stomach, or just in my mind? If I keep cutting, there's a chance I might find out.

\*       \*       \*

This sadness, depression, this thing has existed in me for over a decade. I know it'll be passed on to my children, which in all honesty, I can't even imagine having. I'm already pushing into a size eighteen. Rumor has it that with every kid, you get fatter and sadder. Children always see their mothers naked. Their innocent eyes fall from breasts, stomach, and then thighs. How do I explain my scars when they ask what happened to Mommy?

This body won't have kids. It won't give them a sadness and it won't send them to a college with the Future Racist Intellectuals of America.

I need to stop complaining. I should do a little tap dance, as a showcase of my thankfulness to have this work in your presence, O Thesis Committee. As I'm spinning and cartwheeling in these rehearsed moves, I'll also honor Mother's and Father's hard work to get me here. Yes, yes, I know, my parents didn't send me here to imagine having kids or to sniff out the racist students. Parents' trauma outperforms yours.* They survived, so survival should be in my DNA, right?

---

\*  In medical school, one of Father's professors was convinced that Father didn't know

\*   \*   \*

It's 2:30 p.m. on a Saturday, and Jackson Dining Hall is crowded with the hungovers, the sleep-in-ers, the visitors, the meal-swipe stealers, and the regular lunch eaters. The dining hall closes in thirty minutes, so I pack my plate with any of the day's remains that I can stomach. I push the dry cellentani into marinara sauce. I continue shifting my fork around, hoping this movement will emulsify the pasta sauce and oil a bit better. While conducting this science experiment, two students from my dorm sitting next to me are bragging about prework and the current suffering they've accomplished for classes that haven't even started. Conversations like this—students trying to flaunt their intellectual value—aren't unusual. This University's culture promises rewards for suffering. The greater the suffering, the greater the isolation, the greater your graduation celebration. All we, you, they, and hell even I want is a recognition, concrete evidence of our worth, that exists outside our minds and the obligatory coos from those closest to you.

  Dear Committee, don't let these students worry you. There's nothing

---

proper English. The professor always cold-called Father and corrected his English in front of the class. Another African in the class, an Ethiopian, supported Father and was the only reason Father survived school. He brought Heineken to study sessions and knew how to calm Father down on days his rage was so strong it produced tears. Throughout school, the white students unleashed hell on Father and his friend. They ignored them, studied, and vowed to show them what they knew. Father and his friend graduated first and second of their 1986 class.

  As Father struggled in medical school, Mother struggled with her paralegal certificate. Like me, Mother had extreme anxiety when she was in school. She always stuttered and said the wrong thing. The students laughed. She overheard a male classmate say that he was tired of seeing the faces of niggers who don't belong here. After overhearing this, Mother cried in my aunt Nita's arms until my aunt pinched Mother's arm and told her to stop all that and finish up. Mother did what my aunt Nita instructed and finished up. Years later, Mother conducted a job interview for that classmate. They sat across from one another. Face-to-face. He wasn't hired.

that needs to be changed. Here, the torment is the joie de vivre. I know it's been a while since you've descended from the penthouse suite in your ivory tower. And, of course, I am not one to assume that you all received your intellectual pedigrees from this University. So please, let me help you slip into our shoes. Imagine this: You're here and it's your first week on campus. You haven't made any true friends yet. You're curious to find out more truths about your campus while you're still in that appropriate window of arrival time to panic-call your friends back home. Ring, ring. Hang up the phone. Your high school friends are too busy making their new college identities. Goodbye Scene Kid, hello Beer Pong MVP. Don't worry. Hmm, wait this is all too abstract. I'm still sensing your worries. You need concrete data to show there's nothing to fear. As a measure of good faith, I'll tell you about last year.

*     *     *

My first year, outside of the crying, the anxiety, and the general appetite for self-destruction, there were the dropped classes, the W's,* the constant GPA calculations, the office hours where I stammered and fidgeted, the surprise periods during three-hour lectures, the ghosting of student organizations that took themselves too seriously, there were the frat parties with grinding, face sucking, and spiked-drink avoiding, and, of course, the constant leaping† over the University seal in Churchill—ah yes, it's coming back to me now—there were the failed cigarette lightings during the frozen tundra called winter, the slob sessions in library elevators, empty classrooms, and apartment corners,

---

\* The scarlet letter painted on a transcript every time a student withdraws from a course after add/drop ends.

† In the center of Churchill's floor is a gold tile embossed with the University's seal. Legend has it that every time you step on this seal, you add a year to your graduation.

the Future Racist Intellectuals of America masquerading as allies, the stifled screams induced from 5-Hour Energy–fueled all-nighters, but throughout all of this, most importantly, there was the free food, which made everything better.

If you know any students like me who hold off from eating until their hunger causes dizziness, then they will need to know all the closest food sources. So, here's a pro tip, tell them to set up a separate University email and sign up for every major listserv, every student organization, every grad student orientation, and every religious denomination. Do this, and they will feast for days.

*       *       *

I return from the dining hall, and ROD is waiting for me outside the dorm. She's gazing at the unbought mansion, which is across the street. She's peaceful in her stare, mostly unmoved, except for her eyes, which are continually blinking. She takes out the homemade three-by-five notebook she keeps in her pocket, and scribbles sketches. Her staring returns. The beats of silence between us lasts a little too long. I call, *ROD, ROD*, and then scream, "Hello?"

"It's so big."

"Huh?"

ROD turns to me. Her eyes are blazed in red. I direct ROD up the stairs to my dorm room. She tosses her backpack on my bed and plops down against the frame. She's staring at the ceiling's beveling paint. Her neck's bent upward like the right side of *Guernica*. Trying to help ROD avoid a sore neck, I take out her shattered iPad from her backpack, open the screen to her favorite high show, torrented episodes of *Adventure Time*, and tell her to watch this instead. As she keeps restarting the episode, ROD asks about last night's party. My tongue is on autopilot. It says that last night was fun, and I met interesting people, but when I feel the sting of last night's cuts, I stop and recalibrate the conversation. Instead of relishing in rehearsed joys, my tongue complains about the two science courses I'm perilously fated to take for my University's Foundational Education* requirements. Though there are two courses, for now I will only worry about the first one I'm taking this fall. It'll require more time, which means more work, which means more stress, which ultimately, if I do well, means a higher catharsis, a final relief. (See, Thesis Committee, I've learned something. That means I've earned my scholarships, right?)

LP's jumped ahead from our reflexive thoughts and plans our ending. She's tired of waiting, leaving me to constantly explain that I need to prove that there was is something within me worth my exhaustion and the wasted scholarships, Mother's time and ROD's kindness, Father's sacrifices and this confusion. "I'm already over school and the quarter hasn't even started."

"Come on, don't say that. Another year, another chance. I'm going to bid for a dinosaur class so I can—" ROD flips to her belly and skips to another episode. I ask her, *so you can what*. She pauses the episode and removes the pillow that blocks our view of one another. "What are you talking about?"

"Classes."

ROD laughs out, "Yeah, I'm taking classes. That's why we're here." She's too far gone in sativa. I decide that until she de-highs a bit, I'll read and reread Aunt Nita's zine. The images blur into one another, and every word I read lets me rest in her voice's acoustics. There's beauty in her way of language, a way that Mother made sure to lecture

---

* Because the only true way to show your knowledge is to pretend you know everything, the University requires two years of irritating Foundational Education. It's the bane of my existence that is the required training for being a student here, where they train us to become the jack-of-all-trades and master of some.

out of myself, Brother 1, and Brother 2. She believed or maybe hoped that when it was time for us to leave home and masquerade in white America, improper English,* not the histories of white violence, would be the entity to isolate Brothers 1, 2, and myself from their world.

*    *    *

While I read the zine, Aunt Nita's retelling of her disappearance and evidence of searching where to belong, all I can remember are Mother's lessons that she hoped prepared me for worlds like this University. The earliest lessons, *Act right, you don't get a second chance,* or *Don't give them any reasons to treat you any kind of way,* kept compiling and then leading to Mother's lecture album, *Now That's What I Call Black Parenting: The Trauma Edition.* Hits including but not limited to:

**Track 1—"Never Listening"**

*Aunt Nita, rest her busy soul/
never listened like you're not listening now . . .*

**Track 2—"When I Tell You"**

*If she stayed away from the neighborhood/
she would still be here/
so when I tell you to stay away and not do something/
I'm protecting you how no one protected Nita . . .*

---

* As if a finite rule book should exist for something so alive, so fluid, so personal.

**Track 3—"No Nonsense in This House"**

*When I see nonsense happening/*
*I won't stand by like I did before/*
*and what you're trying to do, little girl,/*
*is nonsense in my house . . .*

Now that I'm out of the house, free to do nonsense within my reasons, I try to not resent Mother for her lessons. She's a product of her time, where they believed being four times as good meant you could earn a chance for that star-spangled American Dream. But there are only so many times you can flip it, reverse it, and play Bop It with yourself, before you're belly up, floating in the consciousness of your self-hatred pooled with every swallowed aggression, and every forced forgiveness of their ignorance.

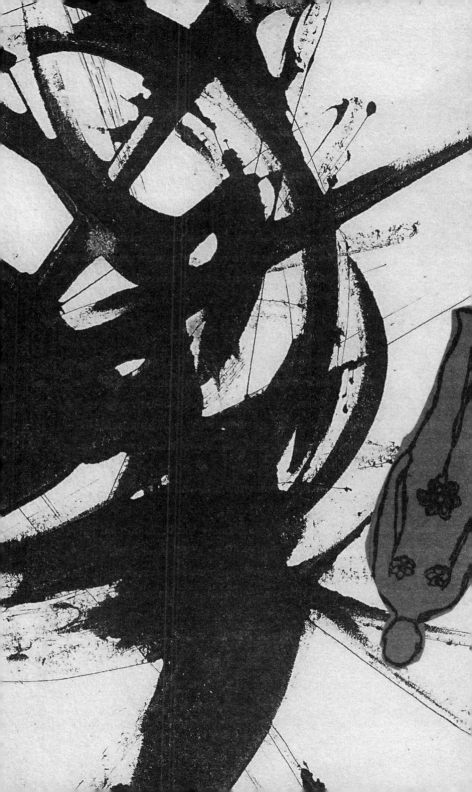

# RETURN OF THE MAC ... AND CHEESE

R OD drops eyedrops into her eyes. Between blinking away tears, she checks her phone for the time. "Damn, the dining halls are closed, and I'm starving. Where do you keep your snacks?" She walks toward my closet, which hides my alcohol.

I jump up from sitting on the floor and block the closet door. "I haven't stocked my snacks yet. There's gotta be something on campus." ROD returns to lounging on my comforter. While on my phone, I open the University email that's reserved for free-food finding. I continue scrolling until I find the open invite for Free Welcome Back BBQ on the main green. ROD's too hungry to walk so we hop on the next campus shuttle. Students and a few lingering parents who aren't ready to say goodbye pack this shuttle. ROD and I are pushed up against one another, clenching the maroon bus straps until we reach the stop that's a short walk to the main green.

While she waits behind a student with Tupperware poking out of his backpack, I leave ROD to use the closest bathroom, which happens to be in Churchill's basement. While in the stall, I overhear, *Tahoe, again,* and other complaints from two students whose summer internships at Morningstar ruined their vacation agendas. Through the slits of the stall's door, as I watch their Longchamp bags bounce against their bodies, I roll my eyes.

There are the rich, the not so rich, and the broke. While enrolled here, I've learned to have envy and then annoyance for classmates whose money pads their life with opportunities, access, and frivolities. On walks to campus, while I'm on the phone with B1 or B2, hearing a retelling of Mother's rant about Father missing another one of B2's elementary school events because of the extra work hours, I'm overhearing student conversations about their current stocks investments and comparing family crests. These colliding realties have taught me that the grass truly is greener on the other side. The reason: while they have the time and energy to water it, we're still trying to figure out if the seeds are in this month's budget.

\*     \*     \*

I return upstairs. There, I walk around the University seal that a velvet rope sections off. Next to a stone column, ROD stands across from two students. Though she's nodding along with them, I see her darting eyes and sucked-in lips, telltale signs that she's annoyed.

"Sahara," she calls out after spotting me. Figuring that there's a reason she wants to escape the conversation, I pretend I can't hear her, and try walking in the opposite direction through a glob of students. There's no reason for both of us to be trapped in the echo chamber of a bad conversation. "Sahara, over here!" she screams. The glob of students separates. A few of them point to ROD. I thank them, even though I already knew her exact GPS location.

When I am across from the students who wear matching boat shoes, I understand her annoyance. These Boat Shoes Boys continue talking at us; I shift my eyes between them, the series of iron-gated windows, and the bulletin board feathered with layers of multicolored flyers that urge students to advocate for their health rights. ROD nudges my arm and repeats one of the Boat Shoes Boys' question: What's my major?

"English."

"Oh," Boat Shoes A responds before smirking with Boat Shoes B. "So, you must not care then about making money—"

"Because you don't come to a school like this just to study words."

"It's waste of your money, isn't it?" Boat Shoes A asks me.

ROD is furiously puncturing holes into her now empty Styrofoam plate. For me, their mockery is just another tally on the board for shit people[*] say. To deal, never cope, because coping means I can process, and $M_O{}^V{}_E$ away from anger's point of origin, I remember Mother's lessons of how to handle their bullshit. I pinch in my anger, smiling as I ask them, "What are your majors?"

"Econ," they answer in unison.

"I simply can't understand how both of you could attend The Institution for Economic Policy, and not study it."

"Maybe we don't want to be responsible for policies that destroy a nation's economy," ROD responds as she cracks her neck. She's had enough. The food helped with her officially de-highing, and now I'm worried for the Boat Shoes Boys. "You know the history of this place and policies, right?" Before either of the Boat Shoes Boys can respond, she answers her own question, "This school is on stolen land. The enslaved built these buildings. The imperialist began teaching, and for

---

[*]  Said people includes Father, who constantly campaigns for me to study medicine, law, or biomedical engineering.

what, huh?" The Boat Shoes Boys are confused—they obviously haven't even taken a course for the major they just flexed for. "For neo-liberalism to appear and cause the worst economic crisis in Chile in the 1980s?" Even though ROD dropped econ last year, she still knows more than they do.* My eyes bounce back and forth among the three of them. Boat Shoes A becomes so flustered that he brings out his new iPhone 5s and begins fact-checking or looking for facts to support the *that's not the whole story* argument he's building in his head.

I'm enjoying watching their popping blood vessels, frantic wiki searches, and waves of white guilt. My joy shifts to awe when ROD's former classmate and my constant crush, Mariah, approaches. Offended that we turned our backs on them, the Boat Shoes Boys slink away.

*   *   *

I first met Mariah during my winter quarter of last year. She sat next to me in Queer Salvation: Art in the AIDS Pandemic,† a class I (and roughly thirty other students‡) desperately wanted to take. For three weeks on MW from 10:30 a.m. to 1:00 p.m., I lived in her brilliance and

---

* In our first year, ROD signed up for an econ course because she was curious and thought it couldn't be that bad . . . it really was that bad.

† Despite my efforts of submitting all the assignments and pleading my case with the professor, there wasn't enough room in the course for underclassmen, and I was never able to officially register. While ranting to ROD about being unable to enroll in the course because of limited seats, and, more importantly, not being in a class with Mariah anymore, ROD realized that Mariah was in her Conceit and Concept: Intro to Conceptual Art class. She understood my crush even more. ROD invited me to work with her and Mariah whenever they had a group project or discussion post. Most of the time they discussed the white nonsenses their classmates said, and I tagged along with their laughter.

‡ While there's never a shortage of classes or professors examining the Poetics of Dead White Men, classes like this, if approved by the department, come once a year.

kindness. Every comment about family and love, her confidence and collectedness, affirmed the beauty I already saw in her eyes. Even as Mariah casually, and frequently, mentioned her partner, it did nothing to stem my infatuation. My brain kept crafting scenes of us spending a Saturday at the Garfield Conservatory, or debating if we were ready to make the next move from snake plants to cats. As I live in this fantasy, protected by its cushiony layers of implausibility, I am worthy. I am beautiful, LP is devoiced, and the brilliant parts of my mind—if they exist—matter more than this scarred body.

"You back yet?" ROD asks. My tendency to zip-line among realities, thoughts, and fantasies leaves ROD constantly having to retrieve me. I think she's used to it by now.

"Almost," I respond.

"—Enough with me. How was everyone's summer, anything fun happen?"

"So hot. I stayed with a cousin in Phoenix, which was nice until the A/C broke week one of a month-long trip," ROD says.

"Shit," Mariah replies. She brushes against me. Her closeness zaps my body. Anxious, my chest and shoulders jump up. Luckily, only ROD notices. "How did you get through it?"

"I'm on a first-name basis with every coffee shop and bookstore that had A/C."

Mariah laughs. The conversation lulls. It's my turn, and to hide their fidgeting, I shove my hands into my jeans' back pockets. "Read and hung out with my brothers."

"Read anything special?"

"Yeah, wait, come to think of it, nothing that interesting."

"Oh, come on, tell her about that one book you wouldn't stop texting me about," ROD comments after yawning, then checks her phone for the campus shuttle's next arrival time.

"Constant texting? It must be good," Mariah responds. "Don't be shy? ██████ is in New York right now. I'll have them visit the Strand and buy a copy."

"*Seven Miles a Second.*" I pause and shove my hands even deeper into my back pockets, rocking slightly back and forth. I try to imagine MP, who is Mariah's Partner, in Manhattan, following up on my suggestion, looking at the book I've picked and pitying me. I know I should describe the haunted life and the illustrations that move with anger; instead, I stammer out, "It's good. I, umm, can't describe why, but it is. I promise."

"I'll text them now to—" Mariah stops speaking and shouts out, *Hold up, I'm coming,* to a group exiting through Churchill's side door. "Sahara, you coming to Shockley[*] for the BSC[†] celebration?"

"I can't." I quickly reply, knowing more time with Mariah is the only chance for my awkwardness to shine. "I gotta get toilet paper and help ROD carry back her order from Blick."

"We'll do it another day," ROD responds. "And Shockley's basement bathroom has wrapped rolls that're easy to steal."

"Come on, then let's go." Mariah begins walking away. My fear of spending too much time with her and accidently embarrassing myself prevents me from moving. But when she turns, and waves me forward, my body feels zapped, again. I follow her with shoved hands in my back pockets both anticipating and prematurely regretting my choice.

\*          \*          \*

---

[*]  Named after William Shockley, winner of the 1956 Nobel Prize in Physics and supporter of eugenics. If Shockley were alive and visiting his building, he would conduct a new research study to discover why there are so many Negroids inside.

[†]  Black Student Coalition.

In Shockley, an emerald rotunda, eight frowning portraits of the University's founding* fathers and their sons ask, "Who let the Blackies in?" For them, my answer is the Common App as I mouth *hi* to fellow students whose names I've forgotten or don't know.[†] As I'm passing from hello to hello, my eyes glimpse the stretch of tables and jump from foil pan to foil pan. I'm guiltily excited that I'll have one more meal that isn't from the dining hall or a cheap, hemorrhoid-causing diner. The combination of steam, savory seasonings, and hunger kick my guilt away. I wait in line and try to decide which food item deserves the first spot on my plate. I can't decide between the Nigerian jollof rice or the plastic wrap corn bread muffins, so I set my plate down, follow what the students before me have done, and grab both simultaneously. After picking something from almost every pan, I look down at my Styrofoam platter of conquests.[‡] The chicken grease creates a small pool of oil that I know will mix well with the jollof rice and collard greens, which are meaty like ya mama. Next to the meaty mama greens are candied yams with a light layer of marshmallows. The sweet stickiness from the marshmallows touches . . . touches . . . wait, it's touching nothing?!? I'm missing the mac and cheese—my only vice behind drinking, smoking, TV bingeing, porn-ing, etc.

I reach for the spoon to pile mac and cheese on my plate, but Mariah murmurs *Don't* under her breath.

"Why?" A thrill that there's now a secret knowledge between us fills me.

---

* It's easy to be a founder when the enslaved did all the building, and you did all the murdering of the land's original inhabitants.

† Often when I must perform familiarity, I must be resourceful and use my childhood trainings of how to be perfect in a Naija world. Key lesson: never admit forgetting a name, face, or Aunty.

‡ Columbus would be so proud of me.

"That shit tastes like spaghetti."

"Spaghetti?"

"Yes, and the game is Guess Who Fucked It Up. I have a theory. More on it later."

I pass the warning on to Hair Braider 1,* who is standing behind me. To hear me, she pushes her twenty-six-inch, indigo, green-tipped wig to her left shoulder. She groans, *damn shame,* and stops reaching for the spoon.

While Mariah warns more people about the mac and cheese, I try to guess who messed up my fifth vice. I'm convinced it's BSC's official gatekeeper, the Lone Caucasian,† the only white board member of BSC. We laugh, and Hair Braider 2 says that sometimes allies can cook. I concede and then propose it was a first-year trying to follow Grandma's recipe, but Grandma didn't want to be bothered, so she hung up the phone. Our laughter loudens and we agree that's a likely scenario. As more people join our circle next to the food, we pause our jokes and warn them about the mac and cheese, saving as many as we can from bubble-gut treachery.

HB2 dabs the grease away from the shined corners of her mouth and mutters, "I wish every day could be this celebration. I only see people when they need their hair done."

The laughter fades. For a second, no one speaks and so HB2 con-

---

* HB1 is the best hair braider and stylist on campus. Piss her off, and your edges will be gone by midterm season. HB2 has upped her styling skills. She's admitted that she used to have her clients' parts as wide as the Red Sea. Though she's gotten better and she and HB1 are the campus's only hopes for affordable hair styling, she isn't planning on doing hair this year. She doubts she'll have the time or energy.

† Legend has it that LC has been on the board for eight years. He's a PhD student and uses his connections to ensure that BSC secures funding for events. If his name isn't part of the proposal, BSC won't get funding.

tinues. "Seriously, you guys. Where y'all at? I feel like I'm always alone here."

I look down at my plate. We all have a reason for not being around. Some more than others.

*Survival*, I think.

Someone articulates my thought. I'm afraid to look up. I'm worried people will see LP and her sadness leaking from my head. What if she's changed the white of my eyes to a different shade of mildewed pain?

HB2 keeps talking, ruminating on survival. "That's what Alicia said all the time before she did it."

I don't want anyone to look at me but I can't help blurting out, "I remember. She used to live in my old dorm.""

We sit in silence and grow uncomfortable. Someone says, *Oh, this got sad.* I'm not sure who. I try to help by tossing some laughter back into the room.

"Well, welcome to campus where guaranteed sadness is included in the Student Life fee."

The others laugh gratefully, and we return to jokes about the mac and cheese, how much toilet paper we can steal before we're arrested, and how to find a sugar momma or daddy so we can drop out and travel. The jokes become more desperate, insistent on drowning out the silence. With laughter, we can remain together.

When an extra burst of our laughter rips through the music, LC, the Lone Caucasian, comes around and shouts, "THIS is where the fun is."

---

* What I wanted to say: She used to live in the room two doors down from me, and over spring break, she killed herself inside her dorm room. No one knew she was dead for days. When we returned to the dorms, the University police only inspected her room because of complaints about the smell. Her death is the reason why I decide to move to a new dorm that's so far away from campus.

He grabs a spoonful of mac and cheese and tosses it onto his plate. He makes room for himself in the circle. The laughter ends.

LC declares, "Every year, I'm so happy to be part of *this*. BSC has so much culture and life, it's a showcase of the University's crème de la crème."

He eats more mac and cheese and wipes what looks like a piece of something—maybe unmelted cheese, maybe egg, hell, maybe unboiled noodle—off his mouth. The piece falls onto the floor, and as his body shifts, his foot mashes it into the burgundy carpet. His body continues shifting until he sets his plate down and then begins biting his nails like a rabid rabbit. He inserts the chewed bits of nail into his front jeans' pocket. Everyone watches but says nothing.

"This University has so many opportunities for students like you. I want to make sure that I'm here every step of the way to guide you and give you access to whatever you need. Think of me as your personal keycard." He adds more mac and cheese to his plate. "Has anyone else tried this? It's not too shabby. I made it myself in under twenty minutes."

Mariah responds, "We will, once we get a little room in our stomachs."

"Aight, aight," LC responds in his best blaccent as he dances away to the Motown music playing in the background.

# REUNITED AND IT FEELS
# TOO GOOD

The event ended two hours ago and the mac and cheese is the only food left. Crumpled napkins and contorted aluminum pans fill a gallery of black trash bins. Half the lights are off. Despite all the signs telling us it's time to go home, we're still here, trying to stretch time.

HB1 has a mini speaker and plays her "Chi City" playlist. Mariah tells her to add "Money Trees" to the queue. A circle of people next to us are planning where to have the afterparty. Another circle is trying to decide a name for our group chat. Eventually, the circles merge into one, causing conversations to fly across the room.

\*     \*     \*

"Call it, *it's lit.*" "We have to figure out where we're going." "No, call it Black Excellence." "Nah, that's too long." "Call it the Soul Circle." "We could swipe in the dining hall? It might still be open." "Call it

Campus Jam." "How about my place?" "Do you have any furniture yet?" "No, but there's room for everyone. That's what matters." "But where are we going to sit?" "We can stand." "We've been standing all day." "Make chat name emojis." "Nah, that's too—" "Call it the Resistance." "—hipster." "The what?" "The Resistance." "What if some white person sees it—" "Y'all we need to hurry up and pick a place my feet are tired." "—and thinks we're trying to start some shit?" "So what?" "Watch a scandal happen, and we get kicked out." "Don't be dumb. We wouldn't get kicked out. They need us for diversity posters." "You know they've used the same photo for like fifteen years—" "How about that breakfast spot by the library?" "—They have our pictures and numbers for their website, they don't need us anymore." "Uh-uh, that spot has rats in the back." "Remember what happened to my ex . . ." "Which one, I stopped keeping track." "The fourth year I was with in my second year." "Oh the premed one, didn't he almost get expelled?" "Damn near, because of a group chat he started with students the University—" "How about we chill on the green?" "—hospital fucked over." "The green? Wasn't it raining today?" "Wait, that doesn't make any sense." "I don't think it's supposed to." "Can we please hurry up and pick a place. My feet hurt." "Get this, he was collecting—" "No one told you to wear those stilettos." "—stories about students' negative experiences and he planned on publishing—" "Let's just sit outside then." "—an article about it. Well, someone in the group—" "You know if all of us sit on the quad we'll scare the white people so much—" "—chat sent screenshots to Dean ███████, and shit got—" "—they'll stop playing Frisbee." "—messy and basically if my ex didn't agree not to publish anything—" "Do we have a place yet?" "—against the University hospital, then he would've been expelled." "Damn, Dean ███████. He stays fucking up." "Who?" "Oh, Dean ███████, I can't stand him either." "I'll catch y'all later—" "He's always smiling in—" "—I'm going home to soak." "—patrol cars like he's Axel Foley."

*       *       *

Mariah leaves the conversation circle to help the BSC members who have started cleaning up. I join her, and stack empty aluminum pans onto one another. With one hand on her hip and her other arm around my shoulder, she tells me, "Every year he brings a bad dish that tastes like hell, and every year someone in BSC has to throw away his concoction of bubble guts. Last year, it was peach cobbler sans peaches. This year, it's this mac and cheese." We both look down at the pan of mac and cheese. Clumps of Velveeta wink at us. "Sahara, this year, it's your honor. Next year, you'll pass the baton to someone else."

I march into the bathroom, and when inside, I remember my primary mission. I pack three giant rolls of toilet paper in my backpack, and then scrape out the mac and cheese. When I return to the celebration, the building manager at Shockley tells us it's time to leave so she can close up shop. Members of the BSC say their goodbyes. There are still some of us who want to continue living in this moment. We finally decided on a place to have the afterparty.

Drum roll, please—/\/\/\/\/\/\/\/\/\/\/\/\/\/\/\/\/—a diner.

The diner of our choosing is Voices of Reason because it's friendly to our perpetually empty wallets. Though we're broke and the food is

---

* According to Mariah, every year someone suggests two things to LC. The first, he does not bring any food. The second, he should step down from his position as the leader. He dismisses both suggestions, especially the last one. He believes he can't leave BSC because he doesn't know anyone as qualified or experienced to take over his position.

cheap, the sounds in this diner are *rich*. As your butt and back squeak against the booth's ripped pleather, speeches* or audiobooks play in the background. These iconic words collide with drunk confessions, exhausted sighs, and roaring laughter.

I stare at the divided wall, the bottom half painted lateritious and the top half melon. Both halves are covered in a massive collection of crooked picture frames that display potted plants, famous visitors, and LIVE, LAUGH, EAT placards. I haven't forgotten my gluttony at the celebration, and as I'm sitting next to Mariah, I'm paranoid that my body is smooshing hers. When menus are passed around, I study the options, and even join in on the conversation of what sounds tempting. Mariah asks if I want to split a large order of fries. I should say no. My mind's estimating that I've already had roughly seven hundred extra calories for today. Mariah's watching me, waiting for my answer. I respond *definitely*, because it is a normal response for someone who is happy, someone Mariah would want.

While waiting for our food, HB1 and HB2 leave for the bathroom. When they return, HB1 one holds HB2 by the arms. "Imma walk her out. I'll be right back." Worried glances are exchanged at the table. No one says what I predict most of us are thinking. Has HB2 reached her breaking point?

"Is she okay?" one of us asks once HB1 returns.

"Yeah, she's figuring out some stuff." HB1's sitting at the end of the booth, tapping her acrylics against the table. "███ was right. We never see each other enough."

"True, true."

"Let's not worry about that. Let's just enjoy ourselves," says another.

---

* Speeches are the only thing the owner will play.

"Nah, that's not enough. We need to do something about it," HB1 responds. "Why has it taken this long for us to have a group chat? All the other groups have one."

"LC doesn't want one because he thought it would deter in-person gathering."

"Fuck LC," HB1 replies. "He doesn't even know what BLM means. This is for us." HB1 orders those of us who don't have it to download WhatsApp and begins adding us to the group chat. She points a fry toward everyone at the table. "None of us will disappear this year." HB1 pauses, listening closely to the background audiobook that comments *that the most dangerous creation is,* well we miss the middle part because we're trying to figure out whose number was accidentally added. HB1 shouts, *shhh.* We hear the end bit of *nothing to lose.* "That's right," HB1 affirms. "We have nothing else to lose, well maybe some dollars, outside of that we're only moving up, together."

*    *    *

One by one, everyone at the table makes the promise that we won't disappear when the quarter becomes hectic. And even I promise and carry the shame that even the joy of this group and this moment is still not enough to keep me here beyond my second year. LP's reveling in the irony. She's explaining that if I simply walked back to my dorm and denied Mariah's invitation, I could've avoided bringing future pain to this group. As always, she's right.

The check comes and I give Mariah my share for the fries. She won't accept it. I didn't have any. "You should've told me you didn't want fries."

"I did, I mean I wanted fries but lost my appetite," I reply as I tuck my crumpled dollars into my fraying wallet.

Outside the diner, we say our goodbyes. Mariah and HB1 are off to meet their partners, and the other members of the BSC are hopping on the University shuttle or scattering toward their dorms. A member, after learning of my dorm's distance, keeps insisting that I shouldn't walk home and should take the shuttle instead. After minutes of back-and-forth, she accepts that I'll be fine, and urges me to message the chat once I'm home. Even though we've already hugged everyone goodbye thrice, we all hug one another again. A University patrol car with Dean ███████[*] sitting shotgun stops next to us. Dean ███████ rolls down his window and waves at us. None of us wave back and instead start the fifth and final round of hugs.

---

[*] Dean ██████, the dean of undergraduate students.

# THE OLD WORKOUT PLAN

The group chat name the majority of us agreed upon is Black Excel, and all day there have been nonstop notifications. The best post from today is from Mariah. She sent a photo of mac and cheese with the caption *now this is how you mac.*

A hundred messages later, I realize I'm one of the few who haven't chimed in. I comment that Mariah's food looks so good that I need it for my soul. The heart emojis start pouring in. *Aces, Aces!* I seem so normal, so chic, so social when chitchatting.

I'm so good at pretending that for a moment I forget that food, when in me, isn't nourishing for the soul. Growing up, food deprived it and plumped the body. Food made Father say, *You're getting too fat.* It made Mother repeat, *One ounce to the lips is a pound to the hips.* It made kid-me believe that no matter what I did, pound upon pound would be added to a ballooning body.

I did find a temporary solution to a permanent problem in tenth grade. I ate a thousand calories a day. I picked up tricks like having coffee with honey for breakfast and lunch, or waiting till 3:00 p.m. to eat so you can binge your calories for the day, then napping to forget hunger, and, of course, sparkling water and Altoids if you want to feel full.

The diet came with benefits.

1.  I got my first kiss.*
2.  I wore a bikini.
3.  LP seemed to shrink her space in my head.

---

* First kiss happened during a band weekend trip to the UP, and it was the scandal of the Geek Century—I, a newly skinny flute player, and always-skinny Drummer Boy performed for the top high school band directors in the Midwest. After the performance, High School Best Friend said she could see sparks flying every time he hit the drums. The woodwinds couldn't believe I'd caught the attention of a drummer; they thought I could've snagged a bass clarinet, at best. HSBF said that Drummer Boy was looking for a serious girlfriend and was falling head over heels for me. I didn't believe HSBF, and I ignored everything she said until a judge pulled me aside and told me it was the chemistry during the performance that won them over. Drummer Boy and I won first place for our performance and we wore our matching medals on the bus ride back to the camp.

That night after our win, there was a bonfire on the beach by the lake. Drunk off sugar, Drummer Boy and I snuck away from the chaperones. We dipped our feet in the water and plastic pop rings tickled our toes. It was the perfect moment. I was pimple-free, feeling skinny in my bikini, and talking to him vis-à-vis. He said it looked like we were about to kiss so I kissed him. Light-headed from my first kiss or missing my dinner of Altoids, I felt as if I could've floated away in the water.

Drummer Boy held my hand and we walked back to the bonfire with the rest of the students. When we returned and two woodwinds saw me holding hands with Drummer Boy, they gasped and shared the news to the rest of the woodwinds, brass players, and percussionists.

During that weekend, I was convinced Drummer Boy and I were going to date. We even held hands during the entire bus ride back. When we returned to Southfield, he told me he had a girlfriend. However, he was willing to dump her if I could prove I was committed to him. I asked how I could prove my love and he replied, "fuck me ;) ." With HSBF, I bought lingerie from TJ Maxx, but the day after lingerie shopping, I got my period. By the time it was over, Drummer Boy had found a new girlfriend.

The diet came with costs:

1.   I was sick often.*
2.   I didn't have energy to do anything besides study, so I had to quit my extracurriculars.

I couldn't keep up with the diet. One meal turned to two, two meals to three, and then three meals to three meals and some snacks. I plumped back up and threw away the bikini.

My resentment for my body lives in every fold, every jiggle, and dimple. I wish I had the cash to treat this body like Mrs. Potato Head, the Beverly Hills edition—remove arms, legs, and stomach, repeating again and again, until I'm perfect.

So, there, that's the truth, which I can't say in the group chat. A truth like this might escape into campus and cause a matrix of consequences.† But I'll trust you with it, Thesis Committee, you understand that the personal is never academic. Hatred, me, and my pain don't matter until they're theory.

---

* One time I got too sick and never had the same lung capacity afterward, which made playing the flute difficult. I went from second chair to last. The next trimester after the demotion, I quit band.

† Second Disappeared Girl, who used to live in my old dorm, didn't disappear in the X-Files or Girl, Interrupted kind of way. She disappeared in a "Fuck This Shit" kind of way. Second Disappeared Girl's roommate told her friend who told her boyfriend who told the RA that they all thought SDG had an eating disorder. Their reasoning? They didn't know of any Black girls who were that tiny. The RA, along with Dean ████████, and SDG's roommate, roommate's friend, and roommate's friend's boyfriend, sat SDG down and told her that it was in her best interest that she take a leave of absence. SDG didn't get a chance to tell them that she'd had malabsorption issues since she was a child, causing for her decreased appetite and slim frame. After a two-hour intervention, she decided to transfer schools. She hated it here anyway and was tired of people at our school diagnosing her after watching one episode of Doctor Oz.

## THE NEGOTIATION

*Inside a legal office, Me and LP sit at opposite sides of a steel double ped-estal desk. Both wear 1980s power suits with shoulder pads that are the length of the desk. Between them is a contract, two pens, and two glasses of water. LP sits with crossed legs as she fiddles her suspenders. To the right of her is a mini calendar where every month has motivational phrases such as "tomorrow could be worse than today," "nothing is better than an unknown something," and "there's no 'u' in happy." Me pats down the ruffles on her bell-sleeved blouse. Both take a sip of water. Dolly Parton's "9 to 5" plays softly in the background. It's time for the negotiations to begin.*

LP: *(pounds her forefinger into the table)* Why not today? It'll be easy enough, even for you. Train, lake, pills. Pick one and we'll make it happen. *(LP sees Me's hesitation.)* Don't tell me you think there's a reason for you. We've been over this. You're a stuffed sad sack.

ME: *(sits back with her hands tucked in her pockets)* Jesus, then why the hell did I unpack?

LP: You weren't listening.

ME: *(rolls eyes)* I'm always listening.

LP: So today then?

ME: No, not today.

LP: *(stands up)* When? Tomorrow, next week. *(Rubs temples in frustration.)* It's always the same shit with you. How about Christmas?

ME: Christmas?

LP: Yes, Christmas. It's not even Jesus's real birthday. You can repack your things after finals. Hell, you can even spend Christmas and

New Year's with your family. *(Walks over to Me and begins bargaining in Me's ear.)* When the celebrations are over, you get on a train to Chicago, and get off somewhere random, like Niles, Michigan, and then that's when you'll do it.

ME: So close to the holidays?

LP: *(Leaves Me's side. LP kicks her chair in frustration.)* What is it going to take for you to agree?

ME: I need one year of being worth something, then I'm all yours.

LP: One quarter.

ME: Two quarters.

LP: A quarter and a half.

ME: Deal.

LP: *(signs contract)* That'll bring us to February.

ME: *(signs contract)* Plenty of time.

LP: *(shakes Me's hand)* Too much of it, if you ask me.

ME: We'll see.

# "SOMEWHERE UNDER THE ARCHWAY"*

First class of the quarter is HSR, High School Revisited. In this Intro to Writing class, we revisit the great novels we were supposed to have read in high school.† It's the first day, and Mr. Adjunct, in an attempt to prove the intellectual worth that his paycheck doesn't show, has set in stone our papers' due dates. People with a last name starting

---

\* "Somewhere under the Archway"
*Somewhere under the archway/*
*Right by Sorority Row/*
*The dreams that I dreamed of/Once in a school day, oh/*
*Somewhere under the archway/Bluebooks fly/*
*Those dreams that I dreamed of/Once in a school day, oh/Those dreams you crucify/*
*Some class I'll wish upon a clock/When I look up, students all around/*
*And answers melt with anxiety/*
*With a silenced tongue that's how/You'll find me, oh/*
*Somewhere under the archway/*
*Right by Sorority Row/*

† First rule about discussion club is that you don't admit what you haven't read.

with I–N have papers due the Sunday before the second week, O–Z's papers are due the Sunday before the third week, and A–H, the Sunday before the fifth week. Then around and around we go until the quarter is over. He tells us that since the papers are based on books we should've already read, he expects, especially from the first group of names, quality papers even with these quick turnarounds. As luck would have it, I'm in the first group, and writing a paper on *The Awakening* this weekend. All, I remember—the main character's husband was shit, her kids annoying, and she definitely, well maybe, died at the end. That's enough to write a paper, right?

\*    \*    \*

High school–me loved writing. I thought I had something to say. The teachers who all slept through their classes or slept with each other loved anything that was interesting enough to make them forget about another year of defaulting on their mortgages. The consistent A's and constant encouragement from teachers who saw you were at least a little interested made me believe that writing could be the one thing I liked about myself.

My first year, the more I wrote, the more I hated myself. I could never craft a good sentence. I was never in conversation with the right forefathers of accepted knowledge. My classmates who attended schools where funding was never in question were already expanding their understandings about pre and post this and thats. As their knowledge expanded, I was still waiting on my used books whose shipping from CheapBooksUSA was delayed, again.

Every assignment, every class, where I am one of the University's trophies, and my skin is a placard that reads BLACKIES THAT MADE IT, I survey my classmates' comments and their stares. I don't know who or when, but eventually someone will need me to explain my presence in their space because they believe that I, not the trust-fund spin-off of *Bébé's Kids*, took someone's spot at this University. As I wait, preparing for their questions, their judgments, their infantilizing intrigue, I fill notebooks' margins, and used books' blank ending pages with my thoughts so they can speak then scream.

\* \* \*

In today's notebook retreat, LP and I discuss my facts of life. She finds it humorous that while Father survived a civil war, I can't survive a lecture. She goads me to leave the lecture and begin planning my suicide. I tell her to *shhh*, because it isn't time yet. I am still unfinished.[*] LP quiets and her silence allows me to pay attention to the discussion on *The Awakening*. Mr. Adjunct asks, "Was Edna's[†] death justified?" Those paying attention are divided. A handful see life as annoying, but in the end still bearable. The others view death as liberating—if and only if your life is restrained. A classmate asks, "Why wouldn't you want to die? Motherhood makes you insane. Literally, there was a mom this week who tried driving through the White House.[‡] You can't tell me that it wasn't motherhood that made her lose her mind."

Though her response is an extreme, half narration of a person's life

---

[*] *Allez vous-en! Allez vous-en! Sapristi!* It'll be all right. My unfinished business won't keep me here for long; it's only a few goodbye letters, a couple of pensive smokes, a last round of shots, and a few good grades.

[†] She definitely didn't make it. That's good to know for the paper.

[‡] A member of the Black Excel group posted about Miriam Carey, a Black mother who was allegedly a threat to national security. There had to be other factors outside of motherhood that made her make her decision. More importantly, there had to be other solutions other than her two police officers murdering her to protect the White House.

and family, students nod and reply, *totally.* LP is enthralled, grateful that we stayed for the lecture, learning the conditions where death can be justified. Since there are students in the class agreeing, LP wants to know why we are waiting. I re-explain that there are things that I still want to try, and she says, *Fine, go ahead then.* She's right. If I'm so adamant about staying here, then I should speak, and prove there's something in me worth this lingering. I'm rereading my responses, which are scribbled in margins. On paper, my anger and intellect are alive, ready to attack. I know classmate's use of *insanity* is a mistranslation that forgets key words such as *choice, disparity, resources, violence, death.* It is a privileged narrative that's unable to fathom the weight of bringing life into a world intent on the deaths of you and your kin. I rehearse my response, then begin speaking. "For marginalized communities, like Black"—fuck, I'm sputtering in spouts—"communities, life is"—I falter, drifting into the thought of Mother. She prayed for children. She believed bringing life was resistance—"a reclaiming," I say, conflicted. Even with knowing my history, I constantly deny this life.

The classmate interjects, "Well, for feminists like me, family is oppression. And what? You're the voice for all African Americans now?"

"No, but—"

"Women have always been slaves to their homes and children."

"Yes, bu—"

"Yeah but what? We never had a chance to pursue our professional or political interests until the first wave. That's wrong, right?"

Classmates turn to me, waiting for my rebuttal. With eyes against me, I mummer, *of course.* Mr. Adjunct replies, *Excellent point.* For the rest of class, he holds the conversation hostage and discusses his unpublished dissertation. Everyone's silent, waiting for class to end. LP's cackling and mocking me for my failed contributions, which I was so adamant about sharing. As I listen to her, I wonder if Mother's prayers were to the trickster of gods. In the year she gained a daughter, she lost a sister. Every pregnancy brought complications that still ravage her body with pain. Raising two Black sons keeps her restless in her prayers for constant protection. Maybe that classmate is right, and there is only one history, one reminding us of pain. But what do I know? I'm still trying to figure out if I have enough to write a paper.

# (HER) TAKE ON ME

Moving through classes as the week passes, the unanswered texts, the ignored calls, the unopened links to morning sermons, lead to B1 pausing his procrastination of his AP Biology homework to text me that Mother's not happy, and I need to call her, *Now.* It's Thursday not Friday, and I am curled in bed, recovering from yesterday's Bar Night.* After B1's text, Mother calls. I ignore. My phone dings, again. I see that it's a text from B2. It reads, *please Call Mom* and includes a gif of Puss in Boots with his wide, green eyes. I groan, shuffling out of bed, tripping over myself as I slip on my combat boots.

---

*  For the students who are under twenty-one and needing a drink, Phi Hi Low-Fi is our watering hole. Three times a week with low prices, stale peanuts, and the hits of yesteryear, Phi Hi Low-Fi converts their basement apartment into a dive bar and discounted liquor store.

Roommate* lifts her pineapple-patterned eye mask, murmurs, *keep it down*, and returns to sleep.

Outside of my room, I call Mother. As I wait for her to pick up, I watch students with cereal bars hanging out of their mouths rush through the hallway to catch the next bus. "Good morning, Ma."

"Good morning, Sahara. Where have you been?"

"Classes, Ma, at classes."

"You have classes all day and night."

"Yes, Ma."

"So, you telling me you're in class twenty-four/seven and don't have time for family anymore."

"No, Ma, but—"

"Nothing." I sit down on the dirty hallway carpet. It's not even 9:00 a.m. yet, and I'm already in my first lecture. "All I'm asking is for you to check in so we know you're safe."

"I'm—"

"Before you left, you promised that you would call and text more. Now, you've been up there two whole weeks. I haven't heard a damn thing."

"Mother, I'm—"

"Uh-uh, stop interrupting so I can finish. I don't know what non-sense you're doing up there, but you have family back home."

In the phone's background B1 and B2 are arguing over whose turn it is with the Wii, an announcer shouts, *GOOAALL*. Father watching his morning soccer means that actually it's not Thursday or Friday, but Saturday. "I'm sorry, Mom," I say. My voice is still groggy, grating

---

\*   Best-case scenario did not happen. Roommate's here and inquisitive. At the beginning of this week, she asked me how do braids work. I replied, "I'm not too sure," then left for an impromptu smoke break.

against last night's streams of Stellas and this morning's servings of guilt. "I won't do it again," I promise, knowing damn well it'll happen again and again, and again until B1 or B2 intervenes.

"Don't tell me any lies. Think about how your brothers feel with you always disappearing."

"I do, Mom. I really do."

# POUND THE ALARMS

Mother's guilt trip keeps me awake. I slip into my dorm to change out of my pajamas and grab my jacket and laptop. If I can't fall back asleep, then I might as well make use of this consciousness. I miss the bus to the dining hall. There's not another for the next twenty-seven minutes. I pass through the nearby park. My boots sink into the mud made from last night's rain. The thoughts of B1 and B2, of Mother and Father, my boots sliding, then shucking off the mud, overwhelm me. I sit on a dewy swing, swaying as I smoke my cigarette. Mother was right. The constant consumption of my self-hatred, the constant conversations with LP, bloat me with selfishness. The bigger I become, the more I harm myself and others. After my conversation with Mother, I'm unsure if my choice of killing myself in February is reasonable or a childish waiting game?

\*    \*    \*

In the dining hall, I deny my hungover cravings for slices of supreme pizza. I drink coffee with dollops of honey diffusing at the cup's bottom. As I sip, a raspy voice calls my name. I turn around and see it's Mariah, sitting alone. She gathers her papers, laptop, and bottle of extra-strength Advil, and takes a seat across from me. She spreads out her highlighted papers with crumpled Post-it Notes attached to them. I peek down and skim the papers, seeing *body poetry, nonlinearity,* and *Chicago* repeatedly mentioned in the margins.

"You should see my apartment windows. They're covered." Mariah spreads out her hands, as if she's charting her next moves for world domination. "Every bit has a scribbling related to my thesis. My partner hates it, but I Love it," she says, with *Love* jumping, then rolling into *it.* "My advisor, this clock-and-gears-tatted, loc-wearing badass, recommended I plan out this way. My writing's never been better. She's so brilliant. You gotta take a class with her before you graduate."

"Cool, maybe I'll try to."

"Please do. She's fighting to get approval for a course. This quarter during registration, if you see something that's all-round Black brilliance, it's my advisor, Dr. ███████."

"Good to know," I say, feeling the same guilt from the BSC celebration. Again, LP's amused, even telling me, I'm on fire with this performance of future plans. Mariah unrolls a long sheet of drawing paper. Questions and quotes fill it. She bites on her pen. She's ecstatic with her ideas. The only other time I've seen so much excitement with working has been in ROD whenever a new, more daring art project is in its first stages.* "How's your senior thesis going?"

---

\* With ROD's ideas that become daring projects, I've learned to expect the most. Last year, she and I spent a spring morning trying to figure out how we would transport her latest project—a massive desk, and a human plaster cast. With two skateboards as our trolley,

"Some days, I hate it. Other days, I love it. Mostly, I'm happy that I FINALLY have a chance to write about something I care about, and not some half-assed prompt a professor came up with. What's your major?"

"English, but I haven't declared it yet."

"Well, if you end up declaring and have to write a thesis,* start early. I'm talking just-received-your-acceptance-letter-in-the-mail early."

"Noted. Are you always here this early to work on it?"

"Nah, I live off campus and don't have meal plan, but a friend offered to swipe me in. You?"

"Definitely not, I'm allergic to mornings. I'm normally here before closing." I finish the last of my coffee. The mug's bottom is sticky and spotted with grounds in puddles of honey. Mariah's so distracted with reading her pages that talking to her becomes easier. If every Saturday could begin like this, I wouldn't mind a wake-up call from Mother. "If you ever wanna come here to work, I would totally swipe you in. I don't live that far from campus."

"Really! I would love that. We could have workdays together." Mariah's enthusiasm makes my lie worth it. I would walk from here, to Evanston, then back again, if it meant somehow I'm useful to her. "Why are you here so early then?"

"My mom called and I couldn't fall back asleep."

"Ah, that reminds me. I need to call my mom."

---

and bathrobe belts and drawstrings from backpacks as our rope, we found a way and pushed her desk through campus until we reached New Grounds café.

* Thesis Committee, this would be the perfect opportunity for us to bond over our theses; however, I haven't found a way to explain to anyone outside of you and LP why I'm writing this thesis two years ahead of schedule. Plus, explaining to my crush that I'm speeding up my graduation timeline because my suicide clock is a-ticking seems like the one-way ticket to the friend zone, row: concerned, seat: 2B . . . or not. Mariah would probably ghost me if she knew what I was planning.

Mariah types a reminder into her phone, then checks the time. "About time." She leaves the table, then briefly returns to ask, "Do you want anything? They just set out the fresh fruit and burger patties."

"I'm not hungry yet, but thanks."

"All right, I'll bring extra just in case."

Mariah returns with pizza slices, a salad, mango and strawberry chunks, burger patties, buns, and a plate of curly fries. While she's dipping her fries in her concoction of mustard, ketchup, and honey, her phone dings. "Fucking asshole," she says after checking it. I nibble on a fry's edge. She's typing on her phone, cracking her neck, hitting her backspace button like she's pounding alarms left and right. She catches me watching. "Sorry, Dean ████████ hit me with some bullshit. He's pushing back a meeting with KYR,* again."

"That's a dick move."

"It is, but it's him. He loves hiding from the facts." She heaves her tote bag, which brims with books. She sets it on top of the dining table and takes out a stack of orange flyers that have KNOW YOUR RIGHTS bolded in the center. "I know that he can't stand me. I've been taping these flyers all over his office door." Mariah hands me a flyer. On it, facts about the University hospital's history fill the front page. The first tick, the fact that the University hospital didn't start treating Black patients until the mid-1960s. The fifth, patients of color have longer wait times in the ER than white patients. The eleventh, Black patients are consistently undertreated for pain. "I'll keep doing it too. He'll keep running and we'll keep chasing till we"—Mariah snaps her fingers— "got him." Mariah's phone rings. "Her ears must be ringing. It's my ma. I'll be right back."

---

* Know Your Rights. A newly founded health advocacy nonprofit and student organization based in the Southside.

\*       \*       \*

Nearly half an hour passes and Mariah's still talking with her mother. My stomach's growling loud enough to shake the University pennants hanging from the ceiling archways. I relent. From the pans, I gather only a handful of fries, an oblong piece of grilled chicken, and chunks of fruit. As I'm finishing my food, I think of Dean ██████ and our shared communication style of avoiding the ugly truth.* I resent that his avoidance allows him to thrive. He has so much power and wealth in this institution. He can avoid emails from students, organizations, hell even his mother. He's seated in the tower, above us all, dictating how to stack these ivory bricks onto one another. The rest of us below him are jumping between truths, playing hopscotch toward our survival in a society where Black death means white survival.

---

* Like its owner, the University hospital has its issues and will give you issues if you're unrelated to donors, a person of color, queer, fat, in a mental health crisis, the list can go on and on, but basically if you're not a rich straight white male, then the hospital will give you problems.

why you dreaming
you got nowhere to go?

# Survive '13

| **A** | **B** | **C** |
|---|---|---|
| DATE 09.23. 13 | DATE 10.5.13 | DATE 10.12.13 |
| N.R. | N.R. | N.R. |
| "Lost in the World" by Kanye West, Bon Iver | "Prayers for Rain" by The Cure | "Tears of a Clown" by Smokey Robinson & The Miracles |
| "1-800 Suicide" by Gravediggaz | "We Might Be Dead by Tomorrow" by Soko | "Good Morning" by Kanye West |
| "Fragile" by Tech N9ne, featuring Kendrick Lamar | "You Know I'm No Good" by Amy Winehouse | "Super Rich Kids" by Frank Ocean |
| "Mind Playing Tricks on Me" by Geto Boys | "Paint it Black" by The Rolling Stones | "Black Balloon" by The Kills |
| "Suicidal Thoughts" by Biggie | "Funnel of Love" by Wanda Jackson | "New Slaves" by Kanye West |
| "Answer" by Tyler, The Creator | "Odd Look" by The Weeknd, Kavinsky | "Tennis Court" by Lorde |

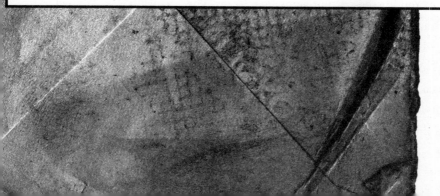

# SHE'S GOT A HOLD ON ME

**M**y first class this Monday morning, Genre Benders. I take my seat at the back of the lecture hall. From course reviews, I've learned that it's wise to sit as far away from the professor as possible. This Mr. Adjunct, while eating tuna salad sandwiches or boiled eggs, only teaches from the rare editions of twentieth-century novels. Those sitting in the front row can count the book lice running across his yellow pages. Though there are plenty of free seats around me, someone decides to set their MacBook right next to me. I look up. It's C1 from the party.

"You missed out not smoking with us," she says while Mr. Adjunct draws arrows on the chalkboard that point to nowhere.

I respond to C1 with a smile and nod, which I think translates to—*Good to see you too* or *Sorry for bailing*—I'm not entirely sure. This is a 10:00 a.m. lecture, so everything inside of me is still waking up and prone to misfiring. I'm not the only one with missed connections. Students ask question after question to try and clarify his analysis of *Nightwood*. Mr. Adjunct's explanations only confuse us more. He keeps talking, determined to salvage the rant he started. He switches to shouting his explanations, believing that the increased volume will convince himself and then us that he understands his preambles and il-legible diagram. The shouts only cause his spit and unchewed pieces of boiled eggs to fly toward the front row of students. To prevent myself from laughing, I doodle, filling every inch of my notebook with words and scribbles, a general palimpsest of my boredom. Mr. Adjunct fin-ishes his boiled eggs and last of his rant. He's erasing the chalkboard. Finally, class is over.

As I walk out C1 tells me, "We should hang soon." Shocked, I debate if I heard her correctly. She insists we find a place to sit. As she digs in her Louis Vuitton bag where the *LV* monogram is a shade darker than her skin, I don't know whether I'm worth her acceptance. On the bench just outside the lecture hall, she rifles through her bag, pull-ing out a matching Louis Vuitton makeup bag, her apartment's sensor key, a monogrammed flask, and a few lingering lipsticks and perfume rollers. Eventually in all her glamour, she finds her phone. "What's your number?" I give it, not entirely sure why me. She has the money, beauty, and Donor Kids all accompanying her. Outside of hit-and-miss jokes, there is nothing I can offer. She shows me my number in her phone, and I confirm it's right. Her eyes, the color of an olive pit, flick back to me, and in them is a touch of anger. "You're not the type to ignore messages, are you?"

"No, of course not," I say, hoping the collective energy of over a thousand unread emails and texts don't scream out, *She's lying.*

Her eyes return to placidity as I secretly promise myself that, of course, that'll be true, starting now. C1 tosses everything back into her tote, and as she walks away, I debate whether to tell her that when she hangs out with me, I'm the type who ALWAYS brings along their partner. When I stopped escaping from LP, I stopped mocking people who never left their partner's side. Now I get it. A partner, a girlfriend, a boyfriend, an FWB, all comfort personified. A breathing blanket. A laughing doll. A kissing pillow. Why question it and separate yourself from comfort? It's there always ready for you.

While waiting for the bus, LP and I imagine lovely scenes. Before I embed myself in these scenes, C1 texts me, asking if I want to hang out next weekend.

My words say, *sure*. My thoughts ask, *why*, I am still here, pretending.

**Imagined Scene #1:**
Me sits at the back of the University bus, listening to music. Unbeknownst to University students, a city bus has just plowed through a stop sign and is headed right in their direction.

Boom, bam, bang.

The city bus crashes into them. Me is one of the casualties. Please send your thoughts and prayers Me's way.

**Imagined Scene #2:**
LP invites Me to her mansion, and Me is obliged to attend. The mansion is prime real estate in Brain Valley, and when LP calls for attention, Me always answers. Upon entering, LP offers Me a platter of delights. Vodka you drink on days you play hookie, double-stuffed cookies, creams for phantom aches, pills for days you need a head drill. Me gobbles down the delights, waits for the pleasures to hit.

# COOLER THAN THEM

It's Wednesday and the last full conversation I had with someone was with C1 on Monday. Between now and then, I've talked only with LP, and she has expanded her real estate. Normally, when she's up and active, she's seductive with her harm. I struggle to deny her reason and desires, the twisted glamour of our misery. She views every moment as a fast-track possibility for my unfortunate demise. If crossing the street, we think of jumping into traffic; if seeing a spare knife in the dining hall, the urge to cut possesses us. The days in isolation, I spent researching. I learned that after I die, my parents won't have to pay back my federal loans. I discovered more of the stakes of failed suicide attempts that you leave hospitalized for seventy-two hours and paying off a medical bill for seventy-two years. LP and I have to get this right. No mistakes that will lead to bills, unwanted attention, and regret.

Now, as I'm with ROD, I'm struggling to shift to the right character. I've spent so much time studying the ways to die that I forgot how to live. I run through the list of what to do. Smile, check. Lie about busyness with classes, check. Ask about her day, check. Still, something's missing. There's a gap in our connection that I know will widen the more LP and I entangle with one another.

\* \* \*

As ROD and I sit inside a bedroom of an apartment converted to artist's studio spaces, LP asks if it's cruel for me to continue this friendship. *Wouldn't she be better alone?* I don't answer and instead ask ROD, "What do you need?"

"Could you close the door?" The complaints from other student artists about the lack of A/C and the recent theft of brushes and quality paint must be too distracting for ROD. I close the bedroom door. To ease our sweltering, I open a window. The sill is propped up with a paint-splattered anthology of Shakespeare's tragedies. She removes her Blick paints from her backpack, unfurls a plastic shower curtain, then tablecloth, her thrifty alternative to tarp. Bored, I jangle with the lever on a broken office chair. It falls off and hits the end of ROD's makeshift tarp that's duct-taped on the room's floor. She stops studying her outlines and peers at me, I mouth, *sorry.* ROD ignores. She's in her art world, where she is unretrievable by any force outside of herself. Normally, my jittering legs, our tendencies to fall into conversations and abandon plans for concentration, mean I'm banned from attending her studio hours. The flow of rejections from art shows has made her procrastinate starting her next piece. She asked me to sit with her so she could have an accountability buddy. While here, I'm not sure how to support. I'm intently watching her, reciting encouraging phrases, repeatedly asking if she needs anything. I'm overcompensating in my care so that when spring arrives, and I'm not there, at least ROD's memories of our love will remain.

"Seriously, I'm fine. You being here is more than enough," ROD responds. She switches from studying the blank canvas, her paints, and sketches. I don't know whether she's procrastinating or on the brink of an epiphany.

"That red looks good?"

"Huh?"

"That red, you know. It looks like a great color for a painting, then you have that nice peachy-looking paint too," I add, hoping ROD will start her painting, and I can leave this room where I'm melting like a Munch painting.

"That's paint thinner, not paint."

"Perfect, you can thin out the red, then."

"That's not how it works. None of these colors are right, and I can't buy any new ones."

"Then make a new one. We'll call it the RODDY HUE."

With that suggestion, ROD's off again. She inspects her colors, trying to decide which to use. She flips her sketchbook open to an empty page and paints a practice stroke. She holds her sketchbook up to the light and frowns at the blue's simplicity. "Too dull, look at it." She flips the notebook toward me, and to me the blue looks nice, the type you could take home and even introduce to your parents.

I tell her, "It's a blue, but you're in your zone. Whatever you say goes."

"My zone?"

"Yeah, your art zone. Every time you're painting, sculpting, or hunting through the dollar store for project parts, you're in a different zone."

"More like aisle," ROD jokes as she adds yellow paint to her concoction. She then sprinkles in pieces of blue and white chalk dust and mica powder, which glitters green into the repurposed container. She gathers a handful of blue and white chalk, places them into a Ziploc bag, then hammers the bag until the pieces of chalk are dust or the size of crystals. "I get it, my shit's weird. Ninety percent of the time, I don't know

now if what I'm making is good, or if anyone will understand what I'm doing, or if I even have a future doing this." She mixes her paint with a wood ruler, smiling at her lumpy concoction, which shines. "Then for like ten percent of the time, it's all energy, excitement, and everything feels so right like there's nothing else in the world I know how to do." She tilts the container toward me. "Looks cool, right?"

I roll closer, then peer inside, seeing the transformation of the previous blue to one that's psychedelic, textured with hues of glittering green. "It's a badass RODDY HUE."

"Thanks." ROD concocts a second mixture of her paint. This time in a large mixing bowl. Before she begins, she covers her hair in a plastic Jewel-Osco bag then sits in the canvas's center. In a circle, she pours the entirety of the yogurt container and mixing bowl onto the canvas, then spreads the paint outward with her hands. While she's hunched over and massaging the paint into the canvas, the Jewel bag falls off her head. I tiptoe over and remove it from the canvas. She looks up. Her sweat glues her minibangs to her forehead. Paint covers her hands, forearms, and elbows in patches. It's even drenching her jeans and smearing her shirt. She's vibrant in the chaos. Indulging in every moment, where the more she paints, the more she is painted. Most of the canvas is covered, and I think she's done, but then she drags her nails through the paint, creating a network of lines inside a kaleidoscopic symphony. She leans against a wall, guzzles water. Wiping her hands with a towel crunched with acrylic, she studies her recent work. She's massaging her wrists and cracks all her fingers, their popping sounding like ticks heating a gas stove.

"Is that normal?" I ask.

"What?"

I point to her fingers as the popping continues.

"Oh yeah, they're a little stiff."

"Maybe it's time for a break."

"I can't. I only have this room for today and tomorrow, then I have another piece planned for tomorrow."

"ROD, let's take a break. It'll give time for the paint to dry."

"I can't. Every art show rejected me. I need newer, better work."

I grab ROD's backpack and take out another plastic bag with wet-wipes in a Ziploc bag and her change of clothes. "Fuck the cafés with their dry-ass muffins, fuck those barista gatekeepers and those racist whipsters.* You are a badass artist, and your genius deserves a break." I hand ROD the plastic bag. "So, change, then we'll get food?"

"Fine." ROD grabs the bag, then snatches me up for a hug. "That's the first time I've been called an art genius."

"Let go, let go!"

ROD unleashes me. My black leggings and top are now spotted with paint. "Dammit, now I have to do laundry."

"Or save it for when I'm a famous artist and sell it on eBay."

"Just hurry up and change, and we'll discuss your Genius merch over burgers."

---

* White hipsters.

# TALKING AIRHEADS AND PSYCHO KILLERS

Dear Thesis Committee, since it's been a bit from your years in undergrad, let me refresh your mind on the shitshow that is picking classes. There are the classes that you want. These are interesting classes taught by professors who are relevant enough to have their own Wiki page. Next there are the *why not* classes, these are the classes that are weird, and fifteen years from graduation they will become your go-to moot point when a conversation stalls. Then there are your required courses. These are the courses where you frown and bear it for ten weeks, then once you survive finals, you wash it out of your memories with vodka.

This class, Naughty Cells, is in a subcategory of required courses that don't require a textbook.* The main learning objective for this course

---

* This class's lack of textbooks makes it a hot commodity. Rumor has it that one student, who never planned on taking the class, sold his seat for $200. The buyer stated that $200 was still cheaper than a textbook for other registered classes.

is understanding why and how cells turn against the body. Though we are weeks into this class, no one has any idea what is going on. Our stupidity doesn't slow down the Naughty Cells Professor from lecturing. Instead, it makes NCP* lecture faster so she can get the class over with.

*       *       *

In the last row, I scribble notes with two Clickers at my side—one for me, the other for Second Black Girl in my class. I met SBG on the first day of class, and by the second week we'd developed a system for NCP's weekly quizzes. Our system is simple but ingenious: SBG drops off her Clicker at the library's front desk and asks the librarian to hold it there for me. I go to the library to get her Clicker, and then click in answers for that week. The next week, I don't attend lecture. I drop off my Clicker at the library, SBG gets it, and then clicks in answers for me that week. I haven't seen her since we agreed on our system, and I won't worry about not seeing her until I get an email with the subject line *Unfortunate News.* Although I hate this class and can't remember the details of SBG's face, her height, or even her year, I'm grateful for her and our system—it ensures I attend at least half of my lectures for this course.

NCP puts today's questions on the board, and they have nothing to do with any of this week's modules she posted on Blackboard.

**Question 1: Infective endocarditis can affect which part(s) of the heart?**

    a. The endocardium

---

\* Naughty Cells Professor.

b. The heart valves
c. Both A and B
d. None of the above

**Question 2: What are some ways that bacteremia (bacteria in the blood) can occur?**

a. Toothbrushing and flossing
b. Chewing food
c. Use of wooden toothpick
d. All of the above

**Question 3: What imaging should initially be performed on a patient with suspected infective endocarditis?**

a. TTE
b. TEE
c. Both
d. No imaging is recommended.

After answering the questions, I watch a student below me. Next to them are six Clickers. Throughout the entire lecture, they search through notes and the internet, and text a group chat to make sure that they picked correctly.*

By the end of lecture, NCP sees that boredom is creating more bags underneath our eyes. She stops lecturing, and after reminding us of our midterm next week, she announces there's a surprise for this week's discussion section. A few students sitting at the sides of the lecture hall perk up. NCP refuses to tell us the surprise, saying she doesn't want to spoil it for us.

---

* The gag is that our answers don't matter. Wrong and right answers are the same. After seeing our responses for the first quiz, NCP said our class needs all the help we can get and changed all the quizzes so they were graded for participation.

Lecture ends. The Twelve Angry Students who have discussion section next migrate to another room, awaiting their surprise. Unlike the lecture hall, with a vastness that mimics an empty orchestra hall, this room is tiny with centipedes orchestrating their escapes as they dart across the orange, coffee-stained carpet.

My stomach knots. I'm standing outside the classroom, watching my classmates file in, bored and unbothered. I hate this discussion section because I must speak. If I don't, then I won't receive any of the participation points that my grade desperately needs. Class is minutes away from beginning. The number of empty seats by the door is dwindling. It's either go and get a seat now or sit next to the professor. I slip into the classroom, unnoticed, and open my laptop. Students carrying last-minute iced coffees trickle in and take their seats. NCP announces that instead of discussing naughty cells, we will discuss naughty scientists. While sipping her iced coffee, a student whispers "sexy, sexy," to her friend. I laugh, picturing Newton dancing to Rihanna's "S&M." My personal laugh track must have run a second too long. The student gives a side-eye for intruding on her publicly private moment. I stop myself from rolling my eyes and note to avoid any eye contact with the side-eyer.

Perhaps NCP thought that after the surprise's reveal, we would jump into discussion or ask more questions. However, she failed to consider the only surprise we want is a canceled class or an early refund check. We're still quiet, waiting for her to cue us in on what exactly will happen. She grumbles in Greek, takes a deep breath, and baits us with another surprise.

This time a student bites and asks, "Is it Halloween candy?"

"No, I don't hand out type 2 diabetes as a surprise." The class is silent. NCP hasn't broken eye contact with the student, and he's turning from peach to tomato. NCP chuckles, then she hands that student a bag of Fantis Mastic candies she brought over from Crete. As the bag of candy is passed around and NCP's opening her PowerPoint, she says, "Next week we will be learning about sugar and cancer." A few students slow their chewing. NCP chuckles, again. Toying with us must be her treat for this Halloween.

Her PowerPoint's opening slide features two pictures, one of Henrietta Lacks and the second of the scientists who conducted the Tuskegee Experiment. Most of the students don't think of Lacks or the Tuskegee Experiment as acts rooted in racism. Their disbelief leads NCP to narrate racist, inhumane acts that fueled scientific progress. With every new detail she provides about the cruelties to Black bodies, a student glances at me. This is the only time I wish SBG* was here in this discussion section with me. At least we could share glances and side-eyes with one another, that say, *isn't this some shit.*

"I believe what scientists did was worth it," is the first comment after NCP finishes her point. The students are quartered in their reactions to NCP's PowerPoint. I see bored students, agreeing students, some annoyed and confused. And now, I think to myself what a mess this will be. So much of this mess I must document for others in the Black Excel group chat to see.

Philosophy Major 1 uses this comment as the basis for his question, What is the meaning of worth? Dear God. That question awakens Philosophy Major 2, who posits, How can we discuss or define worth without truth? Then there's another, of course there's another who wants to flaunt off skimmed readings from another class. This one asks, Who are we in conversation with? Lacan, Marx, Kant? And just

---

* The Second Black Girl in Naughty Cells.

like that, the class discussion becomes a hell with no exit as Philosophy Majors 1, 2, 3 have settled in their quibbles.

Another student enters the conversation and declares, We need risk-taking scientists for the advancement in medical research. Philosophy Majors 2 and 3 agree with this new input. Philosophy Major 1 is still on the fence and wants to redirect this discussion to defining worth. When he figures that no one wants to help him create his dictionary, he finally stops interrupting comments. His silence provides space for a student showboating* in his Cackling Goose Vest to say, Given the socioeconomic standing of the patients, *oh no please, don't let this go where I think*, it doesn't matter. They would have died from some disease anyway.

The Side-Eyer from the beginning of class agrees with the Cackling Goose of a student. My head is down, focusing on my computer, a few students still glance my way. Another classmate with the asinine comment: Lacks changed lives. She probably wouldn't have understood what the scientists wanted to do with them, solidifies their membership within the Future Racist Intellectuals of America, the Boy Scout version of the KKK.

Discussion continues, anger rifles my tongue. I am still sending my classmates' comments to the Black Excel group chat. None of us are surprised by the classism and racism masquerading as a progressive and intellectually stimulating conversation. HB1† and Mariah are encouraging me to speak up against what I'm hearing.

But oh Galápagos, I feel too unevolved. I don't trust my current mouth. I wish I could grow another, a better one with a palate of courageous, eloquent language. Or even new ears, ones that upholster the

---

* It's sixty-five degrees out. There's no need for a vest meant for Arctic explorers.
† The best hairdresser on campus.

old ones and protect me from their racism. I don't care if I look like Frankenstein's comeback creation, I am desperate for a change that will release me from either my silence or my awareness.

In the group chat, Mariah asks:

MARIAH: Is anyone disagreeing?

ME: No

MARIAH: Of course not

HB2: This place is something

HB2: Let me know if you wanna talk about it

ME: Okay

FZ: They wonder why so many of us transfer

GAHDESS: We all should've went to an HBCU

MIC: They really don't know half the shit they're talking about.

HB2: God, I hate it here so much.

HB1: Right, it's nonstop

MARIAH: Sahara, you could tell them about the discrimination lawsuit the hospital settled out of court

LJ: I didn't know that happened

MARIAH: Before your time but basically a Black PhD student sued for being pre-scribed the wrong medication. Somehow she found out they weren't keeping accurate medical records, then she got PAID and left the PhD program.

MARIAH: You could mention that.

Five minutes later, my body doesn't feel anything. Maybe the hug and all the love's GPS system is acting up, and they don't know which room I'm in.[*]

A new student sitting next to me joins the conversation. On her laptop are Pride and Pronoun stickers. I'm hopeful. Last week, she ranted about objectification as we discussed breast cancer prevention. Perhaps she is my white queer ally in hiding. No doubt, this was terri-ble, *okay, okay this seems promising*, but, *oh no not the but*, it brought awareness, and now doctors value the lives of all patients. This doesn't happen anymore.

Well, that took an earnest, misinformed turn. We're back at where we started, at the bottom of the misinformed barrel.[†]

Though there are others in class who haven't spoken, several class-mates turn to me, the class's Negro in Residence, and wait for my input. My history corrects these students. Mother's chronic hyper-tension during her pregnancies, which doctors blamed on her demo-graphic. Doctors blaming Aunt Nita for letting her condition progress

---

[*]   The misdirection is understandable; with its Gothic architecture and ever-changing staff of adjuncts, administrators, advisors, and researchers, this place does feel like the Murder Castle.

[†]   Who would've guessed that Father's rants about crooks and racism in Western medicine would be more informative than this discussion? I should call him and tell him about today; however, a phone call might lead to *Then They Kill You, O*, Father's favorite lecture on white nonsense, medicine, and why I need to become a doctah.

without treatment. Father's rants of fellow doctors dismissing Black patients' concerns. These overheard frustrations and warnings, these haunted memories, are evidence that I, Mother, Father, and Aunt Nita, and those of our skin and of their hatred, listen to history's repetition, where the song's refrain is a denial of all atrocities. I wait for another message in the group chat, hoping someone will give me a script of how to voice what I already know.

Nothing arrives. My knowledge, my problem. I take deep breaths, and start speaking, but the sentence is broken. "They were targeted and mistreated because"—my voice is buried into my computer and steadily quiets as I'm finishing my comment—"of their race and class. This happens often to Black patients seeking treatment." I pause, and one of the philosophy majors assumes I have finished. He initiates a new conversation about the meaning of ethics. Unlike others in class, my comment doesn't receive a rebuttal, an agreement, or even a request for clarification.

NCP raises her hand, cuing the philosophy majors to stop their symposium. She circles back to my comment, asking me to repeat it. This time on my second attempt, I strengthen my voice, so I don't have to speak again, "These patients were targeted because they were Black and poor."

A student rolls her eyes, and if I could, I would perform an enucleation. Instead of placing her eyes on a sterile surgical platter, I would toss them into a time capsule so that they could roll around in the never-ending aluminum box and see the history of violence and trauma against Black bodies.

No one has a response to my comment. The silence slices in half when NCP responds, "Yes, I agree. This is an important part of the discussion. These patients were targeted because of their race and their class."

Since the professor has approved of what I said, the previous defendants of the scientists change their tune. My grandfather was half-Black, so I understand some of the horrors with racism, or My boyfriend has opened my eyes to what's going on in the world. The students are so fired up with newly sparked anger about racism that you would think they were Lacks's descendants. Every new comment is another scene of performed allyship that ends with a commentor looking to me for approval.*

*       *       *

The performances finally end when there's little time left. Today, NCP is full of tricks that she believes are treats, and as we're packing up, she announces the final surprise. Over the weekend, we have a 3,000-to-3,500-word post to write as a response to the class discussion. The requirements are that we must cite six to ten sources, and include our personal reflections.

The bright side? We can divide the work with a partner. I close my laptop, and I leave as everyone begins partnering up. I would rather be alone than a classmate's token to cash out their white guilt.

Thing: A Play without a Word
*Onstage is a large chalkboard and taped on it is THING in giant letters made of rope and silver twine. Next to the chalkboard is Academic who studies it. Kneeling in front*

---

* These classmates must have read *The Blacks vs You: How to Survive* by F. Sandford. This midcentury book contains invaluable information for white survival. Example lesson included, if one Black person agrees with you, then you're not racist and will be invited to every cookout.
  Works Cited: Sandford, Ferguson. *The Blacks vs You: How to Survive.* Karen's Kind Kings, 1955.

of the board are Black Persons 1, 2, 3, 4, and 5.

As BP 1-5 stare out at the audience, Man enters the stage. While Academic studies the chalkboard, Man begins pulling off pieces of rope-twine. Academic pays no attention to Man and continues studying. Man walks around BP 1-5, and as they walk around, they whistle the alphabet song while twirling the rope-twine in their hands. Man stops by BP 1.

Man takes one piece of rope-twine and ties the hands and feet of BP 1.

Man takes one piece of rope-twine, ties the hands and feet and then whips the back of BP 2.

Man takes one piece of rope-twine, ties the hands and feet, whips the back, and then places a noose around BP 3's neck.

Man takes one piece of rope-twine, ties the hands and feet, whips the back, places a noose, and then gags BP 4.

Man takes one piece of rope-twine, ties the hands and feet, whips the back, places a noose, gags, and then constructs a make-shift gun from the remaining rope twine. Man shoots BP 5 in the back until they collapse on the ground.

Man stops whistling the alphabet and exits the stage. Academic stops studying the blank chalkboard to study the Black bodies onstage.

# (WHY) DON'T (YOU) SPEAK

After discussion section, I sit in the library's foyer, waiting for the next bus to my dorm. Most members of the Black Excel group chat have moved on from discussing today's racism. HB2 sent another message that said, *don't worry, you're not the only one who hates it here.* I should need to respond and accept her invitation to bond over our shared hell. My fingers hover over the keypad until my screen shuts off from inactivity.

Thesis Committee, riddle me this: How many *yes girl* or *damn shames* can I send before those words are placeholders for silence? Between now and class, LP and I are mulling over how class discussion has sweetened her argument that I'm not strong enough to exist within this skin. Without any strength, as thoughts and histories, comments and gazes crush me, LP waits, promising me relief. She asks, *Why are we waiting?* I reason that there's still time until February, three months and a few weeks. I remind her that while I greatly appreciate her dedication and understanding the urgency of my desires, steadiness will win this (death) race. This is the first time we'll have complete control over our body and this life, so why abandon the plan and the potential for a perfect ending? LP agrees, then bitterly commands two things of me. The first, I cut till I'm scared I'll need stitching, and even after that, I'll hurt myself a little deeper. Easily, I agree. Her second desire is the hardest demand. It is that I prove that there was something in me worth being here.

I read NCP's requirements for the discussion post and realize taking on this project without a partner buries me in fields of work. It'll be fine. I can do this on my own. I brainstorm ideas, and as my thoughts turn, I'm watching the rotation of students swiping their ID cards to part the entrance's clear gates. I'm thinking of ROD and her dedication toward her artistry. I'm hearing the gates' electronic chime and the tidbits of conversations. I'm remembering how weakly I defended my history in class. I'm seeing students pull off the balancing act of holding books and coffee cups. I'm, I'm, am I, yes I am drowning. I can't do this on my own. As my sense of this world prickles then blurs into pixilation, I know I am too much to enter. I abandon brainstorming to jot suicide plans into margins of my printed-out PowerPoint slides. My plans—overdosing or an intoxicated drowning in Lake Michigan—affix me to an image of my future that I can visualize clearly.

\*　　\*　　\*

*Sahara.* My eyes snap up from my stapled notes. Mariah's touching my shoulder. Her presence clarifies the surrounding world. I stuff my notes into my backpack, leaving the pages to fold and wrinkle against my books. "How are you doing?" Mariah asks.

"Pretty good, you?" I respond, praying that Mariah only stood over me for a few seconds and didn't see anything I wrote.

"Same, you sure you're good after that discussion section?" She sits in the empty chair across from me. Her knees bump against the low-standing glass table between us.

"Oh, that, it's nothing. What else do we expect?"

"More." To make room for her knees, Mariah pushes the table to the side, leaving it to stick out in the walkway. "I've been meaning to tell you ███████ bought a copy of *Seven Miles a Second*."

"Did they like it?"

"They loved it. I can't wait to read it as well."

"I love how it's so . . ." I pause. Worried that anything I love about the graphic novel would be a misreading, a surface-level interpretation, general fodder for you, the Thesis Committee to devalue me, I simply say, "Cool and fascinating."

Mariah nods, and the smile she normally carries has fallen. Before I can cut the silence with a generic *did you have class today*, Mariah asks, "Sahara, can I tell you something?"

"Yeah," I respond, unsure of what she might tell. She starts speaking, then stops. As she searches for what to say next, my excitement over what Mariah will tell me morphs into nervousness.

"Don't worry, it's nothing bad. Just sometimes . . ." Mariah leans forward. My grin widens, and both it and my fear spill across my cheeks. Fuck, Mariah saw what I wrote, or she knows how I feel. I am panicked, trapped in this anxious gaze and frantic thoughts, waiting to be exposed. "It feels like there's more behind what you're saying. Your words are there but you're not."

"Oh," breathes out of me. I'd rather be seen as empty than exposed as the suicidal founder, architect, and sole student of this schoolgirl crush.

"What did you think I was gonna say?" I reply *nothing*. Mariah scrunches her brows. "Like that. You say the half of it. Let yourself say more."

"More," I joke. My discomfort increases. Mariah's glimpsing through my curated emptiness, and I don't know what to do. LP's explaining that Mariah's observation is that I will never be enough. Between her explanations, the relief of someone seeing me tempts me to tell Mariah the truth. What if I did? If I allowed her inside my mind's museum, what would she say or do with what she saw? "I guess averaging four hours of sleep a night isn't the best for my vocab." Mariah's smirk returns. Any inkling I may have had to tell her a morsel of truth disappears. I only want to escape her gaze and this confrontation over my lacking conversations.

"True, and dealing with racists alone doesn't help. Wait, you know what?" She checks her phone. "KYR's having a meeting in like forty-five min. There'll be free food, cool people, and our meetings always end in vent sessions."

"I don't think I can—"

"Shit, Sahara, give it a full consideration before you say no."

"Fair," I reason. This callout from Mariah is slightly humorous, allowing some unease to dissipate. "I think I can make it. I'll mostly be a fly on the wall during it though."

"Lies, by the end of it, everyone always has something to say. You can vent about your discussion section." Mariah stands up and tacks a KYR flyer over a flyer for the University's cocoa and colloquium event.

"Sounds good. I might leave early to meet ROD to study at Sunrise at four."

"It'll only last like an hour or so, you'll have plenty of time. Is it cool if I join y'all?"

"Of course."

"Awesome, I think you'll love the meeting. You'll have a chance to share how you're really feeling."

"If I can think of something, I will."

"Come on, why say nothing when you can say"—Mariah winks then quickly shouts—"*more.*" Students, librarians, and professors gawk. Mariah ignores them and tacks a second flyer on the bulletin board.

# WHERE THEM WORDS AT

With neon posters and laminated lists of patient rights taped on a quarter-cleaned chalkboard, rearranged chairs, and music playing in the background, members of KYR have transformed this tiny classroom into a welcoming spot for gathering. Tables of catered Mediterranean food run along the classroom's left wall. The trays of hummus, falafel, triangular slices of pita bread, salads with sliced tomatoes and chopped onions, heaps of chicken and vegetarian shawarmas, stacked Styrofoam plates, plastic cups, and cans of sparkling water fill any empty space. There's enough food for the seventeen of us here to have seconds, perhaps even thirds, depending on how stingy we get with the hummus. Before the meeting starts, I grab one falafel, a tablespoon of hummus, and a can of sparkling water that I sip first to satisfy my appetite.

Most here are first-years. They fill their plates. Their dollops of hummus, the slices of onions, halved shawarmas, knocking and bouncing into one another in a pinball game themed with mixed textures and flavors. My tongue savors the prickles of the falafel skin that softens as the hummus glides, then mixes with the chickpea pieces my teeth have crushed. Within three bites, my plate is empty. I am still starved. For my second helping, I grab a second can of sparkling water. It glugs with every gulp.

The first-years' awkward bursts of small talk peppered with questions about classes and worries about their first Chicago winters make me curious if I'm the only second-year here. My curiosity evolves to questioning why other members from BSC aren't here. Did Mariah invite me because she sees how lonely I am? In the minutes before we begin, LP's read of this situation is devastatingly true. Either I am here because all Mariah's friends are already proactive, and now, on top of lacking self-advocacy, can't even support my community, or, I am here out of pity like the friendless little sister crashing an older sibling's playdate.

*       *       *

Mariah and two others enter. Over her denim button-up, she wears an orange T-shirt with KYR bolded in the center. She waves at me, I wave back, then place my plate underneath my seat. Going in a circle, we share our names and how we found out about Know Your Rights. When it's my turn and I share that Mariah brought me here, I join the majority, who say she brought them here as well. Mariah thanks everyone for attending, and then introduces us to KYR's Founders. While First Founder discusses why they started this organization, I'm uneasy, as if I am living on the ridges of a ripped portrait. Mariah's seen through me. Her gaze, tattering an image I try to project. To Mariah, I'm like these first-years, lonely and wobbling as they're attempting to gain their footing on campus. I'm humiliated, and I wish she never saw me.

Mariah stands next to a projection screen, waiting for KYR's Second Founder to find his HDMI cord. She encourages us to get seconds and even break out the Tupperware if we want to bring some home. A handful of students take out plastic containers and Ziploc bags. The cord's found, but when plugged in, the screen reads NO INPUT. While Second Founder deals with this sequel in technical difficulties, Mariah fills the time and shares why she joined KYR at the end of her first year. "I'm all about transparency and honesty. They're our best tools for change." I clap along with a few others, guessing what honesty they hide. "Throughout my first year, I don't know what was happening to my body. I was terrified. Whenever I went to the University hospital complaining about my heavy periods and unbearable pain, all the doctors told me to do was lose weight. It wasn't until I scheduled an appointment with an OB-GYN back home in Philly that she finally diagnosed me with fibroids. Even with my diagnosis, my MRI scans, the doctors here still tell me the same things. I joined KYR because I needed a place to advocate with others about my health, and fight for ways to change the University hospital's practices."

Mariah shares more of her history, and while next to the blank screen, she's shining, a twilight of honesty for everyone's eyes. Her openness prompts many to share their rage at the University hospital and campus. The HDMI finally connects, and Second Founder dims the lights. Mariah presents on KYR's history, and what they are planning to achieve in this academic year. "As part of your intake form at the hospital, you are required to list any alumni affiliation you have with the University. This information is irrelevant, and obviously a way for the hospital to see if a patient is related to any potential donors."

"If they are supposed to help us, why is alumni information relevant?"

"Exactly," Mariah replies to one of us. "We are petitioning to have this removed.

"We are also advocating for an increase of allowed counseling sessions for students. Currently, the student limit is four before they are referred out. We are fighting to increase the number of sessions to eight."

Second Founder adds, "The University assumes that after four sessions, the students will feel comfortable to start with someone new. But often, therapy in college is the first time for most of us."

"And they assume we can afford a copay," a student replies.

"Which brings us to our next goal," Founder adds. "We are fighting for a decrease in copays for students with the University health plan. Even if in network, the average copay is thirty dollars. For students who need consistent counseling, that's too high."

*Consistent counseling* prompts a student to share her struggles scheduling her psychiatric appointment during the first week of school. "I was without my meds for three weeks." As the conversation congeals with more honesty, my emotions oscillate between bitterness for their vulnerability, and disappointment that I can't speak. What is a life with constant silence? A game of pretend, a performance lacking an audience, no—perhaps only an unfortunate circumstance with *it is what it is* solutions.

The PowerPoint switches to a chart showcasing a higher mortality rate for Black students treated at the University hospital. The slide ends with the question *How Do I Get Involved?*, then lists the first step of signing up for the Listserv.

As Second Founder passes around a clipboard, LP and I joke with one another. While the University's here to kill us in theory, the hospital's here to kill us in practice. The perfect duo just like us. The clipboard reaches me. I hastily add my signature, hoping that my handwriting's sloppiness will save me from the guilt of ignoring their emails. While the others gather around the food, sharing their numbers and plans to force change at the University, I toss my plate, recycle the cans of sparkling water. I orbit behind a group of students, standing awkwardly in their optimism and plans for change. Eventually, I leave, unnoticed, feeling slightly comforted that at least I have LP to keep me company.

# PENCIL, PENCIL, NUMBER TWO

Alone in Sunrise Café,* I'm waiting for ROD and Mariah to arrive for our group study session. With a navy of papers spread across the blue-tiled table, I'm brainstorming ideas. Desperate for more notes, I add my overstuffed notebook to the table's armada. I'm trying to believe that I can write something worth NCP's time. It's been a few hours since I left KYR's meeting, and in that time, I've thought endlessly of what I will say. If I can't speak, then I can write.

"We're out of coffee," the owner says. I stop outlining, turn my neck to him, and then to the café's door. Mariah's there, holding a stickered coffee canister and carrying underneath her arm a few rolled-up posters.

---

* Students rarely come to this café because the hours are never consistent, and by noon, Café Owner's out of coffee. Instead of making more of it, he'll spend the rest of the day rolling cigarettes and watching *ER* reruns. The owner's moodiness and indifference about students' complaints makes this café the antiestablishment business, which ROD and I are willing to support whenever we can catch it open.

"No worries, I brought my own." The owner doesn't respond. Mariah joins me at the table. I frantically gather my papers. "Sahara, you left the KYR event so early. I wanted to introduce you to the founders."

"Sorry, my mom called."

"Oh, okay. Next time, then." She glances at the messy stack of papers, grinning at the handmade Post-it Notes made of ripped pieces and tape. "Wow, you took my advice seriously." Confused, I respond, *yeah, I had to.* She waits for me to say more. I'm silent and staring, embarrassed that awkwardness pangs every interaction I have with her. "You have no idea, what I'm talking about?" I nod, *no.* "All your papers, it looks like you're writing—never mind. What did you think about the meeting?"

"It was great. I'm looking forward to the next one."

"Hopefully, you can stay after to meet the founders and other members." ROD arrives. She joins me at the booth. From her dented canister, she pours herself a cup of the dining hall's bitter roast of the day. ROD offers me a cup; I decline. Four going on five cups in one day is a bit much even for me. While the three of us work, Mariah's frequent sighs* shift my DIY Post-its. I stare at her, debating how to start a conversation that proves to Mariah that I'm interesting. ROD writes *What's wrong?* on a corner of my printed PowerPoint. I scratch out ROD's message and stop debating how to speak so I can write.†

---

* While most students in Mariah's thesis seminar are solely preoccupied with writing an honors-worthy thesis, Mariah is trying to stack her GPA. During her first two years of college, she rarely saw above a 3.3. At the end of her second year, her advisor recommended that Mariah not pursue a future in academia, and choose a different, more realistic, career, one that didn't require anything beyond her postsecondary education. This advice sent Mariah into an academic rampage, fighting for every A she knows she deserves.

† Dear Thesis Committee, if you have any students struggling to write their first college papers, have no fear, Sahara is here. On the next page, you will find an excerpt from *Writing with Deadlines for Students.* If you enjoy the following guidance, then make sure to add *Sharing Is Caring: Group PSETS,* the next edition in Good Enough™'s Education series, to your reading list.

# Writing with Deadlines

*for*

## Students

Don't know where to start? We recommend opening your syllabus and scrolling down to the readings. Eliminate the readings you haven't done. Typically, after completing this elimination, students are left with an average of three readings.

If you have no readings that you have completed or understood, it is recommended you consult expert sources such as Wikipedia. If Wikipedia has no entries on the readings, go to Google Scholar. If Wiki and Google Scholar don't have your back, go to Reddit. If Wiki, Google Scholar, and Reddit all have nothing you can use, ask a classmate. If Wiki, Google Scholar, Reddit, and a classmate have nothing, you need to read the first and last chapter of the book, and then skim the middle pages for thirty minutes.

Worried about page length and don't know what to do? Good Enough™'s certified action plans include, excessive block quotation usage, changing font size to 11 or 12.5, slight margin changes, and double spacing the front page's header.

Thinking of starting over? If you choose to delete, keep the deleted pages in a spare document. You never know which words you'll need as the deadline and your desperation converge toward one another.

Concerned about your paper's quality? Then preschedule the email, which includes a self-deprecating message, for the wee hours in the morning. Nothing says, Halp, I'm struggling, like a paper submitted between 3-4:30AM.

\*        \*        \*

I stop typing. I'm over the word limit. There's so much more to say. I'm debating whether to continue or stop while I'm ahead. As I'm debating to continue or stop while I'm ahead, Mariah's laptop dings. Her head falls back. She groans. "Come on, this quarter won't let up." She sits up and thumbs the nape of her neck. Her eyes switching from her phone to us. "Are y'all going home this Thanksgiving?"

"I haven't bought my ticket yet."

"Same," I reply.

"If y'all end up staying here, want to come over for Friendsgiving? My friends just bailed for a trip to Atlanta."

"Shit, I'm sorry."

"It's all good. The tickets were a steal. If I didn't have to work through break, ██████ and I would've joined them. So, what do y'all say? A home-cooked meal, a couple board games."

"Minus the board games, a Friendsgiving sounds better than an overpriced red-eye to LA. I'm in."

"What about you, Sahara? You'll have a chance to meet ██████."

"Yeah, sounds fun," I reply, anxious of what else Mariah will see the more we hang out. I fear that with every future encounter, she's pulling back the curtain, catching glimpses of me before my performance is ready.

# V0DKA GET N0 ENEMY

The Café Owner kicks us out. He's ready to close for the day. The three of us say our goodbyes, Mariah promises to text us details about Friendsgiving. On the trek to my dorm, I try to revel in the idea that Mariah thinks I'm worth her time, but LP isn't having it. Loudly, she replays today's embarrassments. Nothing I did in class, nothing I said with Mariah proved that there's meaning within me. Then, the small glimpses that Mariah saw of the real me, she pitied. I'm grateful LP's here to check my delusions and save me from future ridicule. As long as I stay on this campus, sustaining a life that's only a performance, I'm always one misstep away from falling off the stage. With that tumble and truth it would inevitably bring, Mariah and C1, Mother and HB1, ROD and HB2, they and so many more would mock, pity, question, fear, hate everything I am. I can't have that. LP agrees. Perhaps we do need to leave while we're still ahead.

In my dorm room, I lock myself in the bathroom. I slap water in my face and clench the sink's edge, watching the beveled caulking between the sink and the tile wall slowly lift from my hand's pressure. LP is screaming. I'm powerless against her. Desperate to silence her, I turn on music, turn it up to the highest volume, scroll through my phone, searching for C1's message. It's ahead of our weekend schedule, but I ask if she has any plans for tonight. She doesn't and invites me over to her apartment.

With plans for an adventure, LP quiets. I exit the bathroom. On my bed, I see another note from Roommate, telling me to pick up toilet paper and soap for our bathroom. Even though I bought the last two rolls and the last hand soap,* I write a reminder in my phone to get more.

I know what you're wondering. Why can't Roommate, who's constantly taking mini vacations, buy any toilet paper? Your guess is as good as mine. I should tell her she needs to buy it this time, but I won't. If I do, she'll ask me *what's the big deal* and I'll say it's not a big deal. After a stalemate of skid marks, she'll relent and buy, but then my brokenness and the ridiculousness of not wanting to buy another roll will become the pastime conversation between her and her circle of friends. Not worth it. I'd rather hunt for coupons or free toilet paper on campus than have Roommate use me as the centerfold for *Lifestyles of the Young and Broke*.

*       *       *

As I search through my drawers, I'm still bitter and debating. Should I protest buying by stealing the dining hall's napkins? Okay, maybe that's a step too far. I'm spiraling to thieving scenarios to escape the

---

* Even the Charmin bears don't use this much toilet paper. I'm suspecting that she's taking it. Sometimes when I leave for class, there is half a roll of toilet paper left, but when I come back there's a quarter of a roll. What is she doing with all that toilet paper? And no, she's not wrapping her pads in wads of it. Is she stuffing her bra? Suffering from epistaxis? Irritable bowel syndrome?

true problem—I have nothing worth wearing. With each outfit I try on, I'm reimagining C1's glamour, the svelteness of her moments, her constant composure. My go-to choices of black high-waisted leggings, black sheer tops with solid panels hiding my stomach's excess fat, or my oversize denim jumpsuit are all too cheap and ill-fitting. Tonight, I'll either broadcast a FUPA that's so loud and proud that she could lead her own parade, or I'm showcasing Rainbow's bargain couture in a *Vogue* world.

I need to hurry. C1's made time for me, and keeping her waiting could set an irritating tone for the entire night. I settle for my oversize black satin button-up. Satin seems classy, right? But do I leave two buttons unbuttoned or button all the way to the top?* Two buttons, no buttons, class, no class, buttons, class. Does it matter? There's a snag in my shirt's sleeve that further scrunches with every pull of string. The satin's shine is too rich against my dull leggings. There are no clothes or actions that will conjure a glamour like C1's. Tonight will be embarrassing. Next to C1, the prom queen, there will be stares, *and oh, it's gonna be bad, Momma. They're all gonna laugh at me. Hold me, Momma. Please, hold me.*

\*     \*     \*

C1 lives inside New Money High-Rise.† The high-rise has twenty-seven floors, and rent for a studio starts at $1,975. To even receive an application for a unit, all potential tenants must have a referral from a current resident and proof of stable income for the past three years. For col-

---

\* On the third day of queer camp, a true queer said to me, "Have all buttons buttoned if you want to be like me."

† Not to be confused with Old Money Multifamily units, the buildings were bought as investment opportunities by the gouging rich to become richer.

lege students who don't live here, New Money High-Rise is the closest that we'll ever get to Narnia. The key to this wardrobe is a mini white electronic device. The doors into this wonderland are made of glass and have gold hexagon knobs. Here for treats, forget the Turkish delights, there's complimentary lemon- and lime-infused sparkling water or coffee and tea that is served at the perfect drinking temperature of 136°F. The magic of this place extends to the mythical creatures inside. There are the Donor Kids who never go to class but still graduate with honors cords, the International Elite who wear M²C bookbags the size of tampon applicators, and, of course, the tenured professors who use grad students' labor as their personal solar panels. And you thought lions, tigers, and bears were terrifying.

Inside, I tell the woman at the front desk C1's first name and apartment number. Front Desk Woman asks for a last name. I tell her I don't know it. Her eyes switching between my outfit and her computer as she files where I belong. "For security reasons, I cannot allow you upstairs. Have a seat." Her eyes direct me toward the nearest seat, a plain leather lounge chair, which is surprisingly uncomfortable despite the lavishness of the building. I shift back and forth, trying to find the right spot.

As she's waiting for C1 to answer her call, she hears my squeaking and glares over her floral bifocals. Her long, rectangular face is a grumpy Rothko. The top half has wisped eyebrows so faint they're washed into her forehead. The bottom half is a frown that hides her chin. I try to sneak two peppermints from a jar into my purse. Front Desk Woman catches me reaching for them. "Those are for residents, only." Caught mint-handed, I release them. "She's your friend?"

"Yes, ma'am."

"How come you don't know her last name?"

"It didn't—"

"Little weird to not know a last name."

"I'll text her again to let her know I'm here."

"She's not answering my calls." She hangs up the phone. "I'm going to have to ask you to leave."

Who made this wispy-browed granny the gatekeeper for all guests?* I don't protest. I pull my jacket around my arms, apologize for the inconvenience. I even make her excuses for her, so she doesn't have to. "You can never be too careful these days."

Her lips tilt up, but her eyes are frowning. "Have a blessed day." She motions toward Narnia's exit.

"Tha—" The phone rings. She raises her forefinger, stopping my speaking. On the phone, her voice is softer. Her smile, genuine. She looks to me. Her smile flinches to a scowl.

She lowers her finger. "You can head upstairs. Just so you know, your friend's last name is ██████." I'm Nigerian enough to recognize that the first part of C1's name is Nigerian.

The elevator doors open, I scurry inside, and listen to generic jazz play for the sixteen-floor ride. I knock on C1's door. She shouts, "It's open." I tug at the scrunched section of my shirt. It straightens, only slightly. I enter. C1's stretched across her couch, staring at her plasma TV and smoking a cigarette. Her eyes are red and white, like the two peppermints I tried to steal. Her year in Rome and her designer bags led me to expect an apartment draped in bohemian chicness. Instead, it's cookie-cutter cute. The mint-green sectional, the yellow-and-white zigzag rug, the white coffee table, are all agreeable choices. *Hey*, C1 says as she tosses and kicks pillows off her couch, making room for me to sit next to her. I watch the ashes fall into the ashtray that pillows partly cover. "Take anything you want out of the fridge."

"Thanks." I walk toward the silver casing. The only contents inside

---

* HR.

are limes, a case of Guinness, shriveled fruit, and half of a dried-out onion. All I've eaten today are the dollops of hummus and falafel. If a liquid dinner means LP will remain distracted, then that's more than enough. "Is it okay if I grab a beer?"

"Yeah, get me one too."

I grab two beers and return to the couch. C1's done smoking. She takes out two pills and places them inside her grinder. She grinds away. The pills crumble. "So, you're half-Nigerian?" I ask.

"Yep." She opens the pill grinder, checks the size of the crumbs before grinding again.

"The other half?"

"Italian. Why?"

"I'm half-Nigerian too."

"Which side?"

"My father."

"Did he teach you anything about it?"

"One, maybe two things," I respond, remembering Father's love of Fela Kuti, and his discussions with me and my little brothers that us being part Igbo means we must study the right subjects so we can make money.

"Lucky you." She slicks down her leave out. "I didn't realize I was Nigerian until my college admissions coach made me write about it for my personal statement. Before that, my dad never talked about it." She's facing me but isn't all the way here. "Doesn't matter anyways. I can always just visit and learn whatever *I* want." Her *I* bites. I'm not sure whether she's chewing me or herself. "Want some?" She points her joint toward the pill grinder.

"What is it?"

"Do you really care?" She wipes dust off her coffee table then cuts three lines with her student ID. She softens her voice, steadies her stare on me. "Try it. I can tell you're curious." Her seeing my curiosity reignites the belief that despite her wealth and her life's allure, we could be similar. Across from one another, with her knowing what I want, I am her understudy. And if I drink when she drinks, sniff what she sniffs, then perhaps, even if only for tonight, we can be the same? She rolls a ten-dollar bill, snorts, then hands me the rolled bill. I lean in. Before I start, she grabs my shoulder. Her acrylics gather against my shirt's snag. "Don't sneeze or breathe, or else you'll blow the lines away. Anything that's left, you rub on your gums."

I inhale. The crushed pills hit the back of my nose. I swallow the chalky taste and rub my gums.

"What is it?"

She wipes her nose. "Basically, Adderall with a kick." C1 grabs her beer and turns on her music. Drake blares. She's jumping from side to side and snapping her fingers. As she moves against the music, her beer spills onto the carpet. "Let's go out. Are you twenty-one?" Before I respond, she adds, "Doesn't matter. My friend owns a bar. He never cards. It's always a good time." She finishes the few sips of her beer that haven't spilled out from her dancing. "Come on, let's change." C1 leads me into her bedroom and she searches for clothes, first in her French-trimmed dresser, then in her walk-in closet, and finally in the pile of clothing sleeping on her white canopy bed.

This is bad, very bad, so bad that even LP doesn't know where to file this development. I slow my panicking and begin concocting a perfect excuse to leave and not try on clothes with sizing ranging from Barbie to Bratz. "Hey, I left my wallet in my dorm. I need to grab it. I'll meet you at the bar. "

"That'll take too long. And tonight's my treat. I always treat friends I like." C1 walks me to the foot of her bed and tosses potential outfits in my direction. I know that whatever she chooses, no matter how stretchy, will make me look like a sausage being squeezed out of its casing. While I pretend to consider the options, she's found two possible outfits for herself. As she pulls her silk cami over her head, she tells me, "Try something on to see what you like." I move away from the bed and closer to the closet. I take my shirt off and wrap my hands around my stomach, burying my fingers into my flesh.

C1 approaches. "Here, a friend left this over. I'm sure she won't mind." She shoves a piece of clothing toward me. I unwrap my fingers around myself to grab it. The romper's fabric is three times the size of most pieces of clothing on her bed. C1 goes from naked to clothed to naked again, flicking off outfits and ripping off price tags. I stare at her perfection, studying it, part by part. She has long, light brown legs, and every part of her seems hairless. There's a constellation of moles on her collarbone. While in her underwear—of course it's a matching lace set, free of holes—she stands in front of her freestanding mirror and taps her hip bone, which pokes out.

She stops examining her body and turns to me, confused I'm still in the same position of holding the romper in my hands. "Why aren't you changed?"

"I'll change in the bathroom."

"Don't be weird. Just hurry up." Behind the closet door, I pull down my pants and try on the romper. The stretchy fabric clings to my body, detailing every part of my form. C1 pulls the door away and studies me in sections. I try to turn away before her eyes migrate to my thighs. It's too late. All my harm and hatred are on display for her. No one, not even ROD or Mother, has seen this. I try holding back my tears, but fail. As they fall, I stumble into my leggings, and pull them over the romper's fabric, nearly ripping the leggings in my hurry. "Hey, hey, I won't tell anyone. It's okay." She caresses my back until I turn around. As we are facing one another, she lifts her dress, then raises her bra's band. Visible are faded scars. "Have you told anyone? Gone to therapy?"

"No."

"Good. That's all a waste of time. You just need a break. That's all."

She opens her dresser, pulls out a pill bottle, and places it in my hand. "Take one of these when you need to sleep it off." She undresses, again. Before tossing the bandage dress to the floor, she uses it to wipe away my tears. As she buttons my shirt, she adds, "I fucking swear, if you use these to off yourself, I'll be so pissed. Don't do anything stupid because of one bad thought. Promise?"

I respond "I promise" but privately reason that it's never just one bad thought. It's an onslaught dividing my days, to ones of pain, and ones of deception. I place the pills inside my pleather crossbody. C1 kisses me on the cheek and grabs me another beer. I wait for her to ask more or demand my reasons why. There's nothing except my opinion on which outfit looks the best on her. She decides on an indigo blazer paired with a leather minidress and sneaker wedges. While in the taxi to the bar, we drink vodka from a water bottle. C1 tells the driver to keep changing the radio station until she knows the lyrics to the song that plays. Finally, he lands on a station with a song she knows. C1 hollers lyrics and I watch the passing drivers.

*     *     *

The bar her friend owns is a three-storied experience called Dorian. C1 takes us to the basement, where we sit on a long red couch, which lacks a backing. She orders *her usual,* for the first round of drinks. Two shots of tequila and matching drinks called a Tom Collins arrive at the table. She downs her shot, then leaves to say hello to her other friends.

Alone, I inhale this bar's art deco atmosphere, which I suspect drives the drink prices to the teens and midtwenties. The lightbulbs in the basement are blacklights. There's wallpaper patterned with bronze clouds, and spray-painted on the wallpaper are words in Spanish and French. As I feared, I'm too underdressed, serving discount bin when everyone here is in their New York Fashion Week best of dresses, suit sets, or a Grace Jonesian combination of the two. I finish my drink and check my phone. There's no text from C1. I don't check in and ask where she is. She's already seen enough of my neediness today. I can handle this bar on my own. I figure that if I keep drinking for the next hour, I'll look like I belong here, and I'll go home

My hour is almost up and C1 returns. She apologizes for disappearing for so long. She simply lost track of time. "It's been so long since I've seen my friends," she states as she waves over a server. To make up for it, she orders us two vodka sodas and another round of tequila shots. The Bar Owner comes over with the drinks. She kisses his craggy forehead that's marked* with a brutish scar. He squeezes himself between C1 and me. I scoot to the left, silent and sipping as they flirt with one another. They finish their round of drinks and BO, the Bar Owner, tells the Bartender to bring a bottle of scotch. Still on the previous round, I chug the vodka soda, trying to keep up with their sophisticated livers. As I'm chugging he whispers into C1's ears, making her giggle in a pitch so high that all the stray dogs in this city might now run in this direction.

TEHEHE!

TEHEHE!     TEHEHE!     TEHEHE!

TEHEHE!

TEHEHE!     TEHEHE!

TEHEHE!

TEHEHE!     TEHEHE!     TEHEHE!     TEHEHE!

TEHEHE!     TEHEHE!     TEHEHE!

TEHEHE!     TEHEHE!     TEHEHE!     TEHEHE!

---

* Later, I would learn his investor/second wife gave him that scar when she hit him in the head with a wine bottle.

Postchug, my glass is still half empty, or half full, depending on your perspective. I try to listen to BO, but his drunkenness elides his words. I *think* he says to C1, "I love you. I'm better. Let me show you."

Bartender returns with a bottle of scotch and three glasses. BO orders Bartender to get herself a glass while he strokes C1's thighs and then his Salt-N-Pepa beard.* Bartender leaves and returns with a glass. As scotch is poured, C1 declares her love for this bar because it has the best scotch in the city. Though it's my first time trying scotch, I agree with her that it is the best. I guess this tongue is movin' on up to deluxe tastebuds in the sky.

*　　*　　*

We say cheers. The glasses clink. The scotch is too heavy in my hands. I try to gulp it. The quickened swallows burn my throat causing me to cough. While Bartender fills my glass with water and assures me that this happens all the time with scotch, she says, "Your coughs are cute like you." BO and C1 smirk at us and then at each other.

BO turns to Bartender and me. He caresses C1's hand and tells Bartender to grab a bottle of tequila. He lets C1 pick the brand, and she picks something that sounds potent and expensive. I burp up then swallow a portion of my liver.

The four of us take a shot, and though it's a struggle, I finish. Bartender reaches for the tequila bottle. When it's my turn for another pour, my hand covers my shot glass. BO swipes it away. He orders me to drink because *we are celebrating love, sweet love, the world's first*

---

* Oooh baby, baby. They're working up a sweat.

*drink*. He kisses my cheek and pours me more tequila. He and C1 laugh with one another. I'm too drunk to know what's driving the TEHEHEs. I try to lean against the couch but instead fall into the wall.

BO laughs and turns to C1. "My love, I think your friend is done."

"No, she's not. She's having fun, right?"

C1's eyes cut toward me. The ferociousness of her stare metabolizes a bit of the liquor saturating myself. I assert, "So much fun, another round."

I take the shot. My eyes close. Seconds or minutes later they open to C1, she's sitting on BO's lap, drinking, and telling a story. I focus on her words, willing myself sober. "Now this, this is the craziest thing I saw abroad. I know you'll love it." C1 winks at BO. "So, one night while walking to my taxi, I watched two teenagers fucking on the bus." C1 places her drink on the table. Her hands attempt to stage the scene. "There I am, just staring, completely shocked. They saw me and waved. The bus drove away." BO laughs, and C1 vibrates on his thigh like a Tickle Me Elmo. He kisses C1's neck and proclaims, "One day, we'll go to London to be horny teenagers together."

He begins thrusting his pelvis underneath her. I can't stomach them anymore. I leave for a smoke. Bartender follows me. I let her bum a cigarette. She's striking—rosebud lips, an Afro puff of hair so tall it reaches the skyline, a sculpted face, and eyes as dark as a total eclipse. While she talks, I fade in and out of her words.

"Can't stand him. Creep. Free drinks to pretty."

"You free drinks?"

"What?"

"'Cause you're pretty."

"You're drunk."

"So."

"Curious or pissed at daddy?"

"Fuck you,* kiss me."

She stomps out her cigarette and kisses me. Heat rushes to my face. As we kiss, I hope our tongues become tied, connecting us in this moment forever. She kisses my face. I escalate my hopes to prayers that her every touch will consume me.

She unbuttons half of my shirt and pushes my bra down. My knees weaken. My head heaves ecstasy. She licks my nipple, sucks then bites, then moves to my neck. Her curls are pillows for my fingers. As we inhale each other, I count the seconds until she takes all of me. She asks, "How far?" We pause, breathing in one another. I don't know how to explain that this is the furthest I will go. I want more, but the possibility of explaining my body, the evidence of my violence, restrains me.[†] When C1 saw, she promised silence. I doubt that Bartender would as well. Still, I try to enjoy within this confinement. I cup her ears, and initiate another kiss. Gradually, a cold punctures the heat between us. LP's here, draining my pleasure.

Our tongues untie. I step away from her with crossed arms. "I can't."

"What's wrong?"

"I don't know."

"It's okay. We can go back."

In the basement, BO has a bottle of vodka waiting for us. I throw back two shots. When everyone's on their third round, I exit the booth, grasping for tables and barstools as I'm stumbling for the bathroom. My body's swinging back and forth. I grip the wall and slide into a stall.

Head over toilet, too drunk to move, I remain. Enough time passes for people to wonder where I am. I hear one person giggling. Another helps me to my feet.

---

* Securing all the buttons did nothing to show where I am on the Kinsey scale.

† Hail Sahara, Full and Chaste. Blessed art LP who is with me. Holy Mary Magdalene, Lover of God, pray for my sins now and at the hour of death. Amen.

TEHEHE!

TEHEHE!

## DEATH IN THE AFTERNOON

*While inside a posh DMV, Me waits in line. The lights are bright, the counters clean, the carpet fresh. On the walls are plasma and analog televisions playing the same ad on loop. In Me's hand is a card with her fingerprint on it. In front of and behind her are college students, all of whom are either staring down at their cards or watching the ad. Some of the college students are missing arms, parts of their heads, or legs.*

AD: What's your soul worth? Together, we'll find out. With a down payment of your soul, we can put you on track to graduate loan-free. Please ask your clerk for more details.

*Me's number is called. She walks toward the counter.*

CLERK: Welcome to Purgatory. Please give me your card for processing. *(Me hands over her card. Clerk places it underneath a scanner for processing.)* The process should take about five hours. Thank you for your patience.

ME: Excuse me, I would like more information regarding the loan forgiveness program.

CLERK: *(Slides over a handbook that is larger than* In Search of Lost Time. *The cover of the handbook reads* HOW TO BE DEBT FREE.*)* Let me know if you have any questions.

*The clerk turns on her portable television, which is next to the scanner. She watches* Dynasty, *but during the commercial break, she switches the channel to* Dallas. *While Clerk sits on the edge of her seat when she's about to find out who shot J. R., Me watches the Loan Forgiveness ad that plays on the plasma.*

AD: Have you heard about our loan forgiveness program? With the one-time down payment of your soul, you will graduate any higher education program debt-free. Why wait till after graduation to lose your soul working at a dead-end job, when you can lose it now? Still not convinced, then hear from some of our satisfied customers.

*A girl appears on-screen. She's in a hospital gown and missing her right arm and left eye.*

GIRL IN AD: Before deciding to enroll in Hell's loan forgiveness program, I was worried about what I would do after graduation. There were jobs, but the salary wouldn't make a dent in my loans. Then one night after I thought all was lost, I ended up in this DMV and heard about this program. After learning more about it, I immediately knew that this program was right for me. I made the down payment of my soul, and only have five more payments left. Don't worry, the other payments are so easy. I gave my right arm and left eye. It was completely painless. I'm so close to being loan-free and can start living the life I want. This is the best decision I've ever made!

*The girl leaves the screen, Me tries to lift* How to Be Debt Free *from the counter, but it is too heavy. A soft ding is heard in the background and the clerk sighs. She ignores the ding until after the big J. R. reveal. As the episode's credits roll, Clerk removes Me's card out of the scanner, and Clerk reads off Me's decision.*

CLERK: Well, lucky you. You're returning, but I'll see you next Thirsty Thursday.

ME: Wait, before I leave, I would like to enroll in the loan forgiveness program.

CLERK: *(reads the screen)* Well, according to my data, your soul is too empty to give.

# LIKE A PRAYER

Teeth chattering. I wrap myself tighter. I try and piece together a prayer, one that Father will hear. All that is prayed, *Please let this be it. Just let this be it.*

Amen.

# FORGET ME OR NOT

I wake up still in last night's clothes. My head pounds. There's dried vomit on my braids. My mouth tastes like puke and Frost Gatorade, and my body's too heavy to lift. I stay in bed until I hear a moan from below. I look down and it's ROD. She's using Roommate's paisley robe as a blanket. Confused, I lean forward and shake her awake. One, two, three. By the fourth shake, another wave of nausea slams against me. I curl up into a ball. My stomach won't stop its flipping. I use one hand to cradle it and the other to cover my mouth. I rush to the bathroom and during my dash, I step on ROD's arm.

Before I turn on the faucet, I notice my phone sits in the sink. I place it behind the faucet's handles and wonder what else besides yesterday's drinks, ROD, Roommate's robe, and my phone is still displaced because of last night.

*　　*　　*

I scroll through my phone. There are thirty-six missed messages.

1st—Bartender apologizing for not realizing how drunk I was.*

2nd—C1 asking if I'm alive.

3rd—C1 asking if I am up to go to another bar with her and some Donor Kids.

4th—Mother asking why I'm not coming home for Thanksgiving.

5th—Mother asking how, where, and what I will cook for myself for Thanksgiving.

6th—Mother asking if my church is hosting a Thanksgiving dinner.

7th—Mother asking if I go to church.

8th—Mother asking what nonsense I am up to that I can't respond to her messages.

9th—ROD asking where I am so she can come get me.

10th—ROD saying she is coming to my dorm.

11th–36th—a flurry of messages from the Black Excel chat celebrating the final signing of Illinois's Marriage Fairness Act. This celebrating then leads to bets of who in the group chat is the first to get married.

I sit against the bathtub, staring at my phone, which vibrates with a call from Mother.

"Are you gonna answer that?"

"And say what?" I respond feeling slimed with queasiness and shame. "Say hi Mom, I'm between pukes, but I'll call back?"

The phone stops ringing. "How about, hi Mom, I fucked up last night and scared the shit out of my best friend. I called her to come get

---

* How did she get my number?

me, didn't answer any following calls, and she found me passed out in front of the CVS down the street."

"I'm sorry." My phone's back to its ringing, and I'm wondering how the hell I ended up at CVS. "I'll keep ignoring and will tell her I was studying."

"Our moms are the same. She's going to keep calling until you answer."

I lean my head against the tub's edge and pretend to stare at the ceiling, when in truth, my eyes are retreating into myself, rolling through every vein, searching for an answer as to how I can escape ROD's worries. "I can't right now."

"Fine, then I will, again." ROD bends down and grabs my phone, answers it, then puts Mother on speaker. "Hi, Mama Nwadike."

With the lie that the two of us were pulling an all-nighter, ROD momentarily calms Mother's worries. They exchange small talk about classes and ROD's art until Mother asks, "Sahara's not making you lie, is she? If she is, I'll know."

"No, no, of course not, Momma Nwadike. I could never lie to you." I twirl my fingers as a signal for ROD to wrap up the conversation before Mother is on to us. "Once Sahara wakes up, I'll remind her to call you. She's been asleep." ROD hands me the phone. "Hopefully, she'll wake up soon." ROD and Mother say goodbye to one another. The call ends.

"Thanks."

"Just help me find my glasses." ROD leaves the bathroom and begins peering at every nook. "Fuck, they're not here either."

I exit the bathroom and stand by the doorway. "Do you remember the last place you had them?"

"On my fucking face," she spits out. She attempts breathing out her anger; however, it remains in her, incubating. "I had them on my face before struggling to get you upstairs without your RA seeing you, and continually rolling you off your stomach throughout the whole fucking night." She rips back my comforter. "Sahara, I had to leave my studio hours early, and I won't get a refund for the hours I missed."

"ROD, I'm sorry."

"Are you? You don't even seem worried."

"Because it was an accident. I forgot to eat dinner."

"Where did you even go last night?"

"Out."

"Where?"

"To a bar."

"How, you're not twenty-one?"

"I went with a friend who had an in. Can we stop with the questions and focus on finding your glasses?"

"Whatever." ROD tosses my clothes toward the bed's edge, shakes my comforter, then checks for the wedge of space between my bed frame and the radiator. "I don't know why you're mad at me. You should be mad at your asshole friend who left you by a bus stop, and not me."

"I'm not mad. I'm hungover." We tear apart my side of the dorm room and shake out Roommate's robe until I'm convinced the patterns will fall on the floor. I return to the bathroom and pull back the shower curtain. I pick through the wad of wet clothes, and underneath everything, I find ROD's glasses. I clean them off before handing them to her. "Here," and I promise, "I'll pay you back for your studio hours."

"What? I don't want you to pay me back. I want to make sure you're okay." I follow ROD out of the bathroom. We sit next to each other in the chaos of my bedroom floor. I'm leaning on her shoulders as I swear, "I'm fine, I really am."

# I HAVE
# 99 PROBLEMS
# AND I CAN'T
# ANSWER ONE

When I feel that I have ROD's forgiveness, I leave for the library to study for my Naughty Cells midterm. With my hand on my head and my fingers scratching my braids' new growth, I attempt to decipher the charts and memorize PowerPoints. The words, then graphs, then diagrams, then practice questions are bleeding into one another. Instead of answers to my test, I see a forgotten Kandinsky painting.

This is hopeless, but I continue peering at the screen because my grade can't afford me giving up. I close my eyes and recite the facts. I cross my fingers, click my heels as I run through these memory drills. I think I'm close to getting it right this time. I open my eyes and check to see how close I was to being correct. Scroll, scroll, flip, flip. I was way off the mark, confusing T cells with B cells, forgetting what cytokines can't do and what a macrophage eats. This is still hopeless, and there's no other game plan except take a break, and then try again.

I wander the library and return to where I found Aunt Nita's zine. Despite the multiple recall emails, I still have the library's only copy. There are so many books crowding the shelf that you wouldn't notice the small sliver of space where the zine previously rested. I run my fingers along the spines. I imagine the graduate student who used my aunt's zine, searching decimal point by decimal point until he reached the zine's ending of .65. *A work of anti-intellectualism, offensive, amazing what passes for poetry.* Why couldn't he see this wasn't for him?

I sit on the squeaking step stool and roll slightly back and forth as I think of revenge. I could creep into the office of whatever university he is currently schlepping his hatred at. In his office, I would delete his papers and all his backup files, remove the ink from his pens, send a letter of resignation for his fellowship appointments, jobs, and any academic capital he's hunting. Of course, for good measure and a general lesson against capitalist impulses, I'll shake or poke holes in the sparkling water he hoards from University events. A student entering the aisle stops my fantasy. They creep past me, and as I'm scooching out of their direction, I get a kicking whiff of myself.

\*       \*       \*

In the bathroom while keeping an eye on the door, I rinse my mouth with water, then take a clump of wet paper towels and scrub my armpits until the mushed paper towels look like disintegrating halves of soft pretzel twists. God, I'm hungry. But I ~~can't~~ won't eat until I've earned the calories. If I can answer at least a third of the questions right, then I can earn my meal. With every practice set of questions, the list of wrong answers grows. I need the correct answers, an aced test, a successful class. I need just one quarter where there's a testimony to my worth. After that, I won't try to re-create the conditions of my success, I'll finally rest.

I'm getting ahead of myself. Let's pause this rumination so I can return to studying. Before my descent into the books, Thesis Committee, let me apologize. I guaranteed an honors thesis, not the melding of my dietary and study schedule and the pitfalls of my inebriation. However, won't you agree that in this thesis—a soundtrack to my life—I've been doing well? I've given you facts and footnotes, interdisciplinary convos, and met diversity quotas. To guarantee your impartiality, I've even redacted all names of future, present, or former colleagues, students, and acquaintances. I've been twice, no, four times as good. Yet still, to ensure you have no reason to give me half as much, I swear to keep everything purely academic from here on out.

## *Purely Academic*

*The Original Colonial America Flavor*

# Nutrition Facts

About 1 Serving Per Body
**Serving Size        1(Head)**

| Amount Per Serving | |
| --- | --- |
| **Thoughts** | 1636 |

| | %Daily Value* |
| --- | --- |
| **Total Anxiety** 50g | 77% |
| Academic Anxiety 21g | 105% |
| Social Anxiety 6g | |
| **Stress** 600g | 200% |
| **Exhaustion** 2013g | 84% |
| **Total Fulfillment** 44g | 10% |
| Catharsis 0g | |
| Satisfaction 0g | |

*Percent Daily Value are based on a 2,000 Thought Diet

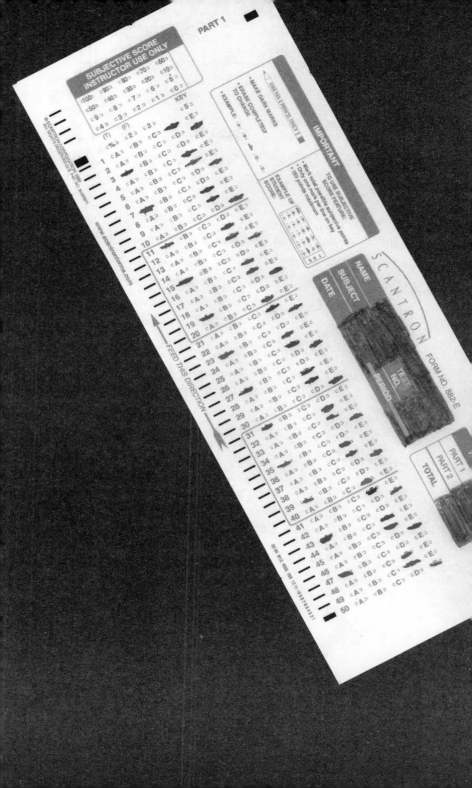

1. Pencils are up, my head is down, and my
nerves swiggle me sideways.

   a. DDI
   b. OYU
   c. VENE
   d. DYUST
   e. OD

2. For the Naughty Cells midterm, NCP has all
of us spaced apart.

   a. DVESEER
   b. OT
   c. EB
   d. HEER
   e. HWO

3. She tells us we have two hours. She takes
her seat behind the lecture hall's podium.

   a. AMYN
   b. ISEMT
   c. ILLW
   d. LIAF
   e. EETSH

4. Coughs and the rustle of flipping pages
interrupt the lecture hall's silence.

   a. SETTS
   b. OS
   c. SAEISBRGRMAN
   d. EWHN
   e. EW

5. I flip through the stapled pages, trying to find an easy question to begin with.

  a. GTE
  b. OMHE
  c. LWLI
  d. TCU
  e. NDA

6. I can't remember anything I studied.

  a. TI
  b. SI
  c. ETH
  d. YONL
  e. GHTIN

7. I wonder if my hours in the library were part of a mundane dream, or if this blanking during the exam is another nightmare.

  a. UYO
  b. NREEAD
  c. IAGAN
  d. THIW
  e. IBTSLLHU

8. Forty-five minutes in, the first student turns in the exam. Time passes and I am still flipping through the pages, trying to crack this test's cipherous language that switches its order every time I reread a question.

  a. TUSJ
  b. A
  c. SETT
  d. MACL
  e. WDNO

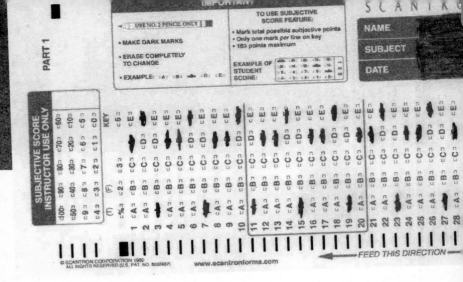

9. NCP announces that there's only fifteen minutes left, I still have a page's worth of questions.

    a. YUO

    b. NKWO

    c. ISTH

    d. UOY

    e. EDSDUTI

10. My stomach bottoms out.

    a. EDSDUTI

    b. HTSI

    c. TSJU

    d. MBREEREM

    e. HATT

11. My breaths stagger.

    a. SI

    b. LLA

    c. YOU

    d. VAHE

    e. OT

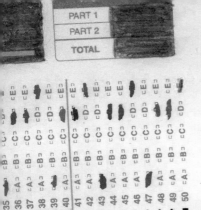

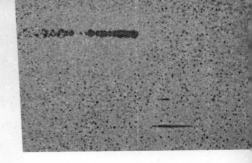

12. LP's awake and cackling at my predicament.

    a. OD
    b. OYU
    c. ERA
    d. LAASWY
    e. VLIIGN

13. I'm the last one left and am on the brink of tears.

    a. NI
    b. YURO
    c. TUOHSGTH
    d. DNA
    e. EGTROTTSAFHUH

14. I rushfill my Scantron's remaining bubbles, and with shame keeping my head lowered, I turn in my exam.

    a. UOY
    b. IDTOI
    c. AMKE
    d. HMET
    e. UESULF

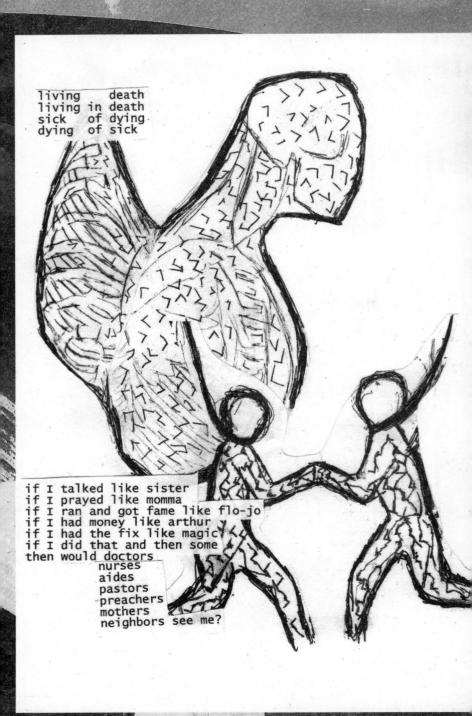

living     death
living in death
sick    of dying
dying   of sick

if I talked like sister
if I prayed like momma
if I ran and got fame like flo-jo
if I had money like arthur
if I had the fix like magic
if I did that and then some
then would doctors
          nurses
          aides
          pastors
          preachers
          mothers
          neighbors see me?

# IN THE WORLD OF A
## BARBIE GIRL

'm on my bed, still thinking about today's exam. I double-checked the few of my answers with the PowerPoints and printed lecture notes, and quickly it's apparent that red asterisks will bedazzle my Scantron.

The sound of my door opening interrupts my dramatic wallowing. Lo and behold, it's Roommate in the flesh, and not in the usual loopy cursive asking me to buy more toilet paper. She's a-huffing, and a-puffing, and a-ranting that none of the elliptical machines at her boyfriend's apartment gym, and then the University gym, were available, and now, she's stuck with a home workout. As she's squatting, wisps of her strawberry hair are damp with sweat. Her talking continues, jumping between sharing the details for her winter getaway and apologizing for being so absent as a roomie.*

---

\* With matters of dorm housing on hand, absence does not make the heart grow fonder. I've been enjoying this absentee Roommate life where there's complete silence from the other side.

"Don't worry, it's fine."

"You sure? You seem kinda down."*

"Oh, I'm fine—just a bit out of it. I had a rough day."

"I figured. Your face said it first. What's up?"

"I didn't do well on a test."

"It's only a test. Ask the professor for a retake."

*Definitely*, I reply, wondering how the hell do I even ask for a retake when I'm too nervous to even squeak in class. Roommate shares the numerous times petitioning for retake worked. I'm not sure if this is her way of encouraging or simply her way of passing the time as she works out. What I do know—explaining to a professor why I failed feels like I'm bringing shame to my ancestors and every diversity initiative. Roommate pauses her workout for a water break. I say, "Great idea," grab my largest water canister, and dart out of the room.

*　　*　　*

The water fountain is hidden underneath the dorm's main stairwell. Every other week dorm maintenance is placing or removing an OUT OF ORDER sign. This week word must have spread that it's working. There's a line of students holding water canisters, pitchers, and ramen cups who all await their turn, as if this water is blessed by Jesus and not precarious amounts of lead. Because I'm a Good Samaritan wanting to help while on my travels away from small talk, I let others in line

---

* While some have resting bitch face, I have resting sad face, which when left unchecked can attract concern, sympathy, or judgment like fruit flies to vinegar. Last year as I walked toward the nearest bus stop, a man stopped his current delivery to ask me if I was okay. I said, *yes*, but my voice wasn't dedicated, and my mind was still with LP. This unconvincing performance led to a back-and-forth that didn't end until I explained that my current sadness was because of a podcast I was listening to. Satisfied with my answer, he finished his delivery, shouting, *you're too cute to be sad*, as he drove away.

cut in front of me, and when it's my turn, I figure before I fill up, I should empty out my tank. So, I leave the line to use the bathroom, and while scrolling my phone inside the stall, I remember I owe Mother a call, and if the choice is between a guilt-trip-filled lecture from Mother or watching Roommate's squatting, then Trebek, I'll choose LECTURE FOR THIRTY MINUTES. Outside on the dorm benches as the wind threatens to blow a few of my loose braids toward Lake Michigan, I apologize to Mother that I am missing Thanksgiving, and explain to her, again, that the break is only a few days and so close to finals that the stress of traveling and having to study between turkey bites would ruin the holiday for everyone, and with hesitation Mother agrees, we say goodbye, I try lighting a cigarette, but the wind has a different plan. With every slip of my thumb against the spark wheel, the crushing yet necessary realization—I will never spend another Thanksgiving with my family—hits me. Eventually, a flame is lit. I finish a cigarette, tuck away my remorse, and return to queue. There, I read a few flyers on the nearby bulletin, between KYR's flyers, advertisements for paid psychology studies, an invitation for "Made in the Microwave Only potluck"—it leaves me guessing which dish is the most likely to cause food poisoning. Then finally after I've exhausted all avenues of procrastination, I return to wait in the water fountain line. After I fill the water bottle, figuring that Roommate has either left, or at least finished her workout, I return to my dorm room.

The room's hot with steam and packed with Roommate's sweat. She emerges from the bathroom wrapped in a towel. Thankfully, she'll be gone soon to meet her boyfriend for a late lunch so they can discuss her officially moving in.

She shoves her phone in my face. "Isn't he a cutie!" My head tilts back, and my eyes adjust to the phone's brightness. I say *aww* to a picture of her with her thumbs up while on her boyfriend's back. "This is when we went hiking together." She then scrolls to her photo album, titled "I'm Only Me When I'm with You," and shows me every outtake from their numerous dates. Her wide smile, her checkmark eyebrows that are so aggressive they could advertise with Nike, and her go-to pose of a thumbs-up are annoying my thoughts.

I didn't ask, but Roommate shares with me all the reasons why this boyfriend is a keeper and might be the one to give her the M R S. He's in a frat and sometimes calls out his bros if they're being jerks, he volunteers at least once a year, he eats vegetables, and he even showers regularly. From everything Roommate's disclosed, I already know the boyfriend's class schedule, dick size, eating habits, siblings' names, and study schedule. If there was an APB out for this boyfriend, then I would have all the vital information needed to track him down. After almost half an hour of her dating details, there can't be anything else to know about this boyfriend, right? No, not right at all. Roommate finds more to tell, such as his upcoming teeth cleaning for his sexy pearly whites. And yes, teeth—when straightened right—can be *so* sexy.

* * *

As she explains why a middle-school dental appointment caused the boyfriend's current fear of dentists, I calculate another escape. A prolonged visit to the bathroom with a few dramatic grunts should scare Roommate enough to have her flee the room or make the post-bathroom atmosphere awkward enough that she won't want to talk. I glance toward the bathroom door and notice that there's no toilet paper. When I left to fill my water bottle, there were two new rolls next to the sink.

"Do you know where the toilet paper went?"

"Oh yeah, I was just about to ask if you could pick some up. This time maybe double ply so it lasts longer."

I'm holding my tongue and know I should tell Roommate it's her turn to buy—and also ask her what the hell she's doing with them—but through a clenched grin, I tell her, "For sure."

"Thanx, roomie." She drops her towel. I avert my gaze and she rolls blue floral printed tights over her legs. "You know, he has a friend who looks like him, and is only into Black girls. I have to introduce you to one another." She zips her khaki A-line skirt that's taut against her waist. "Imagine, no pressure, of course, just imagine how cute your babies would be if the two of you got together." If I had a dollar for every time during this conversation, I had to stop myself from rolling my eyes, then I would have enough money to fund a year's worth of toiletries. Annoyed, I put my headphones around my neck and hunt for a song that will help switch my mood from a track of irritation to indifference. "So, should I?"

"Sure, and our kids would make the perfect multi-culti smoothie."

She laughs. Good. Laughs are good. They hide my anger.

"Sahara, that's such a weird thing to say. If I do set you up, I wouldn't say things like that in front of my boyfriend's friend." First my face, then the ply count, and now my jokes. What else does Roommate want to change? As she buttons her cropped white sweater, she explains, "Jokes like that scare guys away. You only bring out the crazy and weird stuff *after* you've hooked them. For example, I can't say no to BBQ sauce on mac and cheese."

"BBQ sauce on mac and cheese. That's what's weird to you?"

"It's so good, but some people find it weird. So, I won't eat that until I'm positive the guy I'm dating is so hooked he'll try it himself. What's your weird?"

I picture LP sitting on top of my baggage, filing her nails, and waiting for me to introduce her. How could I even tell Roommate about LP when I haven't even told ROD? I share with Roommate a half-truth and tell her, "My jokes."

"Jokes are fun, but you have to say the right, mild ones in front of a guy you like."

"Not too spicy."

"Exactly, not too spicy. Be BBQ, not hot sauce."

Roommate leaves, mentioning that depending on how lunch goes, she might be back to pack up some of her things. Her phone rings, and it is Boyfriend telling her that he's waiting outside to drive them downtown for lunch. She exclaims *yay,* and I join her, *yay,* and then add, *he's definitely a keeper,* hoping that vote of confidence will ensure Roommate moves in with him. She leaves, and I'm relieved. To raise my relief so it doesn't sink into LP, I listen to Ken Collier, a DJ that over the summer Mother mentioned Aunt Nita loving. The music succeeds and moves me past first relief and then to indifference. It allows me to dream a scene where Aunt Nita tells me "fuck the test," and we leave to go dancing. As we time travel between clubs in Detroit and Chicago, allowing our outfits and hair to change with the times, our effervescent joy is so bright that it becomes our calling card letting everybody know, *Aunt Nita & Sahara are here to show you how it's done.* When we land in my dorm for a sweat check, she begins peeking underneath Roommate's covers, and then underneath her bed, shifting around the exercise equipment and the plastic tubs. She figures this Roommate of mine definitely has more crazy in her and has to be hiding it in the same place that she's hiding the toilet paper. I agree and help her as I wonder what will happen once we bring out the crazy.

## HOW TO BRING OUT THE CRAZY

*Man and Me sit in a diner and split a milkshake. Though Me knows damn well she wants a double bacon cheeseburger, her own milkshake, and chili cheese fries, her and Man aren't official, so she is still in the stage of splitting food and pretending she's not hungry. Me wears a sweater with only the top button unbuttoned, a poodle skirt, and ballerina flats. Her hair is straightened and slicked to the side. Whenever she stops speaking, her face jumps back into that warm Chelsea Smile.*

MAN: Hey, so I was wondering, do you want to be my girl?

*Me smiles wider. Her eyes become even brighter.*

ME: Are you sure?

MAN: Yes, you're low-maintenance and you're always there for me. I would be a fool not to lock you down.

*Me grabs Man's hand. The rest of the diner dims. A spotlight appears on them.*

ME: I'm so happy. I can finally show it to you.

MAN: Show me what?

*Me leaves and goes backstage. She returns, dragging a giant yellow drum that has the letters LP etched into the center. The sounds of the drum scraping against the floor echo throughout the stage. Me's outfit has changed. She's wearing stained sweats. As she drags the drum, her wig falls off, revealing her wig cap. Man looks confused.*

ME: Look inside.

*Man peers into the drum, and inside of it, he hears cackles.*

MAN: Is that . . . all you?

*Black slime erupts from the drum and splatters him in the face. The slime burns craters into his skin. He covers his face while he screams in agony.*

ME: No baby, she's part of us.

*Laugh track plays "aww" in the background. Panicking, Man looks around and then darts offstage. He's so afraid that he's tripping over his feet. Laugh track changes to the same cackles that were heard inside the drum. Me puts her wig back on, goes offstage to redress in her sweater and poodle skirt.*

**TEHEHE.**

# STILL
# IN THE WORLD OF A
# BARBIE GIRL

The next day while Roommate is packing her suitcases, NC emails me. To no surprise, I've failed the exam. She wants to meet with me to discuss my options for her class. I want to confide in ROD and tell her everything, from failing a test to falling deeper into LP, but I'm afraid of her response. We're in a new phase of our friendship. We're no longer living in jokes, eating binges, or sarcastic complaints about this University. This friendship was perfect when we were laughing, and I remained in character. But now, as me and everything I pretend to be blurs together, fear fills my time with ROD. I am afraid of her knowing about LP, and our plans to leave. I don't know what she would do with the information, or if she will want to be my friend after the discovery. I want to leave our friendship, and this school, on a high-note. I thought I had at least one year of good laughs and grades in me. However, it turns out that, just like last year, I am again barely surviving the quarters.

I take out one of C1's sleeping pills. I need to forget the past few days, perhaps a long nap will reset my brain. Before I can pop one of the pills in my mouth, Roommate stops packing and narrating her future adventures with her boyfriend. She's waiting for me to join her joy, and I try, believing I'm convincing until her question "Are you even listening?" brings an unwanted intermission. I apologize, she says it's fine, then adds visual props to her story. The addition of her Tumi suitcases and her affixed smile helps sustain my attention. From her duffel, she takes out a turquoise lingerie set. "*This* is my thank-you to him for letting me move in and not having to pay any rent." She places the baby doll bustier against her collarbone. "Sexy right?"

"So sexy, very sexy. It's perfectly sexy."[*]

She squeals out a brilliant idea that a little tlc is the perfect distraction from a little bad news. "It's perfect. You always have the room to yourself." Roommate folds her G-string and places it in her suitcase's front pocket.

"I probably won't."

"Come on, don't you want that feeling of being touched." Roommate pauses to giggle. She blushes as she adds, "And loved?" She rolls her suitcases toward the door. Her flushed cheeks signal that she's detoured to lovers' boulevard while walking down memory lane. "So, who's your go-to pick-me-up?"

"No one."

"There's always someone. You can tell me."

"There's not. I haven't had sex yet." Roommate's flush fades. Her eyes' sympathy mixes with their confusion. "Not a big deal. I just haven't."

Roommate ignores a call from her boyfriend. She firmly clasps my

---

[*]  That may have been one sexy too many.

hands. Her Pandora sterling charms of cameras, doves, and hearts rattle as she says, "You have to, like as soon as possible."

"I'm not sure—"

"Wait, you know what this reminds me of—" She scrolls through her phone, ignoring another call from her boyfriend because my virginity needs her complete attention. "There was this other old virgin who auctioned hers off. You could do that. Honestly, do anything as long as it means you finally getting laid." She answers her phone and tells her boyfriend that she's coming downstairs. As she exits, she says, "Have fun," then winks at me.

## HOW TO SELL BLACK VIRGINITY

*Me stands on top of a wooden auction block, hidden behind a red curtain. She is naked. Her body is oiled. Her face has pink blush on her cheeks, forehead, and eyelids. Her lips are painted with pink lipstick. Her hair is styled like 1959 Barbie. Her eyes are wide because Roommate has ordered her not to blink.*

*Roommate stands by the red curtain. Her blond ponytail is hidden under a black top hat, and she wears a black tuxedo. In front of Roommate is a gang of four white men. Their right hands are auction cards. In their left hands, they hold tumblers filled with brandy. The group of men wear 1980s power suits and top hats that are coated with mercury. Their eyes are glassy.*

**ROOMMATE:** Come one, come all! Come with your throbbing wallets. Come have a taste of chocolate. Come meet a girl so exotic that her very own kin named her Sahara.

*Roommate pulls away the red curtains. Me stares at the men gazing at her body.*

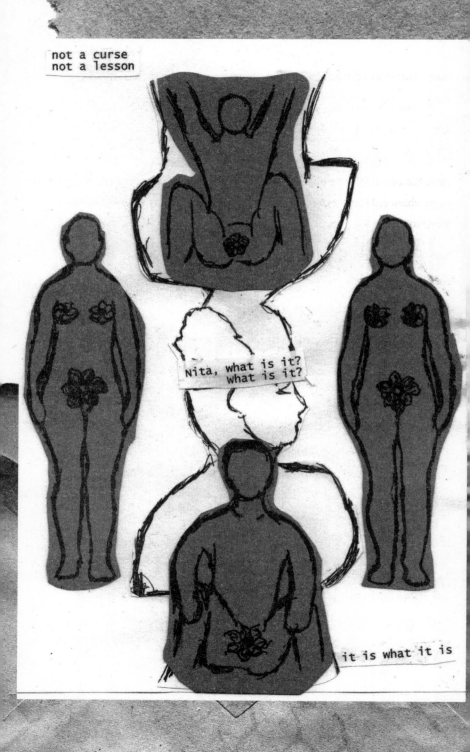

**MEN:** Turn her around.

*Roommate grabs Me, turns her around, bends Me forward, smacks her ass, and then winks at Men. Me is turned back around. She still isn't blinking.*

**ROOMMATE:** Never been with a Black girl before? Well, now is your chance. Don't worry, we won't tell anyone about your little adventure.

**MEN:** *(in a chorus)* Hot, tuh ta, ta, tot. She's no Beyoncé, but we'll take a bite.

*Men laugh.*

**FIRST MAN:** Look at that ass! It alone is a goddess of love.

*Men cackle. Me remains still. Her eyes begin to burn.*

**SECOND MAN:** If she wasn't so dark, I'd date her.

*Men mumble in agreement, then drink from their tumblers.*

**THIRD MAN:** If my grandfather saw that ass or even those tits, there's no way he'd still say nigger.

*The cohort of men laugh even louder. Roommate laughs along with them. Tears drip from Me's eyes. Roommate notices and brings out a new set of eyes from her pocket to quickly replace the watering ones.*

**ROOMMATE:** Shall we start the bidding? Let's start at one date.

**FIRST MAN:** One date.

**SECOND MAN:** One date and a nightcap at my apartment.

**THIRD MAN:** Two dates and a movie night at my apartment.

FOURTH MAN: Three dates, and that's the highest I'll go.

THIRD MAN: Four dates, a nightcap, one present of her choosing, and four months of dating.

ROOMMATE: *(ecstatic)* Well then, we'll stop the bidding there unless someone wants to outbid. *(None of the men raise their auction cards. They grumble.)* Sir, come get your winnings.

THIRD MAN: *(Carries Me on his back.)* Hot, tuh ta, ta, tot! I shan't experience this by myself.

*Third Man sets Me down in front of the other men. Third man's right hand is now a bucket to collect money.*

Kind gentlemen, I only ask that you leave that ass for me.

*Men release the tumblers. The glass shatters on the floor. One by one, they take their favorite parts. First Man takes Me's tits. Second Man takes Me's lips. The Fourth and final Man takes Me's naughty bits.*

# ALONE!
# ALONE!
# ALONÉ

In college, where we are young and feral, the expectation is constant fucking. Despite Roommate's beliefs, I'm 87 percent sure I am not sexually repressed. The other 13 percent of me does concoct scenarios of what would happen if I did find someone. Let's say, I undress, they see my scars, and instead of having a little tlc, I'm suddenly in therapy, or they're too stunned and the mood is killed, or they say nothing and I'm constantly waiting for the other shoe to drop, or I become their pity project. I'd rather stick with me, myself, and I than deal with another unplanned scar showcase.

\*  \*  \*

These lessons on self-isolation as protections started from Mother. After puberty, mother-and-daughter time became Saturday-morning specials about why you need to keep your energy above your waistline.

Saturday mornings while my brothers were away learning Igbo from UB,* Mother and I made meat pies, plantains, *moimoi*, black-eyed peas, and puff-puffs. As she kneaded the dough, she told scripted stories. The content, either from *Oprah* episodes or her life.

Always before the story began, Mother would take a dramatic pause, and I paused what I was doing—normally it was B1's and B2's dishes—and turned around to process her storytelling face. No smile, eyebrows arched upward. Eyes both pained and livened by the lessons she was about to tell. Body wrapped in a green and orange wrapper that no matter how many times she washed it, smelled of fried turkey, plantains, and tomato paste.

The dramatic pause ends. Mother begins. The exact details of where, who, and how, a little fuzzed. But the story's ending point, always crisp. "Kenu,† love yourself because no one else will be strong enough to love all of you." These specials worked. Real romance is too unpredictable. The other parties will always bring external factors that stay with you even after the pleasure has ended. While the real is too chaotic, I can live in the pretend. The fantastical intimacy that quick kisses or quick touches provide are short enough to allow escapes. From this choice, which filled Roommate with so much overflowing secondhand embarrassment then sympathy that they reached the Devil, the only insight I can offer is: it is what it is. Committee, although I can't provide you with any data of past sexual exploits, and even though I traded the ABC Family coming-out special for a Do Ask and Do Tell policy with my close friends, I assure you

---

* Uncle Bigot.

† Mother's nickname for me. When I was four, I asked Mother what my middle name was, she told me, and I struggled to say it and only ended up saying Kenu. Out of frustration, I told her to forget the other name. My new middle name was Kenu.

that I am queer enough to check another box on your diversity quota. As another measure of good faith, I'll provide you with my queer-quaking.* Strap in, and let's travel back in time to 2008. I'm attending Christ the Beholder Academy and am still repenting for past, present, and future sins. We are a year away from the inauguration of our first Black president, the song "Low" is teaching middle schoolers every-where Grinding 101, but most importantly, I've just seen my first pair of good boobs inside the girls' locker room.

*   *   *

The third coolest girl in middle school stood on top of a bench. Her painted-purple toes danced on the locker room's orange thermoplas-tic bench as she announced, "Look, I have something to tell you." Everyone gathered around her. After all, she was Cool Girl #3, the one who told all of us the glory of Victoria's Secret between the pass-ing periods. We gazed upon our idol. She wore only her baggy gray gym shorts rolled up against her waist and a brown push-up bra that matched her skin. She shouted, "I'm a video hoe!" then ripped off her bra and shook her boobs up and down, left to right, backward and forward as she popped her body. Everyone in the locker room began giggling and screaming "eww" and "gross" while playfully throwing gym shirts and ragged white towels in CG #3's direction. I joined in, tossing a sock toward her left boob while my body butterflied with desire.

School ended, I returned home, and then retreated into the base-ment. There, I hid in the storage den as I reimagined CG #3 and felt

---

* Queer Awakening.

the butterflies. From Sara Bareilles, I learned what the infamous butterflies in a body meant: my attraction to girls would be the second secret* I would keep from Mother and Father, following the secret of my depression, my Life Partner and how together we spin plans for the perfect ending.

---

* When I started college, I experienced the second wave of my queer-quaking. And yes, it rocked my world.

With Mother not around, I didn't have to worry about awkward conversations. I no longer cared if Father knew what a bisexual was, or if he's one of the African parents who swears that queer wasn't part of the homeland, but a secret agenda mentioned in airplane pamphlets. I only wanted to accumulate kisses until enough cocooned then butterflied within to radiate in me a life warmer than my own.

# THAT'S NOT MY NAME

Naughty Cells Professor sits in front of her computer. I'm sitting across from her not knowing what amount of terrified is appropriate for this situation. I'm at my baseline threat level of orange. I'm orange when walking on campus, when waiting on food in the dining hall, when sitting in class.[*] There are other colors, of course, like the blues, or the greens when I'm high flying with ROD and the stale edibles from the bottom of her thrifted Kånken backpack. Continuously, I swim through these spectrums. Every experience shading me differently. Never a second where I can reset my thoughts.

As I'm still waiting for NCP[†] to speak, I burn brighter with anxiety. It's been minutes of her only staring at her iMac and scratching her

---

[*] When I'm bottlenecked with anxiety on campus, I'm never present enough to see whether the other students are orange, blue, or pink, as they are living on their own color spectrums.

[†] Naughty Cells Professor.

mottled arms, which are the color of bruised peaches. Next to her are crushed tin cans of sparkling water and abandoned paper cups of coffee. Why am I here? She already established that I failed the test, which is 30 percent of my grade. My fate is signed, sealed, and delivered, leaving me trapped in a panic-filled feedback loop. *Shit, oh God, shit, stop, stop panicking, whatever you do don't cry. Don't let her see you cry. Last year during a moment of exposed weakness, you cried while in a TA's office hours. Outside of Chipotle napkins stained with tears and dried sour cream, all crying got you was a twelve-hour extension, and an email from a TA, clarifying that next time emotional manipulation will not work.*

NCP finally speaks. Her first words, "You failed the exam," offer no comfort.

"Sorry."

"Why are you apologizing? It happened. Now we have to figure out what's next."

"I, I can drop."

"I wouldn't do that." NCP pulls up my discussion post about naughty scientists. She silently reads through the comments she's made in the margins and then scrolls down to my grade. It reads, 90/100. "Did you work with anyone in the class?"

"No."

"Why not?"

"I couldn'—" I pause, debating a lie's worth. There's nothing to lose, nothing to gain. I push back a braid that dangles in front of my eyes. I tell her, "I didn't want to."

"You didn't want to?" NCP sighs. "Their loss. Many of the posts could have used your insight." Shocked, I thank NCP; however, anticipation for our discussion of my failed midterm curtails the happiness over this post. She grabs one of the abandoned paper cups of coffee and places it in the microwave, which sits on a tiered wire shelf behind her. "Sahara, your post was one of the best I've read in years. Decades of teaching have taught me there are some who need their assessments done differently." *Differently* and microwave's timer mix to a blare. As NCP explains my options, my shoulders tighten. I don't want options. I want to do well, like everyone else. "I'll count this post toward your midterm."

"I, well, thank you—"

"And then for your final you'll have the option of writing a fifteen-page research paper instead of an exam. Does that interest you at all?"

I want to lie, and tell NCP I can take the final, and there's no need for accommodations. I want to tell her that I can be, and think, and pass like everyone else. Instead I jolt out of my seat and profusely thank her, then apologize for any inconvenience, then thank her again. She's says, *happy to help*, because, yes, I need help, and can't perform like the students here. I'm halfway through the hallway when I spot one of my Naughty Cells' classmates walking toward NCP's office. I become desperate to know if she offered this accommodation to anyone else in the class, or if this was an act of charity.

*   *   *

At the bottom of the glass staircase, C1, in a custom Ankara suit set, stands with SL.* Her peplum jacket is pushed back and flaunting her flat midriff. Her fresh sew-in hits against her relaxed shoulders. She waves me over. My grip on the silver rail tightens and I slow my pace descending the stairs. "Sahara, you're alive. We were just talking about you."

"I am, I think," I respond, anxious about how much C1 has said about

---

* Student Liver. If confused, see "Pass the Courvoisier, Part III."

me. Would she? No, she wouldn't. But she could, she'll always have the chance to tell any listening ear about the time pregaming turned to a therapy session. Instead of beer pong and playlists, we played cuts and tear ducts.

"See, I told you she was funny," C1 says to SL. "█████ and I are heading to an event for international students, and then we're going to the Dorian. Join us!"

"I can't. I have a Friendsgiving thing, and then studying."

"Friendsgiving. Cute."

Anger flickers in C1's eyes. I assume ignoring all her text messages and her invitations for hanging out has pissed her off. Afraid that her scorn will cause her to slip my secret to SL, I hunt for any compliment that will appease C1 and, in effect, remind her that we're friends, good, no great friends and wouldn't reveal any of the secrets, especially the scabby ones.

Even though the outfit's pattern of orange horses and green grape clusters against a hot pink background looks like an abandoned design idea for a Hi-C fruit punch cover, I tell C1, "Your outfit is so beautiful."

"I know, right. I had a seamstress make it for today. It fits like a glove. Come with us, so I don't have to be the only half-African there."

SL, who's wearing a kilt and has enough leg hair for a set of cornrows on each limb, says, "Sahara, █████ tells me you're part African too. What's your real name?"

"My what?"

"█████ told me all Africans have an African name—what's yours?"

"It's Kesandu. It means 'to spread life.'"

"That's ironic. Is that even how you pronounce it?" C1 quips. Her remark reminding me of every ridicule from my bigot of an uncle. Remarks that left me practicing my name in front of bathroom mirrors, hoping that a perfect pronunciation would unlock the first gate toward my Nigerian identity. "Come with us. My Igbo tutor will teach you the right way to say your name."

I thank C1 for her offer of opening the gates to our culture and excuse myself as politely and quickly as I can. The custom fits, the Igbo tutor, and even an all-expenses-paid trip to Lagos, which I presume is in C1's future, will give her the keycard to an identity, which I am still searching how to open.

As I walk away from C1 and her lapdog, SL continues pronouncing my middle name different ways, chuckling as he shortens it to *Kesan, Kesan*.

A s previously noted, food on campus is precarious, and this is especially true during Thanksgiving. The lack of options means that we students have a harder time finding a good Thanksgiving meal than an econ major looking for their soul. And so, we have Friendsgiving, our alternative to lavish Thanksgiving meals dressed with family drama. Most likely, even if the intentions are good, the food will be bad. We're all overstudied, undernourished, and broke.* However, this Thanksgiving, by Mariah's grace, I have escaped both family drama, and ramen noodle cups.

MP, Mariah's Partner, is a chef who refuses to let anyone else cook in their kitchen. There have been promises of smashed plantains, mac and

---

* Unless of course, you're a Donor Kid, a part of the International Elite, a starter player for the nouveaux riches, or in the league of old money, where your pockets are still heavy with imperial shillings.

cheese that's done right, chicken thighs, and candied yams, rice with pigeon peas, and Stan's donuts for dessert. In preparation for today, I've skipped yesterday's dinner, today's breakfast, and given myself a pep talk that, since everyone will be gorging, then I can indulge as well. I've spun excuses for why I've been absent from KYR's meetings, and planned conversation topics of my love for Childish Gambino's "3005" and Blood Orange's *Cupid Deluxe*. With these plans, I am stocked with enough conversations to be present.

*     *     *

ROD and I dash through the intersection, avoiding a hurdle of cars speeding down Lake Park and Fifty-Fifth. As we watch our breaths, my face is buried in Mother's green infinity scarf, which still smells of her Rare Diamonds perfume. This once-eye-roll-inducing smell is comforting and occupies me with memories of Mother spraying her perfume on the sides of her neck before slowly fixing her sheer Q+ stocking bit by bit. Part of me misses my usual Thanksgiving ritual where Mother and I fight over whether the greens are tender enough. When our fights escalate to prolonged sighs and cabinet slams, Mother pulls her trump card and recites the perfect guilt trip. "You know. I won't always be here. I'm only trying to teach you these traditions now." With this card, I lose all my turns to disagree and spend the rest of the holiday smiling, then serving food on the plates.

"A normal, happy Thanksgiving. That doesn't seem right," I tell ROD while still in disbelief that today has a promise of being fun, and not the second act of a tragicomedy.

"Yours are crazy as well?"

"Yep, there's always a dish blessed with a tear."

"At my house and I don't know how, something always catches on fire," ROD says as her hands run against the iron gates to apartments with ever-increasing rents to keep the right residents in and the wrong ones out. "Last year, my little sister thought she would move things along with cooking her cake in the microwave."

"Oh no."

"Oh yes, and when she put it in the microwave, she kept it in the aluminum pan, and that's how the Thanksgiving Fire of 2012 happened. This year, I bet my mom will start it."

"You have a fire extinguisher back home, right?"

"So many, and the fire department knows our address by heart. On the bright side, Black Friday means there's always a deal for a replacement microwave."

ROD attempts to switch the conversation to a check-in about finals, and after answering *it's going*, I flip the conversation Rolodex to the Thanksgiving fires. Canola oil gone wrong, forgotten turkeys, siblings burning dumplings, sauce bubbling on stovetops, are better topics for conversation than vocalizing my insecurities about NCP's alternative final.

\*     \*     \*

ROD and I arrive at Mariah's apartment. I press the buzzer, and while waiting ROD says, "Remember, Mariah's partner is here too."

"Of course, I remember. They're cooking the meal." We're buzzed in and walk up three flights of carpeted stairs, where gum wads and creaks guide our way.

"Just *really* remember that," ROD responds before Mariah shouts, *come in, come in* between grunts. ROD reminds me to *remember*, again. What does she think I'll do? Proclaim my love as I collect Mariah's personal effects for my closet shrine, which would make Helga Pataki write a prideful sonnet.

Mariah's thesis outlines scribbled in Expo marker on her apartment's windows, to the aroma of all the promised food, and Mariah's stories of thrifting on the North Side to find the decorations that matched her Pinterest board, make this apartment feel like the first true home I've visited since starting school. Mariah hangs our coats on a recently spray-painted coatrack. "Don't worry. It's dry. The smell takes a few days to go away. I got it from the Brown Elephant and *knew* painting it yellow would bring the room together."

"I know, I know, you were right. Yellow goes better than the purple I wanted," MP shouts. We follow the muffled voice to the kitchen, where they are so deep into the oven, I'm worried that they might roast.

"Aha, finally you admit it. This means we're going with the fabric I want."

"No, I didn't say all that." MP pokes a chicken thigh with a fork and comments, *almost there*, before saying to Mariah, "I agreed to Christmas in Chicago, not in Paisley Park." MP emerges out of the oven. They stand a few inches above the rest of us, and Mariah raises herself on her fuzzy-socked tiptoes to kiss their tawny cheeks. This realness of their love upends my daydreams. I wish I could cower inside LP for the rest of this celebration.

"The fabric is a steal and will reinvent our couch after we reupholster it."

"M, it's a deal, because no one wants it." They're teasing one another until MP answers a call on their cellphone and excuses themself to the bedroom. Even with the door closed, we hear MP speaking in Spanish, and giving rounds of greetings. "Sorry, in this home a phone call with a person is a phone call with everyone."

"Trust me, I get it. My dad screams so loud you would think he's talking to friends in Lagos through a paper cup."

"Don't get me started on my mom. Her voice is stronger than any cell tower."

MP returns, and the four of us sit at the table. We pass the time exchanging stories of our families. While ROD shares her fire facts, Mariah and MP's love fills this home, briefly stopping when Mariah grunts. She clutches MP's hand as she asks, "Can you grab my Advil?"

"Tah-dah." From their pocket, MP takes out a small packet of to-go Advil. They place it in Mariah's palm.

"I love you so much." Mariah rips open the plastic container with her teeth and shakes out the two pills, which she then swallows dry. With her eyes closed, she's shifting in discomfort, wincing her lips with every movement. She opens them and sees all of us staring. "Dang, y'all don't have to worry, it's just cramps."

"It's not *just* cramps. You're constantly in pain," MP responds.

"Trust me, I know that better than everybody," Mariah replies.

ROD and I awkwardly glance at one another. Mariah and MP spot our shifting stares. Together, they chuckle. "Everything is fine. This is a no-drama Friendsgiving. We're both a lil' heated after yesterday's doctor's appointment."

"What happened?" ROD asks. I kick her leg, causing the table to shake.

"If, you know, you feel comfortable telling us."

"I've been feeling so off lately, always tired, bloated, and I swear I'm losing clumps of my hair. The doctor here keeps telling me it's just stress. Honestly, it' s fine, I'll hold out till I get back to Philly for Spring Break."

"M, you shouldn't have to *hold out*."

"I know, but they don't— You know what, let's save that rant for another day. I'm here with friends, my love, and this good-ass food. Today, let's be grateful, and tomorrow we'll deal with all that."

MP leaves to grab the chicken thighs out of the oven. Before we commence feasting, Mariah wants us all to give gratitude to whatever is giving us joy, to say thanks to whatever we believe in. Mariah thanks MP for this meal and she's thankful that her thesis cohort actually read her thesis this time and gave somewhat useful comments. ROD is thankful that she's secured summer funding to visit Berlin. MP thanks their aunt for her constant love and support, and then they toss in a prayer to find a job working at a nonprofit that isn't predatory.

By the time it's my turn, my mind grumbles. *What is a prayer that can show progress in my life?* There's nothing real that I can say. I quickly comment, *I'm grateful for moments like this.* Mariah reaches for a spoon, but MP jumps up then screams, *wait, wait, not yet.* Mariah rolls her eyes. "Can we just eat? You don't have to take a picture of everything."

MP sets up their mini tripod and directs us to pose around the drop-leaf dining table. A regular, a silly, a serious, a sexy, an academic, we run through poses until Mariah's had enough and piles the plates with a midwestern portion of food. Everything is delicious, better than anything I've had since I left home. Everyone is indulging, but when half my plate is finished, I know that I can't afford another forkful. I push around my food; between slowed bites, I comment that I wish I hadn't had breakfast before this. MP assures me there will be plenty of food for leftovers, and any friend of Mariah's is welcome to come over anytime for a home-cooked meal.

As MP holds Mariah's hand, the words of *I, have, what* come together to ask *what do I have?* when I see MP and Mariah's love for one another and contemplate if I too was am capable of having a love like this. LP returns, dragging with her a barrel of truth—I can have her, my special something, and we'll stay together till the end.

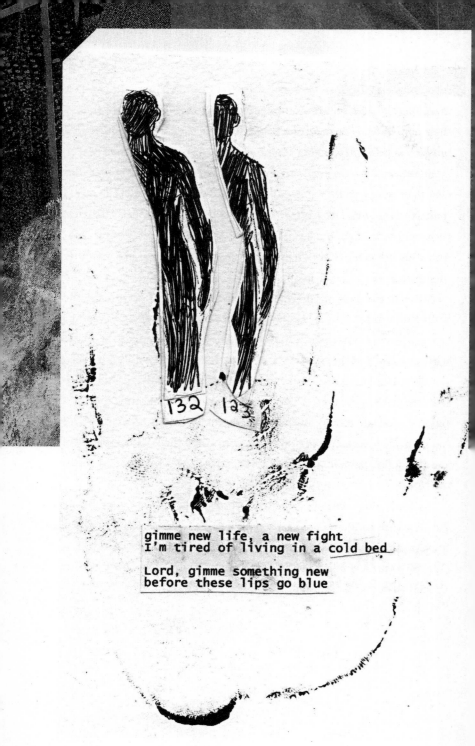

gimme new life, a new fight
I'm tired of living in a cold bed

Lord, gimme something new
before these lips go blue

*Me stands at the altar inside of a cathedral. She wears a high-collar, puff-sleeved wedding dress with a mass of ruffles. While Me's dress is untailored, dinged, as if she's been dragged to the altar, LP wears a pristine tailored tuxedo. Me switches nervous glances between LP and Priest.*

**PRIEST:** *(straightens outs his cassock, which is printed with DNA sequences)* Me, do you take LP to be your Life Partner? Do you promise to listen to her in the bad times, the horrid, and the occasional okay, in exhaustion and in boredom, to understand her and fear her all the days of your life?

**ME:** Do I have a choice?

**PRIEST AND LP:** No.

**ME:** Then I guess, I do.

**PRIEST:** LP, do you take Me to be your host? Do you promise to be faithful and ever present, in the bad times, the horrid, and the occasional okay, to depress her all the days of her life?

**LP:** I do.

**PRIEST:** With the power vested in Me, I declare you one. May the sadness bless all your thoughts.

**PRIEST AND LP:** Amen.

# MEH
# GIRL GONE SAD

The days following Thanksgiving mark a mass migration of students, from living in dorms to living in libraries. The courteous ones brush their teeth in the bathroom sinks and the rest use drinking fountains as their spit fields. I'm burrowed in the bookstacks. My laptop screen tilts backward, moving as if it's ready to pass out from exhaustion. As it's overheating, panting for help, I relent. I place my empty coffee cup behind the screen, and then leave for a smoke.

The smoke break quickly turns to a coffee fuel-up, the coffee fuel-up slips into wandering. I'm a few buildings away from the gray-bricked library. Books surround me in the basement of a cathedral turned bookstore. The book aisles are catacombs for creativity and intrigue. These lives inside the books wait for a reader to resurrect them. Aunt Nita's zine belongs in a place like this, where there's clutter, confusion, no ease in trying to find the book that you need. The hanging steel lantern lights that signal a new aisle, and include labels such as BOOKS THAT REMIND A STAFF MEMBER OF AN EX, POETRY COLLECTIONS

THAT COULD BE INDIE MOVIES, the random teal camel-back couches for sitting and reading, or for napping, the framed dictionary pages with bull's-eyes on the staff's favorite entries, these mini moments of fascination are odd enough to distract your thoughts for at least a few paces. I wander the aisles, gradually becoming too familiar with their idiosyncrasies. I enter the aisle labeled FORMER STAFF FAVORITES. I sit on a couch at the aisle's back and watch a collection of webs swinging from a lantern's line. I can't remember if I've showered or eaten today. My mind is too depleted from studying in extremes. At first, I relish these stolen moments from my work. As my eyes are closed, I rework my final papers' arguments. For my Naughty Cells final, I rethink potential evidence, then challenge these ideas with counter evidence. I'll use my accommodation to write a paper that serves more knowledge than a test ever could. NCP won't pity me and say I gave it the old college try. I'll find a way beyond this present depletion, and show that I have had something to say.

# IF I WERE A HAPPYRICH GIRL, HA, HA, HA, HAHAHA

With a postfinal, prewinter break bliss that intoxicates their days, students scatter and enjoy their lives outside of school. Mariah has MP, ROD has her art, I have LP and all of our gray matters, and together we can be fun and loved. Together onstage, if the light hits us just right, we'll forget all previous acts, and be the life of party. I'm with C1 inside her apartment. She shakes a cocktail in her rhinestone shaker. We don't mention my cuts, Dorian, me ignoring her messages, or her Nigerian identity flex in front of SL. Both here, without work and busy friends, without reason for our presence on campus. What we do have is our finals' exhaustion and this alcohol haul. There's music playing. She's cha-cha-ing side to side, in and out of her living area. I'm cracking self-deprecating joke after joke about barely surviving finals. She's pleased, and my performance has me cheesed. Round of applause if you please, our friendship is back and better than ever.

She pours me a drink. Some of it lands on the glass table. Down on her knees, she licks it up, then cuts two lines with her Sapphire credit card. Who cares what it is. We lean in. She goes first, then ding, ding, I'm next. Sniff, sniff, that's it? No wait, we rub the excess into our gums. C1 shakes another cocktail. The sounds of ice, vodka, and cranberry sloshing ring in my ears like church bells. Ding, Ding.

Her head is on my lap. She passes me her joint, and confides, *BO**[*]* *wants to take me abroad spring quarter.* Inhale, exhale, pass. She runs her fresh white tips through her hair. *Should I go?* She speaks into my eyes. Inhale, exhale, pass. *Come with me. We can make it an abroad independent study. It'll be a fun escape from campus. We need this.*

*   *   *

The University boasts satellite campuses in Florence, Abu Dhabi, and Cape Town. The dedication to increasing their revenue, I mean multi-experienced students, is showcased in Cuvier.[†] Inside this building, which is one of the University's oldest, are pamphlets and administrators who describe the beauteous experiences that studying abroad offers. They're not wrong. From students, the only complaints of going abroad are homesickness, the masochistic boredom from easier classes, and the normally racially rooted cultural shocks. For those whose pockets are never near empty or are willing to finesse or even to say fuck it and add another year of life toward their ledger of loan payments, study-abroad programs are ^wanted needed resuscitations of

---

[*]  Bar Owner.

[†]  The five-story building that is shared between the anthropology and natural sciences department. Named after the Baron Cuvier, this slim, H-shaped building has a connecting walkway, where the walls are engraved with carefully selected details of Baron Cuvier's great contributions to the field of natural sciences. Forget about his hand in exhibiting Sarah Baartman in a human zoo, and then dissecting her corpse. Only praise, then immortalize him for finding a giant sloth.

their college lives. Though a chance away from this campus is a break from being chopped in an exhaustion-fueled turbine, the cost of plane tickets, the added excursion fee on my tuition bills, the surprise expenses that trips always incur, mean studying abroad is priced out of my collegiate experience.

"I'll think about it," I respond, divided between jealousy and forced gratitude that C1 invited me.

She lifts herself off my lap and grabs a bottle of Seagram's gin from her freezer. "So did you bring anything or am I providing mixers too?" I unzip my backpack and remove a lime Faygo. She chuckles, good. Her happy means the night can continue. She pours. I drink. She says, "Going abroad, you know, will make you better. Don't you want that?" I pour more gin in both our cups. I add trickles of pop to mine, and before I can add it to hers, she moves her cup. "No soda for me. Too many empty calories." She retrieves diet tonic water from her fridge, mixes her drink. I hum along to a song I don't know, waiting for her happiness with me to return. Two more drinks, and doo wah, doo wah, doo wah, our celebration is back in full swing. As she cuts new lines, I pour dollops of gin, which I now mix with tonic water. Our talk is small, fleeting, perfect. Unlike with ROD or Mariah, C1 doesn't peel off my surface. She only wants my fun. I'm ready for another go, but C1 hasn't cut the new lines yet, she's still talking about fucking BO, and if I were sixty pounds lighter I might have a BO, and if I keep hanging with C1, I'll probably get a BO too, and I'll call him BO2, and he will be a he because that's what C1 and Roommate assume I need, and I'm too indifferent about living in my life to correct who I want to love. While I'm fantasizing about being with BO2, C1 announces, *Sahara, Sahara, you need to come with me. We'll leave the Midwest. Being here is making me so fat.* Ugh, why, why always with the rude belittling, no bebigging, yes, that's a word.

---

**bebig (verb),**

bebigged; bebigging \ bi-'bIg-guhng
*Transitive verb*
1: **to cause (a person) to feel othered
talking of physical weight**

2: **to belittle a person for their weight**

---

C1 knows I'm from the Midwest—outside of fridge and couch, I'm the only thing that's big in here—fuck her, I should say something, correct, yes correct, Southfield has Mr. Song's hats and Detroit birthed the techno beats she struggle-snaps to, yes set her straight, correct her, no read her, but what will she say, another quip about my name, a remark about my scars. Not worth it, and maybe she didn't mean it, maybe she just doesn't know what she's saying, I'm being too sensitive, we're friends, we must be friends, and friends forgive. *Sahara, we have to finish this second bottle, we're so close.* She's pouring the last of it, and shit, shit, I think I'm too far from good, and am too far gone, and LP is awake, loud, and tells me, *let's call it off, now and not sooner rather than later, let's go home and*—I say no, no, no, this night is good, and normal, I don't want to listen to LP. With C1, I'm good, no great. I'm needed. I'm having fun like Father at Yam Festivals, like ROD with her art, and Mariah with MP. I raise my drink, this, this right here is mine. I sip, and C1 looks for her joint, and when she realizes it's been in her hand the whole time, she laughs and promises, *abroad, this will be our new normal.* LP is completely awake, planning what will happen once we leave her apartment. I try and quiet her, reminding her it's not time yet, but she's up and out, telling me the clock is a-ticking, I need to go before, like ROD and Mariah, C1 starts scratching. For right now, C1's dancing and calls BO, begging him to come over, this right now will never be forever, I leave as he answers her FaceTime.

I walk home, the crosswalk sign turns green to red, I wait in it, LP's right, this way will be quick, a happychance accident. A car brakes. A driver screams. LP says, *it's okay, we'll try again. Doo wah, doo wah, doo.*

# COMING HOME
## AIN'T EASY

S till crashed from last night's high, I arrive late to the train station. As my suitcase's wheels spin inward, I chase after the line of travelers preparing to board the Wolverine. I'm exhausted. I secure the first window seat that I can find. The blurred images of abandoned factories with shattered windows, fields of dried grass with rusted Ford pickups, and ranch homes with chipping gutters remind me that there's more Midwest that exists outside of a bewitching city and a deteriorating suburb. Our train reaches Jackson. We're still hours away. The snores of the woman next to me will not stop falling out of her, leaving me awake and uncomfortable. I scoot side to side, tilt my seat back. When I'm close enough to sleep to feel the dream clouds tickling my ears, an old woman—who has the habit of pacing up and down our train aisle while wearing a white hotel robe and no socks or shoes, exposing toenails the color of graphite—says it's rude for me to tilt MY seat back. I bring my seat back up and begin counting landfills and tattered Confederate flags.

\*     \*     \*

Half awake, I arrive in Dearborn and wait for Mother. Thirty minutes ago, she told me she was on the road; however, the television playing in the background proved otherwise. Thirty minutes turns to an hour, the hour to an hour and fifteen. Any anger for Mother's perpetual lateness is quickly abandoned. As I wait, knowing that this will be my last time home, I know that I have lost the right to be angry with her. Her future rage or grief surpasses any present inconvenience. While at the train station and stretched out on connected plastic chairs, my mind hiccups with the thought that maybe, even if only for moments with Mother and Father, B1 and B2, I can live. When in this break of logic, LP arrives, holding her checklist of my grief's stages. Denial, you mean childhood and my first year of college, then yes. Anger, check. Bargaining, did that with finals, so yes. Depression, been there, <sup>done</sup> <sub>doing</sub> that. Acceptance, LP you're right, I need to accept. I'll hold this guilt if it means a lasting rest.

I wake to several missed calls and texts from Mother asking, *where am I?* I rub the sleep out of my eyes and shake my hangover out of my bones. In the car, Mother's smoking her Sunday cigarette even though it's Tuesday. She uncrooks her pixie wig and flings her cigarette into a pile of snow. I buckle my seat belt. She starts the ritual of hiding the smell of her smoke. She spritzes her Rare Diamonds perfume on the sides of her neck and the top of her wig. She sprays dollar-store air freshener the scent of cinnamon apples and lavender potpourri. I watch the mist fall. Some dampens my right hand and creates a constellation like the moles on C1's body. Mother tosses the air freshener to the backseat and passes the perfume for me to place in the glove box.

As I close the box, she observes, "You look a mess."

"Ma, I'm tired. I barely survived finals."

She kisses my cheek. "That's no reason not to look presentable."

"Ma—"

"I'm just a concerned Momma, that's all." She kisses my cheek and holds my hand. Her rough palms glove my skin. "I'm so happy to have you home. Your brothers are driving me up a wall."

"And Dad?"

"Same as always. Quiet, and I'm still close to getting the locks changed on him."

"Ma!"

"What?" She lets go of my hand to place both her hands on the steering wheel. She lifts herself forward and peers over the dashboard. "You don't understand, but you will. Once you finish planning your wedding, you start planning your divorce." She rummages in her cupholder for her Iman lipstick. At a red light, she flicks off its black cap with her thumb. "I'm telling you this now so you don't act up later. Your uncle is in the States, and he's visiting us for the holidays."

"Which uncle?"

"Uncle ██████████."

As soon as she tells me that UB* is visiting, I'm ready to surrender my winter break and board the train back to school. "Why does he have to visit? He's such an asshole."

"Watch your mouth. He's family and sponsored your father's immigration. So have some respect."

"I will once he does."

"What did you say?"

"Nothing."

Though her driving needs all the help it can get, she returns to

---

* UB, Uncle Bigot. His only redeeming quality is that he's returned to Nigeria and only cares enough to call Father, and send Brothers 1 and 2 spam prayer message chains on WhatsApp.

steering with just her left hand. Her right hand switches between applying her lipstick and twisting the radio knob. She runs another red light as she changes the station to 92.3 FM, the throwback R&B station. Jill Scott plays as we drive. On the doors of the boutiques, bookstores, and electronics stores that Mother and I frequented throughout middle and high school are GOING OUT OF BUSINESS signs. My childhood church is now an empty, gated lot with plastic signs that read SOLD. My childhood and any evidence of it disappears with every visit back home.

"What happened to Mika's Pizza Place?"

"Huh?"

"The diner we always went to on Sundays?"

She turns the steering wheel and doesn't check for oncoming traffic. "Shut down. Turns out they weren't paying rent."

"I really liked that place. They had the best french fries."

"You and your brothers loved that place. Your father and I hated it, but it was the only way to get you three to church."

"Father never came to the restaurant with us."

"Because he couldn't stand that place."

"No, he always chose to get lunch with Uncle ████████ instead of us."

"Your father did come with us."

"No, he never did."

Mother slams on the brakes, trying not to run a light that "magically" turned from green to red. I'm thrown into my seat. "Sahara, stop talking back. I need to concentrate on the road."

Along with her bad driving, the other constant back home is Mother's invented memories of Father's presence in our home. Outside of these constants, nothing feels the same, leaving me the sense that I'm becoming even more of an ill-matching patch woven onto my family's fabric. It's only been three months since I left, and even Mother isn't the same. There's gray hair poking out of her forearms.

She looks shorter while in the driver's seat. When she does decide to check for oncoming traffic, she squints more than usual. I stare at her, holding in these memories of her. "Stop staring at me like that."

I roll my eyes. "I'm making sure you're looking at the road."

"Mind your business."

"I'm in the car too, so *it is* my business." We playfully roll our eyes, repeatedly. Every roll growing in dramatics.

I lean over the console. My elbow's hovering over cupholders that ash and twisted straw wrappers fill. I kiss Mother and lean against her cheek. She caresses my braids and responds, "That's more like it." She unbuckles her seat belt. "But you want something, don't you?"

"No, Ma, I missed you, that's all."

*　　*　　*

At home, B1 and B2 are fighting over the remote. B1 sits on top of B2, who is screaming, *he's crushing me!* Despite these pleas, B2 refuses to surrender the remote. Mother yells the fear of God into them. B1 stops sitting on B2 to hug me. His hug is short because the TV is his main priority. B2 squeezes me then bounces around in circles, asking question after question. "Did Mom tell you that I'm auditioning for the step team? Sahara, did you come back with any souvenirs? Did you miss us? Did you learn anything cool? Did you buy our Christmas presents already?"

B1 answers, "She's in college, dumbass. She doesn't have any money." B1 pauses *The Dark Knight* and asks, "Do you have any cool party stories?"

"None for a high-schooler. And don' t call him a dumbass, dumbass."

B2 laughs. He's eight and still cute, while B1 is sixteen and in his angst. He refuses advice on everything, ranging from using JBC oil on his dyed dreads, which are the length and color of nubby chicken fingers, to which AP classes he should take next year. When he's not popping pimples and listening to Tyler, the Creator, he's in his room playing *BioShock* and planning his escape from home.[*]

B1, a Slim Jim with an appetite, gets up to search for a snack. From the kitchen, I hear Mother scold, *it's not ready yet.* As B1 scrounges for food, B2 turns off the DVD player. B1 returns to the family room with boiled pieces of seasoned turkey meat. He notices the change and sits on B2, again. He's smacking his lips and licking juice off his fingers. "College is cool, right? I can't wait till I'm outta here. Dad's been on my ass."

I don't want to destroy B1's hope of escaping Michigan. He still believes college is part of the starter pack toward an American Dream. I tell him in my best *Little Mermaid* voice, "Oh Eric, it's a whole new world."

"You stay on that weird shit," B1 replies. A grin briefly interrupts his flat affect.

Before I can settle into our orange couch—which is now so stained with oil and spotted with nail glue from sealing my braids, that its new pattern is polka dots—Mother calls for me. I pretend that I'm asleep. "Sahara, did you hear me?"

"Yea, she did," B1 replies.

"Did I ask you?" I mouth *that's what you get* to B1. "Sahara, come help in the kitchen."

"Ma, I'm tired."

"That makes two of us."

While they await my response, B1 and B2 are so still that they could join the decoration cast of fake plants and framed picture-day photos.

---

[*]   Unlike me, he won't listen to Mother's pleas to stay in the Midwest. His eyes are set on California, and even abroad.

They're frozen out of fear that this back-and-forth between Mother and me is the beginning of our first fight during my break. If I want her last memories of me as a good daughter, one that could earn God's forgiveness, then I will do as I'm told. B1 and B2 gape as I get up. "What? It's easier this way."

Mother and I sit across from one another. I'm sitting with my legs spread open. She instructs me to close them and sit like a lady. Instead of asking *what does that mean?*, like I have for the last decade, I close my legs. From years of arguing, we've learned to be careful with our gestures and our words. Our eyes, ears, and tongues are prone to pick things apart to fuel disagreements that turn into screaming matches. Mother believes that any form of disagreement is disrespect. I believe it's genetics. Mother's tongue is fierier than mine. While I pick the greens and feel the graininess of the leaves against my fingertips, Mother cuts plantains. The tune changes to "Give It to Me Baby," causing Mother to grin.

"Aunt Nita loved this song. Even redid the lyrics to 'give me the baby' after you were born."

"Was she a good singer?"

"No, the worst that ever lived. Your grandmother made her mouth along to church hymns." Our laughter warms the kitchen better than our "do you have heat money?" setting on the thermometer. "So much of her is in you."

"Ma, I'm reading her book."

"Really, now." She picks up the heap of plantain skins and pitches them into empty Kroger bags. "How did you find it? I pray you didn't tear up my basement* looking for it because if you did—"

---

* Our basement is always a mess. Around Christmas Mother always tries to rope someone into her holiday cleaning frenzy. Childhood years missing reruns of *Grandma Got Run Over by a Reindeer* taught me to steer clear of Mother's cleaning projects that result in trips of

"How could I mess up the basement? I just got here." I leave the table and prolonging my time searching for the Lawry's, garlic powder, and pepper. "Before coming home for the summer, I found it in the library's queer zine collection."

*Queer* perks up my Mother's ears, leading her to find a new way of asking how gay I am. "Why were you in that section?"

"For a class."

"What class?"

"Why does that matter?"

"You're the one who mentioned the class, Kenu. Why does your school have her book?"*

"I don't know. They like collecting."

"Well, if you can, steal it."

"Ma!"

"Don't get caught. Nita wouldn't have wanted it there. That work was for her, not them. If she was alive—" Mother's chuckles shorten as she breathes in memories of her little sister. "She was only four years older than you when she passed. Kenu, I pray you never experience losing a sibling while you're so young."

Guilt shutters in me. I think about B1 and B2 and their days after my death. LP and I agree that B1 and B2 will grow closer, Mother and Father may try and regrow their love, and they still will have two out of three left. Two out of three is 67 percent, but in Naija culture, the boys

---

her driving her white Subaru packed with trash bags of clothes on hangers, books with damaged spines, and shoes that have no pairs. Most donation centers in the area have been warned not to accept anything from Black, White Subaru Mom.

* She says *book* in a tone of disbelief. I could tell her that she's right in believing it's not a book, but a zine, and then she would ask me about what's a zine and how do I know about it, and I would tell her it's part of my queerstory, and she'll ask your what, and I'll break it down as queer history, and she'll ask why are you part of that, and we will reach another impasse in our conversation.

are worth more than the girls. So, this bumps the percentage up to 75 percent. Of course, the logic is faulty; however, after hours of listening to LP, the math adds up.

I finish helping Mother and retreat to my bedroom. There, leaning against my crooked bookcase, as the used books from my local library cradle me, I'm holding my guilt, remembering that I must accept this truth, which for now, only I and LP truly understand. I write my notes. Dear God and Mother, Father and Brothers, Mariah and ROD, even if I never earn your forgiveness, I pray that one day you will understand.

# WE HAD A FOLLY, JOLLY CHRISTMAS

Christmas morning, after opening presents of socks, ramen, granny panties, black bras probably meant for nursing, and an assortment of $5 gift cards, I escape to my bedroom and stare at the old Gorillaz and Black Eyed Peas posters that are on my beige-maybe-light-blue-or-is-it-actually-gray walls. My room's draft causes the untaped corners of the posters to dance to imaginary beats. I bundle myself with blankets and strategize about where to hide my anger when UB arrives. As I try to figure out the right location for it, I hear Father asking me why I'm back in my room when the family is downstairs.

I return to the family. Mother's taken a break from decluttering the basement. She sits in the family room with Father and quietly listens to Al Green. Father's feet are propped up on his ottoman while he reads the news captions. They recount the aftermath of this month's shootings in Colorado and Nevada. B1 is watching a movie on his phone, which is hidden inside the ACT book he's holding. B2 is pretending he's boogieing down the soul train line.

\* \* \*

In this room, my family is at their normal. Mother and Father sit side by side, joking with one another about their parents and grandparents, debating which ones are in hell. Father passes a piece of his orange over to Mother. She cradles it in her hand, then savors its sweetness. Father and I try to periodically talk to one another. He asks how finals went and I tell him well, then I spew out the random scientific facts that I can remember. Once he hears an interesting fact, Father looks up from his *Midwest Medical Magazine*. Part of him still believes that one day I'll stop my "nonsense" and become a "doctah so I can feed myself."

The segment on 2013's shootings is cut short for a special holiday update of how to cook a low-fat Santa cake. Father scoffs. "America is gun, gun, gun* and food, food, food." This rant divulges his plans to leave this country once B2 finishes college. Everyone in the family hears this rant at least four times a week. At first, they threatened this family's normal. Growing up, I, B1, and B2 were worried these tirades would destroy a family that barely had its gripping. Over time, the repetitious arguments between Father and Mother about his future became extra members of our family that we ignored. I, B1, and B2 learned never to ask if Mother's coming with him, or if he's paying for the international phone cards.

The doorbell ringing preemptively ends Father's rant. B2 opens the door for UB. I greet UB, and see that he has aged into a miserable old man with a frowning, cratered face and deep-set eyes that sink into his skull. I'm positive that even though his too-tight, faded Coogi sweaters

---

* Father's understanding of countries like the United States being about guns and food is historical. As a child living during the Nigerian Civil War, a war with guns that Britain and France provided, the Americans, specifically USAID, brought food to Biafra during the Igbo pogrom.

bunch around his stomach and fat lumps together on his head, he will be the first person to comment on my weight.

I join Mother in the kitchen. From there, I observe Father and UB. While a DVRed FIFA game plays, they speak to each other in Igbo, their tones climb until they hit a peak, and then descend into a spiraling staircase of laughter and sighs. I approach UB and Father carrying a tray that has two Heinekens, a bowl of chin-chin, and a plate of fried turkey meat. While the tray is still in my hands, UB snatches up a few pieces of meat. I set the tray down on the folding tray table between Father and UB. Father thanks me. I return to the kitchen and glare at UB as I'm leaning against the island. Mother pinches my arm. "Leave them be," she says. She places a spatula in my hand and directs me to the stuffing that needs plating.

Since I wasn't home for Thanksgiving, Mother decided this Christmas dinner should have a Turkey Day flair. B1 and B2 and Mother are heaping food into our Waterford serving bowls. B1 lifts the turkey, carefully walking it over to the table. B2 goes back and forth from the stove to the dining table. He sets the table with jollof rice, collard greens, stew, egusi soup, yams, fufu, white rice, chicken alfredo, stuffing, plantains, fried goat meat, homemade cranberry sauce, and puff-puffs. The steam from the food mists B2's oval glasses. He takes a break to wipe off the fog, then continues setting the table, even making sure to quintuply check that forks and knives are clean, straight, and the plates are centered on the reindeer place mats he proudly picked out himself.

UB shouts to B1 and B2, "Come join the men and let the women do what they know."

B1 looks to Mother. She gives him The Eye. It says, *you can go and sit with them*, but a lazy child is an unfed child.

B1 and B2 respond in unison, "Uhh, we want to help."

We finish setting the table and Mother calls over UB and Father.

UB inspects the food with disgust.* Everyone knows this meal is one of Mother's best, and that he will greedily eat every bit and take our unstained Tupperware brimmed with leftovers. When he finishes his detective stint, he says grace in Igbo—the language he knows Mother and I don't understand.

He finishes his prayer and continues speaking in Igbo. Father responds in English to UB's Igbo. UB's monologuing, and Father interrupts. "Uh, uh, my brother have you forgotten your English?"

"Ah, ah, a Nigerian man forgets nothing."

"Prove it, o."

UB glances at Mother. With his fork, he splits his stew's goat meat and mangles the sliced bell peppers. "If you married someone from home—"

Mother's eyes flick toward UB. She's heard all variations of this sentence.† In her silence, her eyes assure her children that we are loved, despite this hate from our family. When her eyes land on Father, they ask, *Are you gonna handle him?*‡ Like UB's previous visits, Father remains silent.

UB straightens his posture. He knows that in our house, he can act however he wants. He tells me, "Go get my Heineken. It is by the TV." I

---

* Though the other Naija women disrespect Mother, they don't disrespect her cooking. Back when she attended Naija parties and Yam Festivals, her aluminum pans were always the first ones empty.

† Variations of the sentence I've heard: *If you married a Nigerian woman, we could've kept speaking our language*, or *you would've had all sons*, or *God would've had more favor on you.*

‡ In tenth grade, the day after UB's Christmas visit, Mother and Father fought with screams. B1, B2, and I watched them. We didn't see the purpose in leaving the kitchen to hide in our rooms. Mother and Father were so loud, there was nowhere else to go, and household screams are more disturbing when disembodied.

The fight ended when Mother started throwing food at Father. Droplets of turkey blood, pink hunks of turkey meat, bell peppers, and white rice lived on our floor for days. Mother refused to clean it up, deciding to have a staycation inside our basement. Down there, she smoked cigarettes and watched her favorite films. Before she could have a chance to watch *Why Did I Get Married?* for a third time, Father cleaned everything, and promised UB wouldn't visit us next Christmas.

oblige. When I return, he asks, "What are you eating in school? You've gotten fatter since the last time I saw you. Remember, my dear, a fat woman is not a beautiful woman."

Mother's eyes are still on Father. UB pops a plantain into his mouth, chews as he complains about the plantain's shape, and then he complains about the thickness of the stew, and then of the dryness of the rice, and then of the moistness of the goat meat, and then of the alfredo pasta being too fattening and American for a Nigerian family, and then of the place mats being too pagan because of their decorations, and then of B1's acne and dyed dreads, then he begins picking a dried-out scab on B1's lower cheek, then he lectures B2 because of his disinterest in playing soccer, then he lectures Mother about her unwillingness to host an upcoming Southeast Michigan Mbaise* meeting, and then lectures me for not studying science. Then he lectures Father for not going back home to Nigeria more, then lectures all of us for not going to church twice a week, and then after lecturing, he returns to complaining. He complains of the cheap American fabric causing his clothes to shrink, then of the American stress that has caused him to lose his hair while his was young, and then of the Westernized Nigeran women back home who don't know how to handle a "real African man."

Eventually, even Father grows tired of UB. Father wipes his mouth with a napkin and asks, "If you know so much about home, family, and food, why don't you invite us over?"

"I don't have a wife to cook for me."

"Because they're always leaving you."

---

* The monthly meeting where other men from Mbaise, a region in Imo state, gather in a basement to complain, rant about Nigeria's corruption, and debate what's wrong with Black America.

"*Nnaa*, this is how you treat me. Your family, *o*."

My father slams his fist on the table. "*Chineke me, this* is my family."

B2 and I stare down at our plates, trying to hide the swallowed shock. B1 excuses himself to the bathroom, snickering the entire way there.

# BEFORE I LET GO

There's an unspoken social contract between Father and me that while home for break, I will take a sabbatical from losing my religion and attend church on New Year's. There, I can never decide whether our beliefs, these rituals, this joint performance of salvation, make us worthy of forgiveness. Normally, as I'm perched beside Father, my sacrilegious questions* distract me from this debate. This morning, after I spent a night rereading my notes to Mother and Father, B1 and B2, Mariah and ROD, I wish I could know if I ever will be forgiven.

*       *       *

—————

\* Blasphemous questions include but are not limited to: Did the first Christians ever think of themselves as cannibals? Why can't the body of Christ have the juiciness of a Double Whopper? If nuns are married to the man upstairs, how do they consummate their relationship . . . you know, get to know Him, biblically . . .)

As I'm getting dressed for Mass I scroll through the missed messages from the Black Excel group chat. Mariah's in the hospital. She and MP are refusing to leave the exam room. The doctor's telling them that he will call security. Mariah's sending us videos of the doctor threatening to call security. One of the new members of Black Excel messages, *Should I tell my RA?* Waves of *no*s are sent as a response. HB1 replies, *We should wait for Mariah to tell us what she wants.* As I'm waiting, I'm rewatching the video, rereading the messages and comments. As our words hold our outrage and fear, none of us know what to do.

"Sahara, you're making your father late," Mother shouts. I rush out of my room. One arm is in my puffer, the rest of my coat swings behind me. "Get the sleep out of your eye." I wipe my eyes and exit the house. Father's waiting in the driveway. His face a tired frown.*

"Sorry."

"We're late." I check the clock. There's still twenty minutes before Mass starts. The drive takes less than ten. Still, I apologize and thank him for waiting. My gratitude surprises Father enough that he decides not to rant about punctuality. As he drives he glances at me, searching for a lecture to give. He asks, "Is the phone your hand?" *No,* I mutter as I continue scrolling. "Then why is it always phone, phone, phone. In your ear and hand, *o*. Tell me the reason, eh."

"A friend is not doing well. We're checking in on her."

"Uh-uh, has she gone to the doctah?"

"She's at the doctor and he says he's not going to run any more tests."

"Foolish man, we will pray for her," Father replies while parking the car.

---

* I figure that's been his expression ever since he immigrated into the States.

\*      \*      \*

We enter the church and sit in our back pew. Our church is so dilapidated that even Jesus's carpentry can't resurrect it. The torn and perpetually wet carpet now lifts from the floor. Most of the pews wobble. The kneelers' screws poke us as we pray. Even the cross behind Holy Father is crooked and rotting from being underneath one of the ceilings' many water stains.* While Father's steadfast in his pre-Mass prayers, I check my phone. No updates from Mariah. The chat's gone quiet. I'm worried and I should check in. Beyond the *are you okay*s and *how are you feeling*, what else will I say? Things need to change—the platitude that pretends action. LP tells me to send nothing; however, even for me, silence is too passive. I message Mariah, *I'm so sorry this is happening. Any updates?*, trying to forget the times I ignored KYR's emails. By the Mass's second reading, there still aren't any new messages in the group chat.

During Holy Father's homily, he implores us to show the youth God's love to prevent any more mass acts of violence. He tells us this is the only way to prevent more violence and pain, and I agree with him. At times, there is only one way. As I'm in the procession of sinners, waiting for communion, I repent, and repent, and repent, hopeful that if the Lord is listening, He will use His forgiveness to ease my family's pain. Between my repenting, I pray for Mother's peace and Mariah's health. For ROD's successes, and B1's and B2's understanding and forgiveness, for Father to hold his shame for me in silence.

Before Mass ends, Holy Father asks for us to stay behind to hear a

---

\* While in middle school, Holy Father, hoping to raise money for the church, had a Channel 11 news crew come and report on a water stain that allegedly looked like the Virgin Mary. After the report, no members outside the church donated money, and we ended up losing a few members of the congregation. The members who left were tired of being part of the St. Water Stain Church.

special presentation of the parish's missionary work in Africa. Even Father, who's such a devout Catholic that his dream vacation is visiting the Vatican, won't stay for this presentation. From Masses where people assumed we were the special visitors from Africa, from parishioners cracking 419 jokes during post-Mass tea and cookies, Father's learned that while souls can be saved, foolish minds cannot. In the parking lot, as Father is forgetting the fruits of the Holy Spirit and ranting about every impatient driver cutting in front of him, I check my phone. It's bright with notifications. Mariah tells us in Black Excel that she and MP are headed home. She's gonna take it easy the next few days. If she doesn't feel better by second week of the new quarter, she'll fly out to her doctor in Philly. She sends a copy of this same message as a reply to the text that I sent her.

Now that I know she's okay, I can check my other notifications. Fall quarter's grades have been posted to my student account. They're a mix of B+'s and A-'s. I am relieved. After I tell Father, his drive to the gas station is fueled with pride. As he's pumping he gives me a thumbs-up. I smile, then recite again, my prayer for forgiveness.

# THAT
# GIRL
# SUICIDE

ear Thesis Committee, I'm almost at a close, so consider these the last sentences of an abstract, which summarizes the conclusion. I promised C1 I wouldn't use her sleeping pills. Even if I did, by themselves these night-night tablets come with a risk. (I wouldn't want a surprise drop-in from Roommate disturbing my slumber.) Tylenol on its own is too painful, long, and could leave me alive. There are no overhead pipes in my dorm, and campus keeps security guards around the clock at their highest buildings. Yes, there are limits to how I can execute this plan. However, it's time to put the one-third of my degree I've earned to work and problem solve. LP and I have decided it will still go on as follows: one night, after two weeks of my last hurrahs, I'll leave my forget-me-nots on my desk, next to my ID and phone. I will walk to the lake, bringing with me only a fifth of vodka and four Tylenol PMs. I will alternate between the vodka and Tylenol. When I no longer feel the cold stripping my skin, I will remove my jacket and shoes. I will continue walking into the lake until I'm swallowing relief, drowning in its embrace.

# THE BODY IS A CAGE

Back in my dorm, I review the syllabi for Double Consciousness, Disorder and Disease, and Colonial Africa. Out of the options for winter quarter, these courses had the most interesting topics for their first weeks.

My phone pings with a security alert, warning students and faculty that the campus police are looking for a robber. The description of the perpetrator says Black and tall. It sounds more like an order for coffee than a person. A student in the Black Excel chat warns that anything Black and tall should go into hiding. Someone else replies, saying he'll put his dick away. HB1 ignores his response and asks if any of us have heard from HB2 within the past few weeks. No one has, causing HB1's worry, and she tells us that if we have the time, we should individually reach out to make sure HB2's okay.

On my phone, I scroll down to the last message between me and HB2. It's the message that read, *don't worry, you're not the only one who hates it here*. The message that remained unanswered. And now, it's been weeks, another quarter is here, another one of us possibly gone. My silence shames me, and instead of texting, calling, or even sending an email with a *thinking of you* subject line, my phone darkens. I settle into my bed with LP floating above me, whispering, *we will disappear too.*

My phone pings again—it's a message from C1.

C1: Hey gurl!!!! Come out with me tonight!!!!

C1: It's gonna be the best party of your college years

ME: Hey, I think I'll stay in.

C1: I'll bring whatever party favor you want ;)

C1: I know you didn't have fun all break

C1: gurll don't leave me hanging

She needs me, and before I was ready, I needed her. Now, since I have my concrete plan and there are only twenty-five days of life left, keeping up our charade feels pointless. I silence my phone and fall asleep with a feeling of bliss overcoming me.

\* \* \*

The next morning, I sit in the first class of the quarter, Colonial Africa class. Six rectangle tables are formatted in the shape of a square. Though we all sit equidistant from one another, my classmates' disbelief over Mansa Musa's wealth truly existing shows that ignorance keeps us centuries apart. Throughout the class and during its break,

I continue refreshing the class registry's website, hoping that I'll find an empty spot in Dematerializing and Designing Desire: A Survey in Character Creation. The creative writing class is over capacity. I still try to add it to my registration cart. As I'm trying to game the system and add the class to my registration cart, I hear, *Kesan, Kesan.* I look up, and it's SL, C1's botfly. He's chewing a bruised apple. Its juices spot his sweatshirt, which reads SWEATSHOP across his chest.

"Kesan, Kesan, we missed you at last night's party."

"I stayed in. Didn't feel up to it."

"You, not up to it?" My phone vibrates with a call from ROD. I silence it. Then, my laptop chimes with an email and notifications from the WhatsApp badge on my laptop. I close my computer. SL says it's probably emails about another student *graduating early*, and he gives me permission to check *MY* notifications. I wait. I don't want a buzzard hovering over my messages. "So, what's the real reason you didn't want to come out?"

"No reason."

"Did you get too wasted to come out?"

"Nope." I shift in my seat. He's staring at me with his painted grin, which is deceptive in its invitation for a conversation. These are my weeks of my last hurrahs. I'll stop pretending with him as well. "I figured it would be too one-percent."

"Oof, harsh, Kesan, Kesan, especially with us *one-percent* footing your scholarships," SL quips. "Look C1 was pissed. You hurt her feelings. If you're gonna take so much, the least you can do is answer her text."

SL leaves for his seat. The professor still hasn't returned from the prolonged break. Heated, I open the Black Excel group chat, ready to report this interaction, which went from micro to macroaggression real fast. In the group chat, I see almost a hundred notifications. I scroll them, seeing a series of *sorry for your loss, what's next,* and *this is the University's fault,*

*God, no, tell us what you need, we're here for you,* I scroll through the messages, hunting for the instigating message. My fingers are on auto-pilot, passing through every message of grief. They are driving toward a destination I'm not ready to see. More messages enter the group chat, increasing the distance to the original message. As I'm scrolling, I collect enough words to know what I never thought to fear.

Umail
Sahara.Nwadike@umail.edu
**Unfortunate News**

1 message

**Dean** ▆▆▆▆ <dean.▆▆▆▆@umail.edu>    Mon. Jan 6, 2014 at 11:13 AM

To: <Sahara.Nwadike @umail.edu>

Dear University Community:
It is with much sadness we share with you that fourth-year University student Mariah Moore passed away early this Monday morning from preexisting health conditions. Please be aware grief counselors are available for those who need help with this tragic loss. You can schedule a free appointment at http://grief.university.edu/. Our mental health partitioners with the Student Wellness Clinic located at ▆▆▆▆ ▆▆▆▆ Ave will have a limited number of walk-in appointments available.

We are here to support everyone during this unfortunate time.

Sincerely,

Umail

Sahara.Nwadike@umail.edu
**Statement on Mariah's Death**

1 message

**KYR** <info@KYR.org>                    Mon. Jan 6, 2014 at 1:13 PM

To: KYR <KYR-list@KYR.org>

We are devastated to share the news and circumstances of Mariah Moore's passing. Throughout her time with KYR, Mariah fiercely advocated for health equality. As an activist, she understood that disparity equals death. At KYR, we are horrified that Mariah died in a system she dedicated much of her life fighting. While we grieve Mariah's passing, we remember that Mariah and her spirit of advocation are forever with us. It would be against Mariah's legacy to not share the facts of her death. We have received permission from Mariah's family and ████████, ██████, Mariah's partner, to disclose the following information:

- Since enrolling at the University of ████████ in the Fall of 2010, Mariah repeatedly sought care at the University Hospital for fibroids treatment. She never received adequate care.

- On January 1, 2014, Mariah Moore, for complaints with her abdominal pain, went to the ER at the University Hospital. After waiting hours, she was denied treatment, and forced to return home.

- On the morning of January 3, 2014, Mariah Moore and her partner, ████████ ██████, returned to the ER, demanding an ultrasound. By the late evening, she was given an ultrasound. There, it was discovered the severe number of growths on her uterus would require an emergency hysterectomy.

- On January 4, Mariah passed from unforeseen complications in surgery.

At KYR, we will not rest until Mariah sees justice. Mariah will be deeply missed by her communities and loved ones. We understand that this is painful news. If you or someone you know has been affected by Mariah's passing, please visit KYR.org. There you will find vetted community practitioners, free recourses for grief management, and links for healing-centric community groups.

Know Your Rights

www.KYR.org

## Autopsy

*Black Person 6 lays naked on a surgical ta-*
*ble. Man enters stage and begins the mummi-*
*fication process. During the seventy days,*
*Man removes heart, brain, mouth, and then*
*embalms BP6 with tears and ink. After the*
*body is embalmed, Man wraps BP6 from head to*
*toe with campus newspapers that read: Unfor-*
*tunate News.*

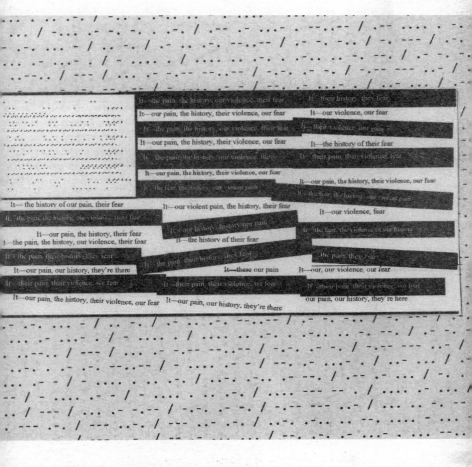

It—the pain, the history, our violence, their fear      It—their history, they fear.

It—our pain, the history, their violence, our fear      It—our violence, our fear

It—the pain, the history, our violence, their fear      It—their violence, our pain

It—our pain, the history, their violence, our fear      It—the history of their fear

It—the pain, the history, our violence, their      It—their pain, their violence, fear

It—our pain, the history, their violence, our fear

It—our pain, the history, their violence, our fear

It—the fear, the violence, our violent pain      It—the fear, the history, our violent pain

It—the history of our pain, their fear      It—our violent pain, the history, their fear      It—our violence, fear

It—the pain, the history, our violence, their fear

It—our pain, the history, their fear      It—our history, history our pain

It—the pain, the history, our violence, their fear      It—the history of their fear      It—the fear, the violence of our history

It—the pain, their history, they fear      the pain, their history, they fear      the pain, they fear

It—our pain, our history, they're there      It—there our pain      It—our, our violence, our fear

It—their pain, their violence, we fear      It—their pain, their violence, we fear      It—their pain, their violence, we fear

It—our pain, the history, their violence, our fear      It—our pain, our history, they're there      our pain, our history, they're here

Umail

---

Sahara.Nwadike @umail.edu
Honoring the Life of Mariah Moore

---

1 message

---

**KYR** <info@KYR.org>                    Tues. Jan 7, 2014 at 11:07 AM

---

To: KYR <KYR-list@KYR.org>

Mariah's family has requested that Mariah's funeral in Philadelphia remain private. We will respect those wishes and have a separate ceremony on January 13 to celebrate the life and legacy of Mariah Moore. Mariah Moore, born and raised in Philadelphia, was a loving partner to ███████ ██████, a daughter to ██████ and ███████ Moore. While enrolled at University of ███████████, she fiercely advocated for her communities and exuberated attentive care to everyone she encountered. She leaves behind a legacy of love and activism that we at KYR will make it our mission to honor. **Join us on January 13 from 11:00 a.m. to 1:00 p.m. for Mariah' s memorial at the Community Church located at ████ ██████ Ave.**

Seen but never protected,

Know Your Rights

---

www.KYR.org

---

# SOMETIMES, I FEEL LIKE A NATIONLESS CHILD

In a fugue with  with  slipping  sanity,  "there's  no  reason  for  her death," floating in   in and out of this   this reality. "Join us in a moment of silence"   in a fugue

fugue   last night I   I   stood   at the shore with   with boots unlaced and thoughts in   "In these times that we place our trust in—"   slipping, "The system fail—" erased my imprints in in  the  sand.     In a fugue with   with, "our communities for support and guidance."

rage   rage and and guilt,   confused. "Let's us join hands." with slipping sanity,   floating in   in and out, Mariah, why are we here. "Mariah—" I I'm trembling   stop   stop this trembling.

*     *     *

I remove my quivering hands from ROD's grasp, and place them in my lap. As I sit with Members of BSCs, other Black students,[*] ROD, HB1 and HB2,[†] Mariah's former classmates, her friends, a few professors, and members of KYR for Mariah's memorial, my hands, the corners of my lips, quaver. I   I'm trying to hold in my tears. This   this grief isn't only mine to to have.

MP stands in in front of stained-glass windows. There are etchings of a cross, the Star of of David, a Crescent and Star, other religious sy symbols that tell us the there is meaning of this life. But   But here there is no   no   reason   no   no   les   lessons never learned.

---

[*] Even Second Black Girl from my Naughty Cells class is here to pay her respects. Before the memorial started, she nodded my way. I invited C1. She said she would try her best to attend.

[†] At the end of fall quarter, HB2 decided to take a leave of absence. She thought that no one would notice. After learning about Mariah's death, she messaged the group chat to let people know she, like so many of us, was at her breaking point.

# MONEY I$ THEIR KING

After a week of ignoring her calls, I finally tell Mother of Mariah's death, the University's denial, and more students coming forward with mistakes and oversights committed by those oathed to heal. I share with her how the rage, new demands, the denial, and confusion mold every interaction, passing conversations, newspaper op-eds, clickbait headlines, campus protests, and events. Students are threating to cancel their University health insurance. The University is making promises, and invited students will discuss the importance of nondisruptive health advocacy on campus. I say to Mother, "We're all so angry." While I watch others fight, I believe the battle has been lost. What are Mariah's death and student complaints against a University endowed with billions, and its hospital, which has existed for almost two centuries? Here, we see, no feel, no know that we are nothing but temporary checks to them.

As I cry to Mother on the phone, she calmly quotes Psalm 34:18. "Kenu, Kenu, my baby. The Lord is close to the brokenhearted and saves those who are crushed in spirit." Mother promises anyone who kills, and murders, the crushers of our spirits will not inherit the kingdom of God. For them, Earth and all its money is the only kingdom. This sadness as it is loosening my grip on the phone, chokes me, preventing my response. In my silence, Mother recites the Lord's Prayer. Her faithwords are frantic as they attempt to calm me.

I stop heaving and shaking. I tell her that I am just tired and stressed. Yes, tired and stressed, and we, I mean I, just need a meal and some rest, and after I'm rest, I mean rested, I will call her back. Before I can hang up the phone, she makes me recite Galatians 5:22. As I recite the fruits of the spirit, she repeats amen.

Amen.

Amen.

```
1. A(men)
A, prefix, meaning without. Men: those who
rule, who hate, who love, who control, who
kill, who free, who enslave, who damn and
save, includes doctor, Mariah, and Men.

2. Amen
So be it
```

Need an Amen, but there is no church. Because in this ivory tower, in this kingdom, in a land far, far away, I do not know how to explain to Mother that they have inherited this Earth and have made themselves gods, and how in this world or country or state or city there is nothing that we can do, and if there was a God and if He did save us, then He only did it to prolong our suffering. So, rejoice and be mad because we don't belong here or anywhere, and since they will find ways to keep killing, we might as well beat them to the punch.

Amen, kingdom come, and we will be done.

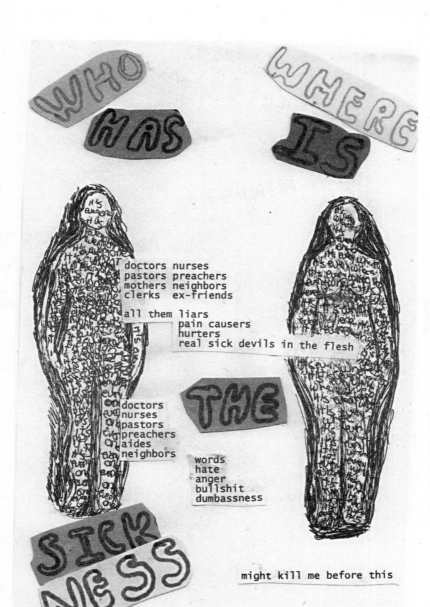

WHO

HAS

WHERE

IS

doctors nurses
pastors preachers
mothers neighbors
clerks ex-friends

all them liars
pain causers
hurters
real sick devils in the flesh

doctors
nurses
pastors
preachers
aides
neighbors

THE

words
hate
anger
bullshit
dumbassness

SICK
NESS

might kill me before this

# WHERE DO EXHAUSTED MINDS GO

Rage's still here. She's banging on the ivory door. Dean ▮▮▮▮ tried ignoring, then saying he wasn't home. She shimmered for another week, then boiled to fury. After *The Windy Beat** ran an article criticizing Dean ▮▮▮▮ for not inviting members of BSC or any undergraduates in KYR to the campus discussion, a petition demanding his resignation circulated throughout campus. Since he is *invested in the health of our students and our campus,* Dean ▮▮▮▮ agreed to lead a celebration of student diversity and health. It's scheduled for MLK Day, and open to the public. He's so dedicated to the cause that he's scheduled the first hour to be a Q&A about the University's progress.

Before I leave to meet ROD for coffee, I fill a flask with vodka, and

---

* University newspaper.

sip a beer. My dorm room's door opens. Roommate flutters in, seeming happier than ever. "Hey you, just grabbing a few things." She spots my flask and smirks as she slides out a bin from underneath her bed. "Getting a start on the long weekend."

"You know it."

"Love that. Change it up from the current campus vibe . . ." Roommate's voice trails off, "So, what do you think about everything that's going on? Crazy, huh." I shrug. Next thing I know she's rambling about understanding both sides. "It seems a bit much, doesn't it?"

"No, not really."

"Hmm, well I guess. I'm ready for campus to become normal again." Roommate sighs and stuffs her ski pants into a quilted Marc Jacobs tote. She checks her side of the room, which empties with every surprise visit. All that's left is bedding, econ course books, and beige hair ties stacked on her desk. With its emptiness, everything's neat. "Take it easy," Roommate says before leaving.

*    *    *

I gargle mouthwash, and then chew on Altoids. I'm running late to meet ROD. My jacket is on. My fingers, gloved. I'm too tired to leave and am dreaming of sleep. In the days immediately after Mariah's death, LP was unsure of what to say. Now, she knows. She explains that nothing will change. With this body and this mind, I will never have control. The best thing I can get is rest. It brings peace and no surprises.

At the Voices of Reason diner, ROD's on her second cup of coffee. Her pancake stack is halved, and droplets of dried syrup bead her fork. I slide into the booth. "What took you so long?"

"I missed the bus and ended up walking."

"I wished you would've texted. I could've waited to order."

"Sorry, it was too cold." I flip through the menu, rereading the options for sides. The exhaustion running through me heightens. I wish today was a day without movement. No Roommate, no ROD, no future classes or forums, no thoughts of the past or present. Just a day of being alone where LP and I can focus, figure out what's best for us. I close the menu, falling against the booth's backing. My eyes are closed. MLK's and Malcolm X's speeches play in the background. "I kept my fingers in my pockets. How have you been?"

"Better, I think, you?"

"Same," I lie. I should've stayed home. I'm not even awake enough to pretend. I check the bus tracker. There's one coming in thirty minutes. I don't know how to start a conversation that doesn't begin with tragedy. I need something generic that ignores the monsters in the room. "How are classes?"

"Really, classes?"

I laugh. I might be too fogged for a conversation, but falling on classes as the conversation starter is admittedly weak. "Fair, I wanted us to try and talk about something that wasn't—"

"I know. It's hard."

"Yeah, it is."

"Talking helps." ROD passes me her phone. "It's an invite for a meet and greet with students, local artists, and community members. Come with me? There'll be a chance to talk about—"

"I don't think I can make it. With everything going on, I'm behind on classes."

"Of course, you're still coming to the forum on Monday, right?"

"Definitely, wouldn't miss it." The bus is more than twenty minutes away. There's nothing I want to say. My time with ROD is always packed with contagious laughter. Our cackle and antics, even our glances are enough to soothe the parts of my mind infected with LP. Ever since I've retreated from shore, LP's resented ROD. I'm starting to as well. "There's a bus coming that Imma try to catch."

"Are you sure you're okay?"

"Yeah, I'm fine."

"It's okay if you're not."

"And it's great that I am." ROD's eyes flinch. I slide on my jacket. "Sorry, things have been—"

"I know. It's okay. See you on Monday?"

"Yeah, see you Monday."

> **HB1:** Hey y'all, ahead of Monday, I'm sending a short list of demands some of us brainstormed and emailed to Dean ▉▉▉▉

> **HB1:** We're gonna give it to him during the meeting so he has no excuse not to read.

> **HB1:** 1. Fire Doctor ▉▉▉▉. Mariah Moore died from Doctor ▉▉▉▉'s negligence. No action will correct Mariah's death, but the firing of Doctor ▉▉▉▉ is the first of many necessary steps to prevent another death due to his negligence.

> **HB1:** 2. Make University Health Insurance free to all full-time and part-time students.

> **HB1:** 3. Have a hiring initiative focused on more Black doctors in the University hospital.

> **HB1:** 4. Removal of ▉▉▉ ▉▉▉▉ from the BSC. It's unfair that LC holds unquestioned authority as the leader of the Black Student Coalition. As a white man, he will never understand and fully have a personal investment in protecting, and then advocating for Black students at this University.

HB1: 5. During welcome week hosting an orientation for students of color. Students of color have a harder time finding community and adjusting to campus life. Allowing an orientation for students of color would help them connect with one another as soon as possible.

HB1: 6. Renaming Shockley Hall. A hall named after a known racist heightens the University's hostile and unwelcoming environment.

# S (NOT) GON' GIVE IT TO YA

Dear Thesis Committee, how do you prove you're progressive without alienating your donors and investors, your students and professors, who want to keep the University as white as the *Mayflower*? Simple, you save all your diversity announcements and initiatives, your newsletters and community service days, for MLK Day weekend, and the last bit of January.*

While sitting in the front row, I'm buzzed at the celebration. My flask's hiding in my bookbag's back compartment. LP and I have decided that if I'm not drowning to my death, then we'll drown in drinks. I'm chewing my mix of gum and mints, listening to chatter as we wait for Dean ███████. The event was supposed to start fifteen minutes ago. His lateness, his choice to hold this meeting in Shockley's smallest meeting room, confirm what many suspected in the Black Excel

---

* If you fully want to lean into your white institutional allyship, then for the first week of February, you can even sprinkle in a few events and Nelson Mandela quotes in your emails' signatures.

group chat. This "celebration," like diversity snapshots on admission brochures, like the faculty's one quota-checked professor, or the diversity statements on the syllabus of a racist professor, is a performance of crossed *t*'s and dotted *i*'s.

\*        \*        \*

"Told you."    "You did. He pulled this with Alicia too."    "To who?" "Alicia."    "She passed two years ago. She was giv—"    "Wasn't her name Angela?"    "—en the wrong meds."    "No, it was Alicia but—" "They shouldn't have—"    "—She passed three years ago."    "—even had this event."    "Girl, right, they obviously don't give a damn."    "What did you expect?"    "They got us—"    "For the diversity quota—"    "Are y'all sure it's Dean ███████ leading this?"    "—they don't need us for anything else." "You know damn well it's Dean ███████. He's this school's—"    "Wait, is that the police, here?"    "—nigga on retainer."    "Why are they here?" "This is gonna be a waste—"    "Dean ███████ probably invited them here." "—of our time."    "Is that him?"    "Mmhmm, that's him with a reporter."

\*        \*        \*

Dean ███████ is all-smiles, slapping the back of a news reporter from the *Chicago Daily*.

His maroon suit and deep blue tie match our school's colors. After Dean ███████ takes his place behind the podium, the reporter snaps pictures of the event, then leaves before it officially begins. "Here at this University, we have always valued all students. As we continue to move forward with this academic year, the University will continue in its excellent legacy of supporting and adapting to student needs." Dean ███████'s thimble mouth is still all-smiles. He uncrooks his gold lapel pin stamped with the University's insignia. "We hear and understand your concerns. Due to recent events and student concern, we have extended the number of free sessions students enrolled in the University's health insurance plan are allowed to attend."

"How many?" one of us shouts.

"There will be time for questions later. However, I will address this concern now. Instead of four sessions, students enrolled in our health insurance plan have seven free sessions before they are referred to a local mental health practitioner."

HB1 shoots out of her seat and asks, "That's it?"

"This is dramatic change. No other University in the nation offers as many sessions as this." HB1 still stands, and she motions for others around her to stand as well. Another student in the front row walks to the podium and hands Dean ███████ a list of demands, which he quickly reads. "Though your dedication to this University is inspiring, these demands are impractical, and go against our University's values."

One of us shouts, "How?"

"It would be unethical to show favoritism to one group of students."

"What about free University Health insurance for—"

"That is not within reason. The University is more than willing to provide practical means of support, such as the extended counseling sessions," Dean ███████ responds to HB1. "If we wish for this meeting to continue, I ask that we hold all questions for the end. As previously stated, the extended amount of free—"

ROD, HB1, and I interlock our hands. HB1 leads with chanting *that's not enough.* Rows behind us follow HB1's lead. While in awe, *I* cower in the presence of HB1's strength. I follow others in our protest. As LP pulls the words off my tongue, my chants become more and more sporadic until I'm mouthing the words, feeling as fake as Dean ███████ ███'s care for us. On the walk over to this meeting, I texted HB1 and promised I would hand out flyers with her. I promised myself that if I could at least stay here, if I could be present and united in this anger, then I could do something good, I could be here enough for Mariah's memory. If I could do this one good thing, then I could rest. But here, as all these voices are interlaced with one another, as frustration locks us in this room with the University's puppet, I want to collapse into LP.

Just shut the fuck up, shut the fuck up because this isn't about you. Become strong enough to be here. That's all you have to do. I try again and I'm chanting, "That's not enough," as I wonder when enough will be enough.

Dean ███████ straightens his suit, then motions to the police officers that they can remain seated. "While I understand your frustration, we must respect each other and this University. If you continue with this hostility, then I have no choice but to end this meeting."

His comment silences us, and Dean ███████ returns to talking at us, reminding us we need to appreciate everything this University offers. As Dean ███████ stands on his stage and prescribes how we should feel, my thoughts jump between Mariah and my aunt, my aunt and her history, the history of this University, this country, our deaths never-ending. I whisper to ROD, *I'll be right back*. I grab my bookbag and dash out of the meeting. In the hallway, I find an empty enclave. I lean against the cobblestone wall, and drink from my flask. As I'm leaving, my phone vibrates.

HB1: Where you go?

ME: lightheaded. needed ta eat.

ME: *to

HB1: okay . . . I'll meet you in the dining hall.

Luckily, I arrive at the dining hall before HB1 can catch me in my lie. I'm out of mints and gum, and so I chug the dining hall's bitter coffee. HB1 arrives at the dining table. Her blond-tipped locs fall against her purple puffer jacket. She slams her tray on the table. "This is bullshit." She unzips her jacket and tosses it and her bookbag on the empty wooden seat beside her. She's stabbing her pasta with a fork. "Dean ████████ is a fucking asshole. After you left, Mariah's thesis advisor shared how she's supported students since Mariah's death. Guess how Dean ████████ responded?" HB1 flips her hair. Her locs rest on her arched shoulders as she digs her elbows into the dining table. "He told her she's not a therapist and that as an untenured professor she should concern herself with teaching. Fucking ridiculous. The University expects all of us to be on a *Happy to Be Here* train." I nod my head. As the vodka suddenly hits me it feels as if I'm bobbing above the surface. "They don't get what it takes to be here. But we'll make them understand. Shit, I'll email Dean ████████ every day if I have to."

HB1 opens her bookbag and from it pulls out a slim stack of flyers. "These leftover from the meeting." She divides the stack in two. "You're still down to hand out flyers with me?" My hands fumble as they try to pick the flyers up from the sticky surface. As I'm collecting them, I knock over my cup. The darkened puddle spreads toward the flyers. HB1 collects them before they are ruined. "You good?"

"Yeah, yeah, of course." I rub my closed eyes, pressing my fingers against my sockets. "I'm making it, I'm good and great."

"Huh?" HB1 grabs a canister of napkins. While she hands them toward me, she smells my breath. "Are you drunk right now?" I reply, *no.* She rolls her eyes then snatches away the canister of napkins. "You're fucking ridiculous." HB1 leaves. I reach for the canister. Napkins disintegrate as I use them to leave up the mess I made.

# BABY
# COME BACK

"Ma, what's it like losing a sister?"

"Kenu, why are you asking?"

"I wanna know. Ma, just tell me."

She yells at B1 and B2 to cut it out before she gives them a reason to be upset. Background's chaos quiets. "It's being robbed of everything you loved. Every day you're left waiting for everything to return, but, baby, it never does."

"How did you get through it?"

"I filled my heart with you, then your brothers. Without my children, I never could've got through it."

"Don't say that."

"Why?"

"It's too much to ask of us."

"You asked me a question. I answered it with the truth. What else did you want me to say?"

"Something, anything else."

"That's all I got. You and your brothers gave me a family again." B1 and B2 return to yelling at each other in the background. "Sahara, I gotta handle your brothers. I know you're in pain, but you don't honor the dead by living like them. It's time to remember how blessed you are to be alive."

"I'll try, Ma. I promise I will."

#Blessed

Me, desperate to see her blessings, sits naked with others in a circle inside a prayer room. The walls are electronic newspapers that roll through headlines. She, along with other members in the prayer room, is sitting in a circle as they wait for God to arrive. As they're waiting, they watch each other and the walls. Time and its headlines move through years, decades, then centuries, and God still hasn't arrived.

# BACK TO LIFE
## (HOWEVER YOU WANT TO LIVE IT)

O gracious Thesis Committee, while I am too drunk—no, drained—to be an activist, I am a woman of my word.* Before all this horror went down, I had a plan to enjoy my last hurrahs. I abandoned my plans and tried living; all that caused was more pain, and exposure. After this interlude of contemplation and a little stagnation, it's time for us to return to our schedule. It's time to have fun, fun, fun.

C1 meets me at my dorm. Inside her Ted Baker tote are nips of tequila and whiskey, and handles of vodka and gin. She apologizes for missing Mariah's memorial and offers this alcohol haul as her token for my forgiveness. I accept and stash the alcohol inside my closet. "I can't believe that happened. She seemed cool."

"She was."

---

* That is, when my word deals with me and LP.

"You okay?"

"I'm better." As I sip my nip, she searches for a place to sit. There's nowhere. Dirty clothes, beer caps, and crumpled papers cover my floor. My half-opened bookbag occupies my desk chair. I apologize for the messiness. To make room for her to sit, I push clothes and books off my bed. Her eyes dart from the floor's new pile to my bed's tangled and pilling sheets. "It's impossible not to have a mess when these rooms are so small," she says after she perches on Roommate's chair. "I don't know how you do it."

C1 sets her quilted Chanel boots on the chair. She's hunched over, not even drinking, still staring at the room's mess. "I'll find an outfit and we can pregame somewhere else." C1 unhunches her body and lets her boots hit the floor. As I'm crouched on my floor, searching for clean clothes, C1 relishes in the details of her and BO's current love high. They plan to spend a weekend together in St. Lucia. She's counting down the days till their love getaway. I'm disinterested, unsure whether she's angered or reveling in my lack of responses. Outside of *amazing* or *I can't wait to see the pics*, I don't have anything else I want to add. When her monologue shifts from her celebrating their love to her indulging in the details of snorkeling, then windsurfing, then, "*holding each other as the sun sets*," I know I'm only here to witness C1's happiness. "Don't worry, we'll go on a trip too this spring break. My treat, you need it after ever—"

"No need. I already have plans for spring break."

"Oh, that's nice." C1 stands up from Roommate's chair. She picks through my desk's mess. "Hopefully the plan is getting your room together."

"Something like that."

"Whatever, we should be going soon." In the bathroom, as I change into a baggy black-mesh turtleneck and high-waisted black leggings, I hear C1 ruffling through my papers. Anxious, that she'll find my letters on my desk, I forgo any attempts at eyeliner and exit the bathroom. Her mumble of, *cute,* is the only approval I'll receive for my outfit. "███████ says he hasn't seen you in class."

"I'm thinking of dropping it."

"You probably should before add/drop ends."

"Add/drop, classes, it's like we're in college or something."

"Ha, funny, you—" My phone rings with a call from ROD. I ignore and take a swig. ROD calls again. We take a shot. After her third call, C1 removes my phone from my hand. "Hello, hello Sahara's line." I struggle to grab the phone out of C1's hand. I stumble over a stack of books and fall backward. C1 laughs and puts my phone on speaker. "Sahara's occupied. Can I take a message?"

"Yeah, where the fuck has she been?"

A pen hidden inside a sweater pokes my back. I'm rolling on the floor, giggling as the heat rushes to my cheeks. "I'm down here," I yell. *What the fuck,* ROD replies. I sit up. My palms are pressed against a boot's eyelets and broken earmuffs. "I'll call you back."

C1 hangs up the phone. I stand up and open a whiskey nip. As the plastic bottle is between my teeth and I slowly tilt my head back, allowing a stream of liquor to burn my throat, ROD calls, again. *She's such a stalker.* C1's ready to press the ignore button. I swipe my phone away from her. "Hello, hello."

"Sahara, what the fuck?" C1 hovers near me, holding in laughter at ROD's rage. "███████ told me what happened. What's up?" C1 taps her finger against an imaginary watch on her wrists, goading me to hang up the phone.

"Nothing happened, nothing's up. Classes been crazy."

"But you have enough time to go out?"

"It's Friday. The new Lord's Day. Even Dean ███████ is probably going out."

"Where are you going?"

"This place ███ likes." I fumble with the phone and accidentally put the call on speaker. "It's called Spectre."

"I'll come too." C1 kisses her teeth and mouths, *don't let her.* I don't want ROD to join us either. I need a night of only fun, no ROD, no confrontations, no life, only fantasy.

"The place is pretty far and tickets are probably sold out or super expensive. But next time," C1 replies.

"I'll look into it and see if I can swing it."

"Fun, well Sahara and I have to go or else we'll miss the train. See ya." I say goodbye, then hang up. As I'm mixing a to-go cocktail inside an empty Gatorade bottle, C1 says, "That's *so cute* she checks in on you." She opens her hand, signaling that she wants to taste my vodka, pink lemonade, and fruit punch Gatorade concoction. "Especially if she's not controlling and lets you live your best life." We leave my dorm, and as we slug through the snow, C1 begins planning our trip together. On the 6, she shows me photos of her in a bikini with her white friends. "See, this could be us in Turks and Caicos."

## TURKS AND CANKLES

*Curtain opens on C1 and Me sitting on a beach. C1 wears a white bikini. Her long blond wig blows in the wind. Meanwhile, Me wears a baggy red dress and a white apron. A yellow and white headscarf hides her 4c hair. As C1 relaxes on a lounger, Me applies "Oh Yassum You" sunscreen to C1's back.*

C1: Isn't this so great? A little fun in the sun.

ME: *(wipes her forehead)* Yeah, so great.

*Spotlight brightens. Though uncomfortable, Me continues providing care to C1.*

C1: *(staring in disgust)* You're getting sweat everywhere. Take a break.

*Me collapses. Underneath her is a giant puddle of sweat. Me closes her eyes, and as she rests, fit Black men and women wearing blond wigs and white swimwear march onto the stage. One hands C1 the cookbook* Cook Me Thin. *The others fan C1.*

ME: *(opens eyes)* What's that?

C1: *(She and her fanners simultaneously smirk.)* Well, if you're not doing your job anymore, you can at least look better.

*Me's puddle of sweat inches closer toward C1 and her fanners. While backing away from the encroaching sweat, one fanner slips in a puddle of it and snaps her neck. Fanners in white Speedos carry her off the stage. A new fanner appears from offstage and resumes C1's fanning.*

ME: How?

C1: Simple.

*Another new fanner enters the stage, pushing a giant-size pot that sits on top of a burner. A group of fanners hoist Me inside. One of them turns on the burner.*

C1: *(Me reads the cookbook.)* This is amazing, right?

ME: *(Face and body melting. Her words are gurgles.)* Ye—e—s, so—o gre—e—at!

# ICKY HUMPS

At Spectre, as C1 and I wade through waves of heaving bodies, we are baptized in sweat. We swipe away grazing hands that are desperate for a feel. She introduces me to a group of her friends. I lurk in their circle, listening to comparisons of this club to another, better spot. I escape from them and lean against a concrete wall. C1 finds me and presses into my palm a pill stamped with a heart. She smiles. I swallow.

ROD texts she's on her way. Instead of worrying about ROD's arrival or C1's disappearance into the sea of others, I dance. As the music jolts through my body, it possesses. I am disconnected, unbridled, ungrieved. I am in a fantasy. With others on the dance floor, our bodies curl in and away from one another. My breathing heavies. I'm hot, thirsty, desperate for a touch. I dance with Some Man. He pulls me in harder, too hard, no just harder. His hand enters my leggings, then underwear. I'm wet like the sweat against our necks. While in me, he yanks my braids, licks my neck. I am falling in love with his violence.

His fingers exit me and rub my hip bone, then thighs. He's touching jagged scars and slit skin. He promises, *It's okay*, and I think he's falling in love with my violence. After the song changes, he disappears.

*       *       *

Alone on the dance floor, more people pass by me, wait no through me, wait no by me, no, through me. After passing through me, they swipe me away like smoke. I float to the smoking terrace. Outside, the cold air returns me to my body. Shivering, I light a cigarette. I need to find C1 for another drink, another pill, another anything. I close my eyes and see LP and Mariah dancing with one another. LP unzips her body, then drags Mariah inside. Between the cacophony of screams and laughter, LP urges me to jump. I clutch the steel rail bars. The cold metal aches my fingers then wrists. I stare at the concrete below me. One jump is all— "Sahara, I've been texting you," ROD says. "I thought you and C1 already left."

I flick my cigarette onto the ground. We briefly hug. "Let's go back inside." With another drink, another song, with more touches of pretend love, I can handle her being here. I grab her hand and lead her toward the door. She snatches her hand away.

"What's up?"

"Sahara, what happened between you and ██████?"

"ROD, nothing."

"She told me you were drunk in the dining hall."

"Buzzed, not drunk."

"It's not funny."

"You're right, it's freezing."

ROD rubs her thumb against her forehead. "I traveled almost two fucking hours, Sahara. All you got is jokes."

"I have cigarettes too." ROD's eyes dart as she holds her mouth open. Before she can yell, or judge, I add, "What do you want me to say?"

"Anything that's not a dumb joke."

"Do you want to go inside? I'll introduce you to ███████'s friends."

"███████, really? She's a fucking cunt, Sahara."

I rearrange, then tweak ROD's reply to the truth, *Sahara, a fucking cunt, she is.* ROD's eyes well. She wipes her nose, which drips from the cold. This is too real. Why can't she pretend we're fine, and there's only the club's echoes no grief between us? "I'm grown. If I want to go out, I'm going out whenever and with whoever."

"That's it? You're gonna treat me like shit 'cause ███████ is your new best friend."

"ROD, it's not like that."

"Whatever." ROD shoves her hands into her gloves. From her parka's front pocket, she pulls out her beanie, which falls onto the snow. I kneel to pick it up. "Don't," she says.

"I don't under—"

"Sahara, just don't. I lost a friend too. And I'm losing one right now because you're too selfish to be there for anyone but yourself." Other partiers join us on the balcony. They and their chatter walk between ROD and me. When the space clears, too much is still between us. She leaves. As the snow melts into my braids, and the wind numbs my brows, I kick away the indentations of ROD's footprints. This is what I needed, right? No ROD, no real, only a final fantasy.

# STEP IN THEIR WORLD
# (MONEY'S DELIGHT)

It's 3:00 a.m. The city zings. Cars run red. At a drugstore, New Friends buy booze, chips, candy, and eggs. We migrate till we stand in front of a museum. Huddled by a bronze lion, our hands are shoved into our pockets, waiting for our turn to smoke. Someone passes to me, and I take in whatever's inside. New Friend next to me spews words. More New Friends join in. The group spewing turns to bellowing, singing, and screaming.

Old Friend straightens my posture. She instructs me to stand still. It's time to play the Burroughs game. I stare at an audience rich with white faces. The instructor places a beer can on top of my braids. The audience throws eggs. One, two, three, finally the can's shot off. There's egg on my face. Yolk dripping from my braids. I drink, and others play.

3:00 a.m. turns to 4:00. Old Friend turns to me. She nudges me awake. I join the restarted group singing. I don't know any of the words, so I melodically scream.

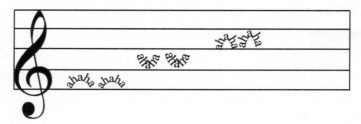

A New Friend tries to climb the bronze lion. He falls down, and tries again and again, and another New Friend pulls him off. Angry at the tug, the New Friends fight. The rest of us are divided between laughing at the violence or singing louder.

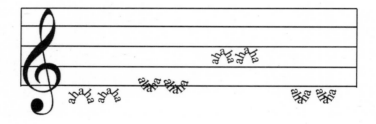

I run into the street, yelling for a taxi. One stops. Its tires scream. Its driver swears. We pile in. The ride is long. He's taking the streets. Why blame him? He sees the money, the waste, the wasted money. We are living dumpsters, dumpster scholars piled in metal taxis instead of metal bins.

I fall out of the taxi. As I'm walking to my dorm room, everywhere hurts. I sit on my bed, crying and paining. Nothing's right. I need something, anything, to feel right. I take one, then two Tylenol to make the pain disappear. It's still here, growing. Three, then four. The pain strengthens. Five, Six. Empty bottle.

Paining me.

# IMAGINED ME

I wake up. My mouth is dry. My thoughts, blurred. My hand still clutches the empty Tylenol bottle. Last night didn't lead to a passive escape. I have another chance to try again. I check the messages I missed in the Black Excel group chat. HB1 updates us on the recent progress since last week's town hall meeting. The University is hesitant to fund an orientation that's solely for students of color. A few professors and deans are worried about the message an orientation of that nature will send to the rest of the student population. The response to the University's reluctance is BSC and its allies have called for sit-ins at the University hospital and outside of Dean ████████'s office. HB1 needs all of us there to show our support. The University's network of Black Front Desk Women support her cause, and allow her to enter every dorm to hang flyers, and gather all those who promised that they would come.

A knock echoes from my door. I hesitantly open it. "Did you get the message in the Black Excel chat?" HB1 asks.

"Yeah—yeah, I did."

"You coming? Some of us are in the lobby. We can wait for you."

Quickly, I brush my teeth and join them in the lobby. It's fifteen degrees out and we're all bundled in scarves, or blankets that double as scarves, and have pocket warmers stuffed in our jackets. As we exit, a woman working behind the front desk hands us small cups of hot chocolate to drink during the walk over.

In the hospital, we sit in the lobby, silent, smelling the iodoformed air underneath the fluorescent lights as we wait to be seen. Once noticed, we hand out xeroxed flyers to those who are willing to receive them. Old grandmothers with IV drips, people delirious with fevers, nurses with wrinkled scrubs, all take one and sit with us. We in a collective stillness, remembering Mariah and all those we have lost.[*]

## BLACK BOTTOM

*Me and LP stand across from one another in an abandoned ballroom. Pieces of the crumbling mosaic ceiling fall between them. The marble floor corrodes with every new beat of blaring jazz. LP tucks her right hand into her zoot suit, which is blacker than ink. She snaps her left hand's fingers with a frantic pacing that rattles her gold watch. Me's eyes dart from LP to the crumbling ceiling and eroding floors. She begins frantically dancing. Her dress's fringes, which are encrusted with pills, shake and create clouds of white dust as her knees knock back and forth, and her arms flail.*

LP: *(removes her hand from her pocket to tap her watch and grins her Chelsea Smile)* Keep up, Keep up, Keep, Keep Up.

---

[*] Dear Members of the Thesis Committee, I apologize for the previous scene. If I could change time, I would've left with HB1, and sat with her and everyone else who supported the sit-in. In truth, I ignored the knocks and HB1's messages. I remained in my dorm, tangled between covers and clothes, waiting for the strength to leave my bed.

ME: *(shuffles to the right, then the left)* I am, I am, I am.

LP: Faster, baby, Faster

ME: *(panting)* This is as fast as I can go.

LP: Come on now, that's nothing.

*LP's hunched and slapping her knee. Me's dancing through clouds of dust.*

ME: *(coughing)* I need a minute. Come on, give me a minute.

LP: *(The ceiling and floor crumble faster. Me's dancing quickens.)* Ticktock, ticktock, our time is up.

*Me's dancing slows. The ceiling and floor completely collapse, sending me and LP to rock bottom.*

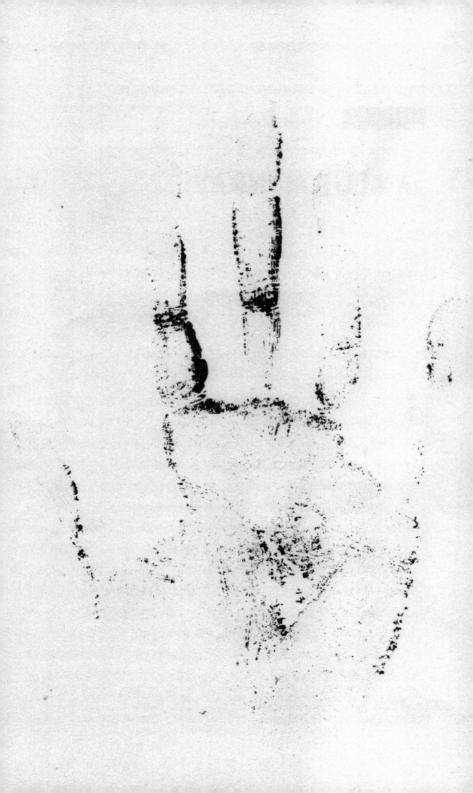

# A BLUE MONDAY

'm good, I'm fine, I'm close to divine. Everything's coming up fine, and will work out in due time. I'm blessed, yes so blessed. Roommate's never here and staying with her boyfriend. I'm blessed, oh so blessed. ROD and HB1 have left me alone, since her trip C1's busy with BO. I can sing as my thoughts ring, la la la, tah, teeh, tah, tah, ha, I know what it's like to be free and completely me. I can cry, cut, pee in sheets. I can squirm, choke, and plan again. Next ticktock with enough pills, I won't miss my shot, until then I rest, no prepare, no rest and prepare for one more go. While in my bed, my me, I read Advisor's bolded emails that warn me if I don't attend my Double Consciousness class today, she'll notify my RA of never attending my course. I can't have that happen, I can't let RA see, I need to get up and pretend one more time. I need to think of a game, a joke, a song, a trick, there has to be another that this mind won't forget. Come on, LP and the rest of me, we can play, play this final game of pretend, right? Yes, yes, we can play, come on, let's play.

I skip around my floor's minefields, creep into the bathroom, and flush the toilet that's been mellowing for too long. I sit in the tub with my clothes still on, not ready to see the damage I've done to this body after a week no two no some, but I must, I must, it's time to pretend one more time. I turn on the showerhead, the water hits, clothes drench, I struggle to peel them away. I need to get to the skin, wash it close to clean, I clean, then scrub the layers of dirt, scabs, and skin-gunk that sleeve my body, I finish then dress. Come on now, come on, just one more dance, come on now, don't leave 'em waiting, get on up. I get up, again, after returning to the bed for an hour or so, I've missed the first two hours of lecture, and by the time I arrive in the hall, there's only fifteen minutes left, when the professor's back is turned, I slip into a wooden-arm desk chair in the last row, from there I see Double Consciousness Professor's arms are sleeved with tattoos of gears and burning clocks, half of her head is shaved while the other half is in locs, her skin, russet. DCP ends the lecture, and I try to slip out of the chair, but a piece of splintered wood snags the side of my leggings, causing me to tug until a hole in the cheap fabric is ripped, after I'm freed from the desk, I notice that DCP watched me the entire time, I walk down the aisle's rubber stairs, my gait shaky, I want for someone to grab me by my braids and drag me through campus until we reach my bed, I approach her and make sure to stand several inches, maybe it's even a foot, away, LP screams at me, she tells me that I'm still not clean, not meant to be seen, LP keeps screaming while I am in front of DCP, I'm too tired, no preoccupied, wait no tired to concoct a smile, did I even brush my teeth? LP laughs, TEHEHE, TEHEHE, TEHEHE, DCP interrupts, if you were here the last weeks, you would've heard my warning of getting here early to avoid the seats in the back, sorry I missed all your lectures, I was sick, she stares at me, then I see the concern that connects her brows.

She replies, "How are you feeling?"

"Better, much better."

"That's good. You haven't attended this course, and attendance is mandatory, but—"

"I understand. I'll take the W."

"Wait, Sahara." I turn around, grinning so that I seem unbroken. Before leaving my dorm room, I removed my letters to ROD, B1 and B2, Mother, and Father from underneath my clutter, and set them on top of my desk. I am ready to try one last time. My hands are stuffed inside my pockets, fiddling with nips, and the envelope that stores Mariah's letter. I've accomplished 60 percent of what I need. All that's left is for me to finish this conversation, pick up my Tylenol PMs, and drink at the shore. "This quarter, especially with everything that's happening in response to the death of one of my advisees, I understand if classes were the last thing on your mind. Let's figure something out that works for both of us."

"Thank you," I respond. Time slows so rapidly that it reverses. Will I always be a person in need? I step away from DCP. My fiddling with nips has caused the drinks to leak. She looks concerned, then confused. I remove Mariah's letter. It is destroyed. Tears rupture out of me. I repeatedly cry, *I am so sorry.*

*       *       *

DCP guides me toward her office. I'm promising DCP *that I am fine.* She's silent. Her grip tightens. I'm panicking. LP's screaming. This is all too real. I don't know how I will escape out of her office. I'm cowering in her corner chair, smelling of leaked vodka and tequila. She asks, DCP asks if there's anyone I can call. Initially, I say no, and DCP then asks if I live in a dorm, and if she can contact my RA. The fear of remaining here gives me enough strength to hold in my tears. I wipe my cheeks with my jacket's sleeve. Again, I assure her that I'm okay.

I even muster a half grin. I think it's working. I'm close to escaping. Everything will be okay. I reach for my backpack. DCP's smiling as well, standing by her open door. I think she's preparing to say the generic, *there's on-campus counseling if you need it,* instead she closes her door slightly and hands me a box of tissues from her bookshelf. "I don't feel comfortable with you leaving alone. If there's no one you can call, then we'll have to figure out some alternatives."

"I'll see if I can get a friend." Initially, I call C1. I know she'll have no questions. We'll chalk this up to another one of my Sahara moments. I'm sent to voicemail. DCP overhears the automatic greeting, she asks if there's anyone else. I text ROD, knowing I don't deserve her response. Minutes pass and she hasn't answered. DCP suggests I call. ROD hears my faltering voice, and after asking for my permission, DCP talks to her in the hallway.

"She's on her way," DCP says after she returns. While we are waiting, she's standing by her bookshelf. On it, everything's sorted by color. From the middle shelf that transitions from blue to white bindings, she pulls out a teal folder. "This is a list of affordable or no-cost off-campus resources I have been giving students. Did you know Mariah at all?"

"Kind of. She was a friend," I respond, remembering the day at the dining hall when Mariah told me about this professor. As I hear her past joy, I bend the folder's edges, fixating on the rill of wrinkles to keep me in this present.

"Have you talked to anyone about it?"

"No, but it's fine. It's just how this school is. I'll be fine, just tired."

"Nothing's ever a just. You need to process what's happening." DCP taps the folder's center. "This is here when you're ready."

"Sahara?" ROD pokes her head inside the office. DCP opens the door fully. As I'm hunched, knees knocked together, ROD approaches slowly. Her concern brims her eyes. She kneels by my side, asking *what happened.* I burst into tears. I rub my fingers against my forehead and hide my face. I apologize to ROD and DCP, and tell them I only need some rest. ROD carries my bag as we exit DCP's office. She's holding on to me as I walk to my dorm. "Sahara, whatever it is, it will be okay. We'll figure it out," ROD promises as we walk to my dorm. Even when she's not speaking and is searching for clean sheets in my closet, I tighten my grip on those words.

I throw everything off my bed, "Can you please st—"

"Yeah, I can." ROD climbs into the bed with me. I sob in her arms. The next morning, I wake up to ROD unrolling her CVS receipts, hunting for coupons for cleaning supplies. Both ROD and I agree that my room is, *Mr. Clean's wet dream.*

# MY FUNK IS PLAYING AT MY HOUSE

ROD hangs clothes, and I'm crouched on the floor, filling pink dollar-store trash bags that are the size of a toddler's sock. Among the curled pads, food wrappers, dirty underwear are bloody razors. She doesn't mention them, and neither do I. Her silence is a relief that I can interrupt when I am ready. The small bags fill quickly. As I'm collecting the floor's junk, I'm amazed at the mess I've made. It's a little over a month since Mariah died. I don't know when this all happened. A bag rips, spilling out the trash. *Fuck, again?* I think as I start over. ROD finishes hanging my clothes. She ventures into my closet and pulls out enough empty liquor and beer bottles that they overflow the recycling bin.

"How long?" She stands by my desk, next to the teetering heap of glass bottles.

"I got a little carried away this quarter."

"No, how long have you been planning?" I look up from the bottles to ROD's hand. She's holding my note addressed to her. I'm not ready. My head falls to the messes beneath me. LP's scolding. She tells me that I waited too long, and have made everything worse for myself and ROD. I'm writhing with shame, wishing I had the strength to kill myself before my breakdown in front of ROD and DCP. "How long?"

"A while."

"Why?"

"I don't know." I add a beer can to the already overwhelmed tower of past escapes. "It's been this way since I've been a kid." The tower collapses. ROD's eyes shift from bottles and cans haloed around the bin to the razors I haven't yet rethrown away from the ripped bag. I finish recollecting the trash, and my floor is still nowhere near clean. I'm kneeling on the floor, and ROD sits by my side and groups the cans into a separate pile. She pauses, turning to me with welling eyes. "Don't ever do it, okay. 'Cause if you did, I would start an apocalypse to bring you back," she says as she bombards me with kisses on my chin and cheeks.

"Gah, gross," I scream, then wipe away the slobs of her snotty tears on my cheek. "You would end the world for me?"

"The world's shit without you." ROD holds open a giant black trash bag that we nabbed from an unattended janitor cart in the dorm's lobby. "I'm serious, don't ever leave like that."

"Okay, I'll try."

"Will you really?"

# ROCK-BOTTOMED GIRL

W hen you've been splayed out at rock bottom for so long, and have failed both in living and dying, even the most hardheaded and terrified will admit that it's time to temporarily approach this whole life situation from a different angle. Thesis Committee, the key word here is: *temporary*. LP's been with me since childhood. I doubt that a therapist with some elbow patches, and strategically placed *uhmms*, will be strong enough to separate us from one another. Even if they separated me from LP long enough to fight against her, what would they advise or force? Would I join the fables of forced hospitalizations and surprise meetings with deans to force academic leave, of awry medication treatments and worse depression? Becoming one of the many student horror stories that warn us of what might happen while we are at the deepest point of our vulnerability? What if I'm told I'm unfit to remain here, and I am forced to return home. I would rather

O O I O O
O O A O O
O O M O O
O O A O O
O O M O O
O O I O O
O O R O O
O O E O O
O O A O O
O O D O O
O O Y O O
O O I O O
O O W O O
O O I O O
O O L O O
O O L O O
O O W O O
O O I O O
O O L O O
O O L O O
O O I O O
O O L O O
O O I O O
O O L O O
O O I O O
O O E O O

disappear with LP than explain to Mother, Father, B1, and B2 why I was incapable of simply learning for four years.

ROD sits with me in the waiting room. Even though I've taken the right precautions—picked a therapist from KYR's recommended list, had ROD read said therapist's therapy statement, dressed in clean clothes so I seem well adjusted, and agreed to debrief with ROD in case anything went wrong—I fear that coming here was a miscalculation that will lead to more harm. And so, I lie on the intake questionnaire. I say I'm the medium level of sad. I'm only mildly stressed and sleep six to eight hours. I've never had suicidal ideation. I do not engage in any behaviors of self-harm. I eat a regular amount of food, and never feel hopeless. I feel the appropriate amount of overwhelmed. On the questionnaire's second page, I follow the first page's pattern of always in the middle. The questions don't matter, I only need to show I'm perfectly fine.

It's completed, and according to this new data, I'm the medium level of happy, the typical stressed, overworked, malnourished college student. Before I enter for my appointment, ROD whispers, "This will be good, but if anything happens, I'll be here." I hate that with her, my professors, and my attempts, I am never enough, always needing something more. I sit in the blue armchair that's against marigold walls. LP and I know this isn't right. We need to consider the facts. ROD's outside because she pities me. If it's not pity, then she's outside because she doesn't want to carry the guilt of me killing myself while still being her friend. She wants me to get help so she can end the friendship without a guilty conscience. If those two reasons are false, there's a more practical argument. I am too bothersome and chaotic to be present in our friendship. I distract ROD from her art and school. There's more evidence in my patterns of mistakes and the letdowns that support this decision as an outlier in my downward spiral. I'll never be together enough to be a good friend. So, why am I trying?

*    *    *

Therapist starts our session. As she reads out my responses to the questionnaire, I'm planning how LP and I will get out of this session without any suspicion from Therapist or ROD. "Sahara, where are you?"

"Huh?"

"A minute ago, you didn't seem fully present."

"Sorry, I was thinking about all the work I have to do after this session. It's okay if we don't use all the time, right? I might have to leave early so I can work."

"I would prefer you stayed for the session's entirety. What assignments do you have?"

"The usual. Papers and discussion posts." I stare at the brass bowl, which rests on the table next to her. An assortment of mini paper notebooks, stress-relief balls, and peppermints fill it. Therapist accepts my answer and returns to the introduction. She explains her sliding scale for students, which checks off the worry of new debt. With that worry away, LP switches to explaining how Therapist will have me forcefully hospitalized.

"Last name is—"

"Nigerian."

"I know, I'm Nigerian too. I was going to say it's powerful."

"I don't even know what it means."

"If you want, I can tell you."

"Sure."

"It means you're from a strong lineage."

"Cool," I respond, and I'm not sure whether she's here to sniff out my lack of Nigerianness. I straighten my posture, in an attempting pre-empt of any judgment that I am a lazy disgrace of a Nigerian.

"How do you feel knowing what your name means?"

"Nothing really. Just a word from a language I can't speak. It's cool to know, I guess, but I'm not attached to it."

"What do you feel attached to?"

"My family, my friends, school . . . I'm grateful for all my parents' sacrifices so I can have the privilege of studying here. They've been through so much, and all I want to do is make them proud."

"If you don't believe that, then you don't have to placate what you feel. That helps no one."

"That's true, thank you." I gather my coat and backpack. "I don't think I need this anymore."

"So why did you initially schedule the appointment?"

"I promised my best friend that I would."

"Then at least until your session is up, let's honor your promise."

"Okay."

"Sahara, I've been a therapist for seventeen years." She hands me my questionnaire. "And in those years I've learned when a new patient fills in mostly middle bubbles, they're hiding something."

"I'm not."

"Really, even I hide things from myself, my husband, my neighbors, lots of people, if I'm not ready to talk. Let's say you aren't hiding anything."

"Okay."

"Then, can I ask you again, where you went during the start of the session?"

"Sure."

"So, where did you go?"

"I was thinking."

"And what do your thoughts say?"

"They remind me of everything that's wrong."

"With what?"

"Me."

"What happens after the reminder?"

"I think of ways to escape them."

"Do you ever end up hurting yourself?"

"Sometimes, I—" LP screams for me to be quiet. As I rub my palms against my thighs, I agree with her not to tell Therapist about the pills. "I cut. It's so high school. I'll stop soon."

"You don't sound too worried."

"There's nothing to worry about."

"So why are you here?"

"I told you. I promised my best friend. I didn't want to disappoint her, again."

"Do *you* think this will be good?"

"I don't. At least I'm trying to keep my promise, right?"

"I think you owe it to yourself to try. Let's make one more promise, together. How about we see each other two times a week." From her bowl, she fishes out a notebook. "Between the times we see each other, write down some of your thoughts, and we'll go through them together."

"Why?"

"I want to see and hear what you're seeing and hearing. If you try it out and hate it, then you don't have to keep doing it."

I cradle the notebook in my palm. The exterior is fuchsia. The paper inside is cream with brown lines. I've had notebooks before. I've written my thoughts in paper margins while in lectures. I've scribbled on napkins, and unread syllabi. Always, I've reused, and forced my thoughts into the slimmest spaces. Never have I been given a space of my own until now.

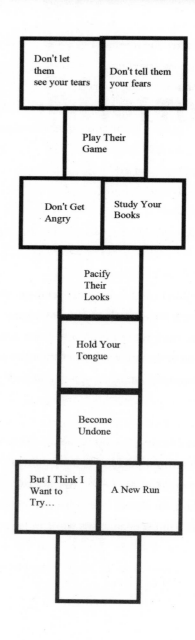

# The Academic: Black Girl Edition

Don't let them see your tears

Don't tell them your fears

Play Their Game

Don't Get Angry

Study Your Books

Pacify Their Looks

Hold Your Tongue

Become Undone

But I Think I Want to Try…

A New Run

# I NEED A RESOLUTION

Therapist and ROD think I should attend my classes. In the first week of therapy, I lied to Therapist and skipped. Within the first half of our session, she caught on. She said, *this won't work if I'm lying.* I asked, *isn't every lie based in truth?* She replied, *we're here to get better, not to philosophize, but if I'm so inclined to, then maybe I should attend class.* I appreciate her calling me out on my bullshit enough that for this week, I'll start with one class, the lab section* for BIO131: Disorder and Disease. I sit in the back row of a library conference room converted to a classroom. Squeezed inside are four rows of rectangular steel tables and black folding chairs. In groups of three or four, students are working on a P-set† predicting the bubonic plague's rate of infection. At the front is a SMART board and a TA wearing a baggy

---

\* It's in R. D. Wright, the on-campus library that's directly across from a bus stop, and a decent walk from my dorm.

† Problem set.

shirt that reads TOXICROBOTICS. Every time the SMART board falls asleep, TA's fingers tap it awake.

*    *    *

Group by group, the students who have finished the P-set leave. I'm the last one left, rereading the problem examples on the SMART board, hoping I'm on the horizon of understanding. Between yawns and overarm stretches, TA watches me. After being inactive, the SMART board turns off. TA doesn't bother to tap it awake. He approaches me and hovers over my paper. He removes my pencil from my hand. As he's solving my problems, his shirt with holes around the collar and sweat stains burned into the underarm, drapes against me. "If you cared enough to come to class, this would be easy. It's basically a child's game." TA solves the first problem. "Do you want me to explain?"

"I got it, now." TA slings his aggressively buttoned messenger bag over his shoulders then exits. Another class enters, I remain in my seat, refusing to leave until I can figure out how to solve the problem.

# MS. CELLOPHANE

With this whole therapy thing, I am enjoying how it's a one-woman show. I tell Therapist of LP, of suicidal plans, of school, of courses, of Mother, and of Father. I tell her of B1 and B2, of finding Aunt Nita, of being unworthy for ROD's friendship, of ignoring C1, of HB2 going on leave, of my consistent silence, then of Mariah.

"Mariah, should we talk about her today?"

No, we won't. This is the only time I have to tell the truth to someone other than LP. So far, LP hates that our folie à deux is morphing into a ménage à trois. Because Therapist, our extra person, is always questioning LP's intentions. There's only an hour, enough time for my approved topics. My next bits on school and dying, of the University and its killings, of being a bad Nigerian and spoiled American, of hating Southfield and my take that my death is my chance at agency.

"When I heard about Mariah's passing in the news, I was devastated. Does her death have any impact on your suicidal intention?"

That's not on today's lineup. I open with UB treating me like a mutt, and past plans with LP, of this morning's cut feeling more satisfying than this morning's cigarette, of—

"Sahara, let's talk about Mariah today."

I don't think our sixth session will end without me speaking about her. There's about half an hour left. I think I can wait her out. Therapist and I stare at one another. The silence ices inward. The Midwest in me wants to appease, but I don't have a joke or redirect, not even story coded in deprecation. "How do you hold her death?" Therapist's entering my stage with a new script. I expected, *how do you feel about her dying,* not this.

"I don't understand."

"I have a feeling that you do. Just say the first word that comes to mind."

"I guess confusing and uh close." My eyes trace the blue and yellow geometric shapes patterning the carpet. "I don't understand, I mean I know how it happened. I don't understand why it had to be her."

"You mentioned close. What does that mean for you in the context of Mariah's death?"

"I have to always remember her." I stop studying the carpet and its overlaying shapes. I look to the clock. There's only ten minutes left, yet it feels like we're just starting. "I have to because if something happened to me, then maybe since I remembered someone, someone will remember me."

"What about Mariah, her family, and her partner, would they remember?"

I mumble, *yes.*

"What about your family, would they remember you?"

"They would only remember—"

"Remember what?"

"The painful parts. Outside of that, I don't know if I have anything worth remembering."

"What if you did, could you then start holding life close to you instead of death?"

# I AM (K)NOT MY HAIR

In my dorm room, I wonder where I could hold or find life. Honestly, it might be in my hair. The months of buildup have evolved into braids of their own. My hair is a city of knots and dry patches. Three hours in, my arms are sore, my fingertips numb from unraveling, and I have enough toothpick punctures to give a person with trypophobia a case of the faints. I'm not even close to finishing a quarter of my head, I have better things to do with my time. After a back-and-forth where Therapist exposed every fault in my logic, she convinced me it's better to tell someone about your peanut allergy, than die from anaphylactic shock because there are peanuts in your salad.* In the context of school, this means that instead of failing all my classes, I need to tell my professors what's going on, and see what they might say. With my

---

* Her words not mine. I'm still in the camp of picking out your peanuts and ignoring your throat's swelling. However, Therapist thinks communicating to others is a good experiment to try.

permission, Therapist sent a letter to my professors explaining my situation. Two-thirds of my professors[*] agreed to let me do makeups for my missed assignments and papers. I have a backlog of work. Instead of writing responses to Du Bois readings and figuring out what's on the syllabus for Colonial Africa,[†] I'm tangled in Kanekalon.

I finally reach a braid's root. I'm yanking on it, trying to get it free, and once it is, I toss the discarded pieces of hair onto my floor that pieces of cut and unraveled braids, ranging from the size of Laffy Taffies to TI-89 calculators, cover. My body aches from being stuck in the same position. When I relocate to the mirror, with popping and creaking bones, I see all the hair that's left to take down. Honestly, fuck this. I start cutting the braids as if I'm a determined Edward Scissorhands working on my first Black client. I'm not sure how much I should snip, and if my erratic cuts will even help with removing the buildup, but there's no turning back. Braids descend into the sink, the bathtub, the toilet, the trash can, the dust bunnies' corner between the lower door hinge and wall. The battle is over, and yes, my hair's serving Cynthia doll, but at least it's free.

\* \* \*

As I exit the bathroom, Roommate enters. She gawks at my head and switches between staring at the Kanekalon carnage and searching through her desk's drawers. I slide on my headphones and begin collecting the discarded braids. The floor and bathroom are clean, I'm sitting on my bed, minding my business, but Roommate's stares are drowning out Le1f's newest EP. I lift up one headphone. "I wanted a hair change."

---

[*] Professor for Disorder and Disease said my best bet is doing well on the final.

[†] It's probably the general anthropology nonsense of masquerading a white savior complex as academic intrigue.

| A | B | C |
|---|---|---|
| DATE 02.13. 14 | DATE 2.19.14 | DATE 2.25.14 |
| N.R. | N.R. | N.R. |
| "Back to Life" by Soul II Soul | "You Don't Own Me" by Lesley Gore | "Starships" by Nicki Minaj |
| "Free Your Mind" by En Vogue | "Keep Ya Head Up" by 2Pac | "Get Lucky" by Daft Punk |
| "Brown Skin" by India.Arie | "Show Me Love" by Robin S. and Sandeville | "Sexy and I Know It" by LMFAO |
| "Feels Good" by Tony! Toni! Toné | "It's My Life" by No Doubt | "Flawless" by Beyoncé |
| "Let's Go Crazy" by Prince | "Get Ready" by The Temptations | "Imma Be" by The Black Eyed Peas |
| "Go Your Own Way" by Fleetwood Mac | "Bust a Move" by Young MC | "Get Free" by Major Lazer |

"Oh, really. I didn't notice. It's uh, cute." She's rifling through her drawers. I'm praying that she's not looking for jump rope and weight bands for another convo and sweat session. "Got it." She waves her passport then places it in her PETER AND PAUL produce bag, which has two Robin Hood figures running with a sack of vegetables on their backs. Roommate's lingering in the room and quiet as I'm creating a playlist. She enters the bathroom, and while the door's open, she asks, "How's your quarter been?"

"Long."

"I know right? I can't wait for spring break. We're thinking of going to Peru for camping. Are you planning anything fun?"

"Rest."

"Oh, that's it."

"Uh-huh."* Roommate's so quiet that I almost forget she's here. When the bathroom door closes, I snatch off my headphones and pretend to search through my desk. There's no flushing or faucet running. I hear plastic crinkling and Roommate rushes out of the room. I run to the bathroom. Two rolls of toilet paper are missing.

---

\* Sure, there was C1's offer to travel with her abroad, and even if I had the money, the ridicule and pressure, my constant performance to sheathe the displacement I feel with her and her friends, would make the break LP's dream vacation.

# THE RE-EDUCATION OF MS. NO PILL

H ave you thought about ways you hold your life?"

"I thought about it. I know you asked a week ago, and I still don't have an answer. I've been trying to focus on school. Here, I don't have any life."

"Why don't you go on leave like ███████?"

"I wouldn't have it in me to come back."

"Okay, have you thought about transferring?"

"I'd have to apply to school again. What if the next school is worse? What if I don't get any scholarship money? I don't know whether the problem is me or this University."

"Why does it have to be either or?"

"It just is."

"What if it's both?"

"So, you agree there's something wrong with me."

"Sahara, I'm not going down that thought path with you. Your mind operates differently, and sometimes medication can help with its mechanics."

"Medication."

"Yes, are you open to trying medication?"

"If I say no, will you have me forcefully hospitalized?"

"Sahara, I will never force or reprimand you for your medical choices. Though I hear your distrust of treatment, especially considering the recent events and your family history, I do believe medication can help you in a way we haven't yet tried."

"So, on my own, I'm beyond saving."

"No. I didn't say that. Sahara, failure and death aren't the only two options for your life. Your depression might tell you they are, but if you fully believed that, then you wouldn't be in therapy."

"What do you want me to do then?"

"I don't want you to do anything, but it could be helpful to realize no one is forcing you to attend this school. I've had patients who by the fourth session decided to leave this school. You've decided to stay. Why is that?"

"I can't do that to my parents."

"Try and forget about them for a moment. Trust me, I can understand this is a hard ask, but for a moment, let's take your mother and father out of the equation. Without considering them, do you really want to stay here?"

"I'm not sure. I want my degree. I want to be capable of taking a test without panicking. I want to finish and prove this place didn't win. I don't think pills are the answer."

"Sahara, pills, therapy, none of this is magic. You might stay on campus, you might try medication, you might keep seeing me for the rest of your time in school, you might do all of this and still have days you cut and feel suicidal. What matters is that you're trying, and you're using the support that's around you."

"Shit, and after all of that, there's no guarantee?"

"I know, annoying, right. Is there anything in life that's guaranteed?"

"Death, taxes, and racist shit."

"No argument there."

sister

REAL LOVE

never forget any of me
yes girl even the crazy me

nd while we're at it
ever forget

cing
ging
k
hair-do
py
aling

aking in
y
aring
king
ut to get some
lthy
ghing
ing

me
me
me
me
me
me
me
me
me
me
me
me
me
me

remember me
every     me
tell of  me

# SORRY
# IS THE HARDEST WORD

After the session ends, I join ROD at the Voices of Reason diner. We share a pizza with sauce so dry its only purpose is to paint the pizza a pale red. The layer of cheese is hardened and cracked open. The taste is cheap, and for us, this means it's bearable.

"I dream of pizza with sauce that moves."

"Oh, and crust that flakes," I add after munching on semiedible cardboard.

"And meat that's from this decade." ROD inspects the sausage. Her eyes are ovals of skepticism.

"I dreamed a dream when slices were good."

"And their bread was soft."

"And their cheese inviting." We stop and cackle, sounding like witches having a kiki on their brooms. I think ROD and I have stabilized our friendship. The guilt of how I treated her, the embarrassment of how much of me she's seen these past two quarters are here, interrupting these moments. I'm trying to believe that she loves me, and that I, even the nasty bits of me, can be loved. "I'm sorry." *I know,* ROD responds. "I messed up this year." ROD repeats, *I know.* Was LP right, and now that I'm in the clear, ROD is ready to leave this friendship? "I promise, I'll be there. If you need help loading a thirty-pound marble for your next art project, I'm there. If you need a CTA buddy, a study playlist, or—"

"What?"

"If you want space, we can do that too."

"Come on, don't be ridiculous. I love you." She picks the rubber meat off the last pizza slice. "I don't want anything. No, I lied. There's one thing."

"What?"

"I'm having an art showcase during finals week. I would love it if you were there."

"Of course, I'm there in the front row, screaming, clapping."

"There won't be any rows, but I appreciate you."

ROD's beaming. She sends me the Facebook invite for the art event. I read where it's located and gasp. "Dude, it's in a real gallery. This is huge."

"I know! It's my first time being in somewhere legit. I can't believe this is happening."

"Of course it's happening. You're so talented. I only have therapy in the morning, so I'll have a bunch of free time, if you need help with anything."

"Sahara, it'll be finals week. No one has a bunch of free time."

"I'll make the time. I'll even reschedule the therapy if you need me."

"Stop it, that's too much. How was therapy by the way?"

"Uh, at the beginning, she seemed more concerned than usual. Then before leaving, she asked me if I've been feeling impulsive at all. Weird, right?"

ROD cackles. Her eyes shift to my hair. "It's the haircut."

"Is it that bad?"

"It's really bad, really bad."

"My therapist did start the session asking why I decided to cut my hair, and then mentioned medication. Shit, she must've thought I completely lost it," I reply as I piece together more of my recent session. "Ugh, I should've worn a hat, then she wouldn't have been so focused on starting me on meds."

"What's wrong with being on meds? If it helps it helps."

"I don't know. It feels like too much, you know."

"You've snorted lines, popped Molly, and huffed who knows what with C1, but meds are too much?"

"Damn, okay. I guess that's true."

"I know I love you so much. I call you out on your bullshit."

I raise my white coffee cup and toast to *No More Bullshit*. ROD and I clank our cup's blue trims against one another. While she's away in the bathroom, I snap a picture of my hair. With assignments, class, and therapy breakdowns and breakthroughs, I've been more concerned with fixing what's in my head than what's on top. I zoom in on the photo, and it really is that bad. My lazy wash, the unsteady cuts, the attempts to DIY an Afro bang, and the short supply of my deep conditioner has left my hair parched and patched. I send a picture of my hair with the message *Halp!!* to the Black Excel group chat.

HB2: Put a wig on! I have some for sale with free shipping.

HB3: Let me practice braiding it.

GAHDESS: Practice?

GAHDESS: ☺

AR: Nah shave it all! Then I'll smoke you out to celebrate! #baldlifefreelife

HB1: Oh, look who's back.

GAHDESS: Nah, headwrap it. #nubianqueen

HB1: Tho you're flakier than that dandruff. I can't have you walking around like that.

AR: And I, oop.

HB2: You gotta mention the dandruff tho? 😅😅😅

HB2: If I were on campus, I'd help you out, free of charge.

HB1: I'll give you a Finals Week Special

AR: Didn't you just have a Midterms special?

HB1: yes because I'm about my business

HB1: The Finals special includes deep conditioning, fresh cut, and style

ME: !!!!!!!

ME: Sorry for disappearing. A bunch of life happened.

HB1: If you actually end up coming to the appt, I'm all ears.

\*      \*      \*

The next day, as I'm kneeling over HB1's bathtub, my knees are pressed against a plush red bath mat. She massages my scalp then applies her deep conditioning treatment into my hair. I pray this treatment isn't secretly Nair. Outside of the hellos and asking what style I want, we still haven't had a full conversation.

HB1 leads me out of the bathroom and into her kitchen. On her floor, which is half carpet, half cream tile, sits a royal purple office chair. Next to the chair is HB1's treasure trove, a pink styling cart packed with banana clips, pressing combs, multiple blow dryers, braiding hair, edge control, flat irons, plastic caps, face masks, gold and silver braid jewelry, wig brushes, brush brushes, wide-tooth combs, combs as skinny and tiny as spaghetti noodles, rubber bands, hair ties, styling strips, and spritz.

The chair faces a blank wall, and as I sit, HB1 says, "If you want to watch anything on Netflix, I can turn on the projector." HB1 puts a plastic cap over my head, then takes out clay, lavender oil, and apple cider vinegar. "Can I put a face mask on you?"

"Yes, but don't hate me if you end up touching my pimples."

"Sahara, I would never hate you. Keep your eyes closed and relax." She places clumps of the mask on my face, and slowly smooths them out in circular motions. Lavender fills the air. HB1's touch warms the cool clay. The silence between us is gentle. I peek my eyes open, and I see the swooping outlines of her pixie wig.

"I'm sorry for not being there when you—"

"It's fine. We could've used you there for support. It's all still a mess. We're still trying to at least get ██████ out of the BSC." HB1 taps my shoulder so that I open my eyes. "Hopefully there's another meeting soon so we can get his ass out."

"Oh I—"

"Only say you'll be there if you actually can show up."

"Okay, I'll let you know closer to the actual date." My phone vibrates with a call from C1.

"Do you need to take that?"

"No, I'll call ██████ later."

"Oh, ██████, as in ██████ ████████?"

"Yeah, you friends with her too?"

"Used to be." HB1 leaves for her bathroom, returning with a hot washcloth. She lays it flat on my face as she tells her tale. "During my and ██████'s first year, we were part of the BSC. She was super excited to explore her Blackness for the first time, and we were so excited to be part of her journey, but then shit went left."

"What happened?"

"She kept bringing her boyfriend around, like every damn where. He's this old-ass dude with a real creep vibe. None of us got why they were together, but we didn't say anything. Then one night, she invited all of us to his bar for free drinks, and a bunch of us went. Like hell yeah, free drinks downtown, this was basically an episode of *Sex and the City*." HB1 removes the facecloth and wipes the mask away before rubbing moisturizer into my skin. We return to her bathroom and wash the conditioner out of my hair. Over the water's roar, HB1's words ignite her story. "A couple drinks in, her boyfriend starts saying all this problematic, kinda racist shit if you listening closely, then starts feeling up on all the girls and grabbing ██████ in any kind of way. We ask him to stop, and he yells at us and he makes us pay for the drinks. The bill's in the hundreds and we're broke, he tells us, 'Make sure you tip thirty percent.' I'm pissed, trying to stay calm, everyone else freaking out that they didn't have the money and they don't know what he's gonna do to us."

"Oh, no."

"Oh, yes. I'm the oldest of four, so I'm basically always the mom of the friend group, figuring something out. I tell everyone else to leave and that I'll handle the bill. I put down an empty Visa gift card, look him in his old-ass face, and tell him and ███████ that I was going to the bathroom upstairs and will be back to sign for the check. After I get up, I look back and see them all cuddled up on one another, then my ass runs outta there so quick."

"I wouldn't have even thought to do that."

"I know, ingenious. The next day ██████ apologized to me and said he didn't mean it. I told her that she couldn't bring him around anymore, and if she didn't feel safe setting those boundaries with him, I would help, and would be there for her if she decided to leave him, because she deserved better. After that, she snapped at me, and told Dean ████████ that I did hair out of my old dorm. I almost got expelled. Thank goodness I didn't have a digital trail of my payments."

"Wait, really?"

"Yup." HB1 blow dries my hair, then clips my ends. "Then get this, she comes to my dorm to get her perm, and acts like nothing happened. I may have left it in too long. I don't regret it. She wanted to be bold and come here, so she left with some bold hair. So yeah, girl, that's it. I'm not a fan, but that's my business." HB1 applies mousse on my hair, then wraps styling strips around my head. She places a soft-hood hair dryer on my head, tightens its elastic strings before attaching it to her dryer. I doze off, thinking of C1, her moments of kindness and her flashes of cruelty.

# S R, I, I, I

Doctor starts me on 10 milligrams. After my body adjusts to the dosage, the plan is for me to take more pills bit by bit until I've reached 40 milligrams. I keep taking these meds, even though it's causing vivid dreams, an upset stomach, a three-drink limit, stank breath, spitting up, insomnia, decreased masturbation, hot flashes, dizziness, diarrhea—did I mention the vivid dreams?

Despite these side effects, I told Therapist and ROD I would try. Trying includes me not becoming folded into thoughts, which means me throwing away razors, keeping the room clean, showering every day, eating enough food to fill me but not enough to clog the sink with all the spit-up, telling Mother that there are days I get sad, trying to believe Mother when she says she loves me, writing down LP's words on paper then destroying it, putting an ice cube or snapping a rubber band on my thigh or my wrist, writing down things I did, even if I spent most of the day crying, telling Therapist of my fucked-up imagination, screaming into a pillow when LP becomes too loud, promising myself that if I can survive this night, then I can survive the next one and the other nights thereafter, D.A.R.E-ing to be different and saying no to drugs . . . for now.

---

Healthy Things Done Today

✔ Showered for more than fifteen minutes

✔ Washed face

✔ Brushed teeth twice

✔ Oiled body

✔ Wore clean clothes

✔ Went to class

✔ Took meds

✔ Replaced bathroom napkins with toilet paper

---

# YOU HAD A A FRIEND IN ME

It's two weeks into medication and I've lost five pounds. Who needs Atkins and AA when you have antidepresskins? Last night, I ate glass noodles, corn, and carrots, and watched the sink swallow the specks of food. Last week, I tried drinking, and ended up passed out in the dorm lobby. Front Desk Woman helped me upstairs before RA returned from wherever RAs hide. FDW told me that if she sees me drunk like those white kids again, she'll scold the Black back in me. When I told Therapist, she couldn't help but laugh at FDW and her old-school ways. "Sahara, it's good that you have people who are watching out for you."

"I guess. I wish that they weren't seeing everything."

"Outside of that night, how's your drinking?"

"It's okay. I haven't been drinking as much as I want."

"You won't be able to drink like you used to for a while,* and that could be a good thing."

---

* Upon hearing this news, my liver became so excited that it agreed to stop filing for divorce from the rest of my body.

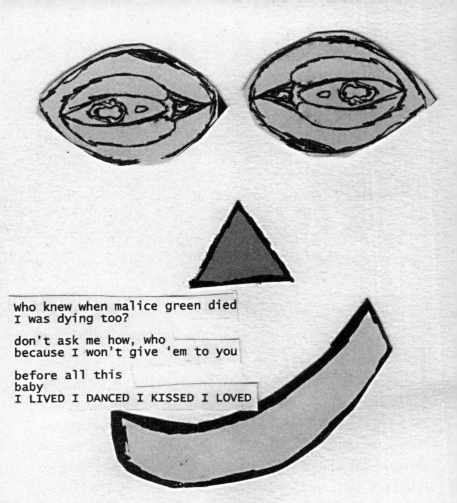

who knew when malice green died
I was dying too?

don't ask me how, who
because I won't give 'em to you

before all this
baby
I LIVED I DANCED I KISSED I LOVED

never gonna give a sorry
but you can have these worries

"Well, at least I'm losing weight."

"If you weren't, would that be okay?"

"No drinking and no weight loss and still dealing with flare-ups from LP? Seems like a hell I don't wanna be part of."

"Sahara, while we are working together, it's important that we're working toward having you feel comfortable with your mind and your body."

"Okay, yeah sure, but before we do all this body positivity stuff, let's make sure I still have a body to love. Deal?"

"Deal."

\*　　\*　　\*

Dear Thesis Committee, since my breakdown in front of DCP and ROD, I've been forced to reframe my life's central argument that I am unworthy. This thought renovation means that I'm trying to say no to everything that gives me comfort. Some nights, as I'm failing to stop LP's tracks, we worry that if I only know my pleasure through my pain, what happens when the pain is gone? Will there be anything recognizable left?

The temptation to become undone is ever present. After weeks of ignoring her calls, declining her invitations to go out, I'm meeting with C1. On the bus ride over to Dorian, I fantasize feeling the euphoric glow within my chest as the alcohol burns away my cares. I arrive at the bar, and since it's the middle of the day, I see it in a sober light. Wallpaper's peeling from the walls. There's a bartender sweeping up pieces of shattered glass from behind the bar, and another's pouring water into the vodka, not caring I and a few others are looking. This place isn't Oz, Narnia, or even a place on Eater Chicago. It's a bar trying to keep up with all the others on the block.

She guzzles the last of her whiskey sour. I sip my water, ignoring two shots and a whiskey sour in front of me. C1 passes me a shot. "Come on, don't waste it." The tequila burns. The warmth isn't the same. "So, are you coming?"

"To what?"

"If you weren't ignoring my texts, you would know." C1 orders a round of cocktails for us, then shows me the villa in Maui that's been booked for spring break. Her plan is for us to split it with SL, and a few other Donor Kids we meet after clubbing. "So, are you coming? I'm tired of waiting for a yes."

"I'm sorry. I can't."

"You want to stay on campus? No wonder you're always sad."

"Campus is *free*, and the trip's not." I cuff my ears, pretending to hear wise whispers from below. "What did you just say, wallet? I should stay my ass at home."

"Whatever. I thought you would've figured out your finances by now." The cocktails arrive. C1 sips, and I check my phone for the next departing bus. "You have somewhere to be?"

"Library and then a movie night with ROD."

"Cute, I'll get the check then." The bill comes. She calculates my share, the cost of the tip, and includes the cost of the show ticket she said she was willing to cover. I withdraw what I owe her from the ATM. I need the money I've given her, but I would rather have psych students shock me with electrodes to earn extra cash than remain her charity case for another day.

# THE NOTORIOUS L.I.E.

I'm heated, snatching books for my Colonial Africa research essay off the library's shelf. I approach the checkout desk, wanting nothing more than to leave and start working so I can forget the interaction with C1. I'm first in line, waiting and watching the grad student attendant, who rushes between placing callers on hold and calling a coworker whose shift it is. According to the voicemails he's leaving, he was supposed to be off almost two hours ago. As he opens a breakfast bar with his teeth, he tries checking out my books. The computer blares. He informs me, "Your library account is temporarily suspended." He runs his fingers through his thinning hair and clicks to my student account. The temporary restriction on my card is due to a book being overdue. I ask which one, feigning shock that this is happening. He shares the zine's title, and then the cost of $310 for it not being returned nearly three months after it was recalled. The block on my library privileges was the last resort for them to get the zine as soon as possible.

\*       \*       \*

It's in my backpack, but if I return it, then I'm still in the hole for $310, and there's no cubic centimeter in any reality or in any hell where I pay a fine for a book Aunt Nita never even wanted in a place like this. *This isn't possible,* I respond. He's waiting for me to leave, and that makes us two peas in a pod, because I've been waiting to exhale. I'm finally breathing everything out, and he's just going to have to wait as I'm trying to drain out my panics, and anger, that I'll have to pay for something that is part of my family's history. With the lighter in my back pocket and the gasoline pumping in my plasma and drowning my sheaths, I could burn this gray-bricked gulag down. Shit, shit, shit, this is my fault. I should've dragged myself out of myself enough to pay attention to the library emails. But with all the emails of guest lectures, new collections, and who-gives-a-fuck academic appointments, ignoring library emails is habit, one that's now expensive. What's next? Call Mother and listen to her lectures. No. Call Father and leave a voicemail. No. Call B1 and ask for a loan for library fines. Hell no, he'll have interest rates worse than private loans. Calm down, Sahara, remember what Therapist said: when your body is in high alert, deep yoga breaths. Here they go, now inhale and— "Excuse me, miss, do you think a mistake has been made?" the attendant asks while the line of disgruntled, students grow.

"Yes, yes, it has." I channel Mother's selective memory and Aunt Nita's life within me, then add, "This is my first time even trying to check out a book from the library."\* He's preoccupied with a new horde of grumbling and begrudged students behind me. "I'm not leaving until this is figured out."

---

\* This is technically true, considering Aunt Nita's work is a zine, and not a book.

"You can't hold up the line. There are people waiting."

"Well, I'm not leaving."

*Are you serious, what's taking so long,* students behind me continue complaining. He mutters, *they don't pay me enough for this shit* as he clacks on the computer. "Must be a mistake in the system. I'll make a note to remove it. Is there anything else you need?"

"No, thank—" The attendant checks out my books, calls the next person to the front. I gather my books and lies and dash away before the attendant's frustration turns against me instead of remaining in my favor.

---

Umail

---

Sahara.Nwadike @umail.edu
**Office Hours Availability?**

---

**6 messages**

---

**Sahara** <Sahara.Nwadike@umail.edu>    Tues. Mar 4, 2014 at 3:21 PM

To: DCP <DCP@umail.edu>

Hello, I hope you're having a great week. I was looking over the syllabus and saw that you are willing to offer accommodations for students. Are you available anytime this week for office hours to discuss a possible extension for the final project?

Sincerely,
Sahara

---

**DCP** <DCP@umail.edu>                    Wed. Mar 5, 2014 at 5:11 AM

To: Sahara <Sahara.Nwadike@umail.edu>

This week has been good but busy with organizing a conference panel. I'm afraid I won't be available for my office hours this week. I am more than willing to offer you an extension of a week; however, I fear that still will not be enough time. If you are willing, I would recommend you take an incomplete in the class and use either next quarter or the summer to finish the final. Please let me know as soon as possible of your decision.

---

**Sahara** <Sahara.Nwadike@umail.edu>   Wed. Mar 5, 2014 at 1:03 PM

**To: DCP** <DCP@umail.edu>

Thank you so much for this offer, and after much consideration, I think taking the incomplete for this course is my best option.

---

**DCP** <DCP@umail.edu>                Wed. Mar 5, 2014 at 2:49 PM

**To: Sahara** <Sahara.Nwadike@umail.edu>

Okay, I will contact your advisor and finalize the logistics of it all. I am excited to see your project. Do you know yet whether it will be critical or creative?

---

**Sahara** <Sahara.Nwadike@umail.edu>       Wed. Mar 5, 2014 at 2:56 PM

**To: DCP** <DCP@umail.edu>

So far, it's a creative assignment formatted like a mock thesis.

---

**DCP** <DCP@umail.edu>                Wed. Mar 5, 2014 at 3:13 PM

**To: Sahara** <Sahara.Nwadike@umail.edu>

Looking forward to reading!!! Good luck with finals :)

---

## MY SOMETHING CONTINUED

*Me and LP, after renewing their vows with Therapist, sit at the back of a bus. "The Sound of Silence" plays and Me pushes back her white veil to stare at LP, who wears a tailored tuxedo. Me unfastens LP's bow tie and cummerbund. As she is being undressed, LP snarls, mocks, and waits for Me to recoil in fear.*

LP: I'll hurt you.

ME: *(folds the white bib)* You have.

LP: I'll kill you.

ME: *(slips off LP's trousers)* You've tried.

LP: I'm never leaving.

ME: *(She stares at LP's naked skin, a palimpsest sequence of words and DNA, which raises LP's skin. Me touches the skin, caressing every jagged piece of flesh.)* I know.

As the bus moves forward, Me begins rearranging the language on LP's skin. Every touch causes LP to fidget and snarl, laugh, and question, but Me continues with her arrangement, leading LP's outbursts to slowly decline.

EBON

I love you
I love you
I love you

sister, even though that ba
got your loud mouth
your fussy ways
your mean stares
and your greedy lips
if I could, I would
hold her forever

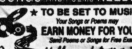

I'll keep

helping
seeing
worrying
praising
loving and listening to her

while living and dancing in my new heaven

# M.O.N
## ARTISTE

I take the 6 downtown to buy paintbrushes from Blick, and three bunches of crazy daises from Jewel. I return to my dorm room, carefully unwrap the bunches of daisies to then fashion a new bouquet. I place the paintbrushes at the bouquet's center and rewrap everything with the plastic that originally held the flowers. The bouquet is a little loose, so to secure it, I wrap tape around the flowers' stems, and the bouquet's plastic. With the flowers secured, and a swiped newspaper from the dorm's lobby covering my tape job, I'm ready and catch the 170 bus for ROD's art show.

Crowded cafés and partitioned art rooms in basement apartments, classrooms turned galleries and summer sidewalks where the emergence of art that sprang between sidewalks like weeds left us sweltering in our intrigue, have all been showcase locations for ROD's art. This show is different. Instead of chipped walls with taped art bios, the appearance of passionless but allegedly intellectual art, the walls here are pristine, with the art bios printed on foam placards. Here, there is no pretend. There is beauty in the real.

I stand next to one of the white pillars, staring at a suspended queen-size quilt hanging vertically. Lilies with names embroidered in red are on the front. On the quilt's back there are no names or flowers. Only the words *There are so many more,* printed in repetition, every line in red. I walk closer to the quilt's front, unsure if the name I'm seeing is true. My hand tightens on ROD's bouquet. The soft crunches of newspaper return me to the present, and away from LP's looping of only pain. Seeing Mariah's name still hurts.*

Instead of remaining in front of the quilt, I walk away, searching for ROD's work. After a few detours of admiring and interacting with other work, I finally see ROD. She's standing next to her art, talking to a group of onlookers. She's in her art zone, her zone of creation, where her knowledge and curiosity, her dedication and care, are beacons. Smiling, I study her painting, titled *Their Game.* Her piece is laid out on the floor. At its center is a papier-mâché tower. For the tower's surroundings, she's painted a vibrant game board where every neon square has a museum or University's blanket statements for change, the overheard racist remarks, professors' and museum directors' problematic takes, headlines of the University's past atrocities and empty apologies. The group leaves. ROD spots me. "You made it!"

"Of course, I'm here." We hug, and I hand her the flowers. Her smile blooms. "Thanks, dude, you didn't have to."

"I definitely did. A special bouquet for a special day."

*Special* cues for ROD to examine the bouquet again. She notices the

---

* There are nights I reread our messages, and as my fingers hover over her number, I wonder what would happen if I called.

paintbrushes living in the center. She presses the flowers close to her heart. "Thank you. Have you seen the other works yet?"

"A few."

"You have to check out more. Everything is for sale, and all of today's profits benefit KYR." Another group approaches ROD's work. One of them asks her about her process. I step to the side, then wander through the gallery, feeling the joy and pain, the progress and stagnation. In this gallery, I am here, seeing other lives, all of us at one meeting point as we rotate against axes of our destructions. All of us, the viewers, the artists, the organizers, like butterflies to nectar, we are here, living and moving w $^i$ $_{(n)}$ t h this art.

And you, interminable Thesis Committee, will never, no matter how many times you analyze, no matter how hard you pretend, no matter how much you fund, you will never feel the entire beauty of our gathering and creations, of our survivals despite our destructions.

# CAUGHT HER RED-HANDED, STEALING FROM THE BATHROOM FLOOR

After her art show, ROD and I enter my dorm room. The bathroom's door is wide-open. I poke my head inside. Roommate's there, removing the toilet paper from the gray cylinder. Roommate sees me and pauses, placing the toilet paper inside her tote bag. "What are you doing?" ROD pops her head in as well and asks, *What's going on?*

Roommate stands up, fidgets with the handles of her camel Kate Spade tote. "Nothing, this roll is wet and needs to be thrown out."

"Bullshit. You're taking the toilet paper. Why the hell have you been stealing so much of it?"

ROD and I step farther into the bathroom, cornering Roommate. This is a reckoning two quarters in the making. She stuffs the roll in her bag and pushes herself past. "With all my trips and living downtown, everything was getting expensive. All economists agree that reducing household expenses is the best way to save. And you basically have a single for the price of a double, so I figured the toilet paper was your thank-you."

"You figured wrong. I'm not buying all the toilet paper for you and your boyfriend's apartment or your trips."

Roommate pushes herself between ROD and I. "Whatever, I'll borrow them from Shockley. They're bigger anyways."

Roommate leaves, and I shout, "I knew it, I knew she was scheming or swiping."

"And not just wiping," ROD quips. Laughter fills our lungs. Between her gasps, she says, "You have to include Toilet Papergate in your project."

"Honestly, I might. Wanna hear the opening?"

"Of course."

"Wait, not here," I say as I move toward the bathroom.

"You want to read it to me in the bathroom?"

"It's our spot."

ROD rolls her eyes and follows me into the bathroom. There, I stand in the bathtub and ROD sits on the toilet. I clear my throat and begin.

"Dear Thesis Committee, It has come to my attention that smoking kills, along with police, loner white boys, and looks. While embroiled in the process of trying to live, I have written this honors thesis. It is dedicated to the first-years who haven't yet died from alcohol poisoning, exhaustion, or overdosing. This work has been a labor of love and of hate. In it, you will find juxtaposition, verisimilitude, French, Freud, and anything else I've wasted $60K a year to learn. I would like to thank my advisors: Mr. White Supremacy, Mr. Capitalism, Ms. Racism, and, of course, my Life Partner for all the guidance they have provided during this process. Yours truly, Sahara Kesandu Nwadike."

"I love it. It's your—"

"Truth."

(Shout-Outs)

# ACKNOWLEDGMENTS

There are so many individuals who were an integral part in the creation of this book. Their support constantly reminded me that writing and community are forever intertwined with one another. Thank you to my grandmothers, Juanita and Bibianna, and their everlasting ingenuity. Thank you to my mom for always telling me that I am enough. To my dad and his constant determination, which inspired me to never surrender a dream. To my sisters, Athena and Michelle, and their willingness to listen to every half-started story. To my friends, who provided so much laughter and care, food and flowers, during this process. To my impeccable agent, Larissa, who fiercely advocated for this book and calmed my every moment of anxiety. To my editors, Millicent, Ore, and Ann, who nurtured this book and helped it grow in so many breathtaking ways. To Jamilla Okubo, who created such a beautiful book cover. To Leah Carlson-Stanisic and everyone at Harper who helped with bringing this novel to its final stages. To LAMBDA and all the 2019 fellows who brought so much joy and community when I needed it the most. To my professors Laird Hunt, Goldie Goldbloom, and David MacLean, who saw and encouraged my writing's weirdness. To Faridah and all the mentorship she provided. And to my readers, thank you for giving me your time.

## ABOUT THE AUTHOR

**J K CHUKWU** is a writer and visual artist from the Midwest. She holds an MFA in literary arts from Brown University and was a 2019 Lambda Fellow. Her work has appeared in *Black Warrior Review*, *DIAGRAM*, and *TAYO*.